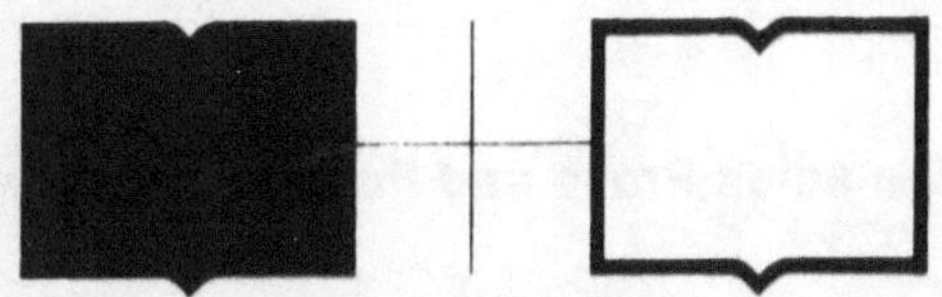

Toronto Reprint Library of Canadian Prose and Poetry

Douglas Lochhead, General Editor

This series is intended to provide for
libraries a varied selection of titles of
Canadian prose and poetry which
have been long out-of-print. Each
work is a reprint of a reliable edition,
is in a contemporary library binding,
and is appropriate for public circulation. The Toronto Reprint Library
makes available lesser known works
of popular writers and, in some cases,
the only works of little known poets
and prose writers. All form part of
Canada's literary history; all help to
provide a better knowledge of our
cultural and social past.

The Toronto Reprint Library is produced in short-run editions made
possible by special techniques, some
of which have been developed for
the series by the University of Toronto
Press.

This series should not be confused
with Literature of Canada: Poetry
and Prose in Reprint, also under the
general editorship of Douglas Lochhead.

UNIVERSITY OF TORONTO PRESS

Toronto Reprint Library of Canadian Prose and Poetry
© University of Toronto Press 1973
Toronto and Buffalo
Reprinted in paperback 2015

ISBN 978-0-8020-7518-5 (cloth)
ISBN 978-1-4426-3136-6 (paper)

American editions:
A Canadian Girl in London.
By Mrs Everard Cotes. (Sara Jeannette Duncan).
New York, Macmillan, 1908. 365 p.;
Cousin Cinderella. By Mrs Everard Cotes.
(Sara Jeannette Duncan).
New York, Macmillan. 1908. 365 p.;
Cousin Cinderella. By Mrs Everard Cotes.
(Sara Jeannette Duncan).
London, Methuen, 1908. 316 p.

COUSIN CINDERELLA

THE MACMILLAN COMPANY
NEW YORK · BOSTON · CHICAGO
ATLANTA · SAN FRANCISCO

MACMILLAN & CO., Limited
LONDON · BOMBAY · CALCUTTA
MELBOURNE

THE MACMILLAN CO. OF CANADA, Ltd.
TORONTO

COUSIN CINDERELLA

BY

MRS. EVERARD COTES
(Sara Jeannette Duncan)

New York
THE MACMILLAN COMPANY
1908

A CANADIAN GIRL IN LONDON

CHAPTER I

I WILL first introduce our father, as seems suitable.
He is Mr. John Trent of the Minnebiac Planing
Mills. I could say "the Hon. Mr. John Trent" if I
liked, but father does not care about its being dragged
in everywhere. Minnebiac is a place in Eastern
Ontario with the accent on the "bi." It is not the
only seat of father's interests, but it was the original
one, and we have always lived there, so it counts
for most with us. Father never had a great
deal to do with politics; but he made lumber pay
from the very beginning, and he simply created
Minnebiac, and there were other reasons, so about
ten years ago they made him a Senator, so that,
of course, we can claim to know Ottawa. Our
mother must have been the loveliest thing when
father married her; but now she isn't strong, and
none of us would think of asking her to under-
take anything more than just to keep as well as she
can. We ourselves are Graham and Mary Trent, —
mother was a Miss Graham, — and there never were
any others, so they were able to bring us up very

much as they liked; and I do not see how it could have been better done. We had the best influences, and even in Minnebiac were never allowed to play with interesting children or in the street, though how we longed to on big, light, empty spring evenings after tea, words can never tell. At that age we went to a private school where there was a backboard for punishment that had come out from England, and I think the teacher, too; but she is lost in the funny cloud that hangs like the drop-scene of life just in front of the time when you couldn't read. As I remember, however, even her misty outline suggests something remote and superior, anyhow, old and different; a brown front emerges, and a high forehead. I think she came from England, but I am certain about the backboard. After that Graham went to Upper Canada College and to the Military Academy at Kingston, and I to Miss Vincent's in Toronto, where one was taught æsthetics as a regular course, and thoroughly prepared for life. I mean such things as Domestic Science were obligatory; and girls simply cried to be allowed to take Beautiful Thoughts, though, of course, practically everything was extra. Father never seemed to mind the expense, and I must say I was very happy at Miss Vincent's. There was a time when I wanted enormously to be finished at New York, but father said no, I wasn't an American — and now I am just as glad. It is simpler to be a natural product and to finish where you begin, I think.

The South African War had a great effect on father, who came originally from Yorkshire, especially after Graham was sent home wounded. It was odd, too, because all the time Graham was at Kingston, hoping hard to get a commission from there in the English Army, father more or less discouraged it. He would have it he wanted Graham in the business. But the moment the war broke out he began to worry about the waste it was, all that drill and riding Graham had had at Kingston, if nothing was to come of it; and he was perfectly delighted when Graham made up his mind to go out with the first contingent of Canadian Volunteers. Mother and I were not delighted, though we pretended to be. Mother's grandfather was a United Empire Loyalist, so she had to make more of a pretence than I, who am further removed from George the Fourth. However, he went; and in six months they offered him a commission, and shortly afterwards a D.S.O., and he took them both, also typhoid fever, and finally a piece of shell in his leg which is still there. We got him back then. In the meantime father's partner had suddenly died — it was the longest funeral ever known in Minnebiac — and it was simply impossible to do without Graham in the business. So he resigned his commission. We thought father would have difficulty in getting him to do it; but, to our surprise, there was no trouble. He said very little one way or the other about his experience as an officer, though he told us a great deal about what he saw and did as a private soldier. The only thing I remember his saying definitely about the officer part was that he wouldn't resign what it had taught him for something. It was in Minnebiac, the day he wrote to the War Office in London, and we were walking back from the Post Office together. I was still at Miss Vincent's then, but home for the holidays.

"They were decent enough chaps at bottom," he added; "and there was one thing they could do rather well."

"What was that?" I asked.

"Drop down dead," said Graham; and I would have given anything to know who he was thinking of, though after all — if he was dead ——

"You've got to learn their ways," he went on. "They've got a lot of little ways, and it's a pity not to know them, for they don't seem to make any sort of allowance. But when it came to fighting, it was always all right."

It is a shady road along the river between the town and our place; and the afternoon woods were full of the sound of the saws devouring the timber.

It is a delicious sound; they sing their way through it with a kind of mounting cry, that wanes and waxes and wanes again with a perpetual call and a perpetual lullaby; I like it better than any other note that you hear out-of-doors. It is always there, of course; but sometimes you listen to it. Graham listened for a minute then.

"There's a lot of Canada in that," he said, "and Canada, Sis, is a pretty good alternative."

We continued our way home; and next day Graham went into the business.

So that Graham, of course, has not seen quite so much of life in Ottawa as the rest of us. He has been there off and on; but he never seemed greatly taken with it or excited with it, though they were always very nice to him at Rideau Hall on account of his Distinguished Service Order. I like to write it out in full like that, because it isn't an ordinary thing for one's brother to have, in my country. Graham stuck to soldiering as far as the Militia was concerned, and is a Captain in the Minnebiac Rifles, so he has to wear it when he dines in uniform with the Governor-General; and it always pleases me to notice the effect upon the A.D.C.'s.

"What's that your brother is wearing?" one of them has asked me before now, as if it were something out of a cracker.

"The D.S.O.," I would reply. "Don't you know it?"

This was very nice for father and mother and me, and I didn't care how often it happened; but any-one could see that Graham took no great satisfaction out of it. What he loved was Minnebiac, where he built himself a kind of workshop for composing and carving things out of wood. A mantelpiece he made, with a design of fir-trees, comes back to me like a line of poetry, or a bar of music. He gave it to one of the foremen, who thought a great deal of it. Graham was a kind of missionary in Minne-biac, of simple purposes and fine ideas in wood, the people there, though so near to nature's heart, being dreadfully fond of gilt and plush. He would have done well as an *ébéniste* of the First Empire; he had the conscience and enthusiasm. Or as a Japan-ese cabinet-maker with his life before him, and no accounts to keep. As a little boy he made clothes-pins, and signed every one of them. He loved the touch and the feeling and the idea of wood. Instead, however, he was the Son of John Trent and Son; and with the business extending the way it has done and seems bound to do, he has been obliged to reserve the poetry of it for his spare time; which perhaps is as it ought to be.

For a time all went well; and few men, I must say, had less to complain of in life than Senator Trent. His health, as long as he didn't touch certain starchy things, was excellent, and mother's never bad enough to be more than a subject for kind enquiry. He had a finger in every sort of national pie. There was nothing he couldn't help to endow if he wanted to, from a Home for Dyspeptics in the grape country, to an independent newspaper in Toronto. He had become so rich that none of us liked, except quite privately, to mention money. He was one of the legislators of a country he couldn't say enough in praise of. But a year or two ago the old microbe started working in father again. They began to talk about Canadians in England as if they were very fond of us indeed, and were longing for an opportunity of showing it; and the Toronto papers were full of their wonderful opinion of us, cabled across for practically the first time. Most people thought it was probably true, though nothing to get excited about; but father didn't seem able to take it that way; he would get worked up. He made his secretary cut out all the speeches delivered in England about that time on the subject of our future greatness, and paste them in a book, which he intends some day to publish at his own expense; so that whatever happens, they will be obliged to recognise over there that they did see it and say it once. It was as if he wanted to triumph over them in their very words; and he wouldn't give them credit for half-realising what they were proclaiming.

"Yes," he seemed to say to the people of Great

Britain; "you're talking as if you had found out the truth at last, but the day after to-morrow you'll think it was a fairy tale, and be sold again."

Father has very little patience with his own countrymen — in one way, that is. In another way he thinks more of them than you would imagine.

It might be expected that feelings like these would induce him to go over there often and explain things, and show what he himself had arrived at by believing in the fairy tale; but, no, father is curious in some ways, and back across the Atlantic nothing will induce him to go. He adopted Canada forty years ago in the most specific kind of way; and I believe he feels that to go back again even for a visit would be to admit that for him the bargain wasn't perfectly ideal. As a matter of fact, it has been ideal. He has been as contented in Minnebiac as if he were king of it. There may be things to see, and know, and enjoy beyond Minnebiac; but he doesn't seem to hunger after them. He likes to run across to the States now and then, for the sake of criticising their political arrangements, and coming back, as he always makes a point of doing, about three days before he need; this seems to give him more satisfaction than going. But he never goes to England. People do seem to escape like that from the British Isles; I've noticed other cases. With quite a pleasant sentiment about their early cells, and great affection for the warder, they simply don't want to set foot there again.

But it was easy to see that father felt differently about Graham and me.

"They're nothing but a pair of colonial editions," he would say, looking at me; and mother would reply that what greater advantages we could have had she was sure she didn't know, and tell her boarding-school story. (It was only that when mother was at boarding-school in Montreal, as a girl, she was sent a hamper with a pot of jam in it, and the head mistress thought proper to distribute this jam among all the girls there, which she did with a spoon, making each girl open her mouth for a spoonful. Mother was shy the first time the spoon went round and refused it; and the second round finished it just before it came to her. Mother didn't mind the injustice; but it left her with a great contempt for the educational facilities of her time, which she was fond of comparing with mine.) And she would point out how much I had been in Ottawa, helping her to entertain, and how I had accompanied her twice to New York, and once to the Coast.

"Five days and nights in the train," said mother, summing up the advantages of travel.

"And Graham has had South Africa," she would add, as much as to say, "I suppose we don't want any more of *that*." But she would always have to admit that she had not been to England herself; and father would say that that was the great drawback. Mother wasn't equal to going too. He would have liked to send us all.

Then suddenly one day it flashed upon me why father really wished us to go. He had a secret unacknowledged reason — he wanted to send us as samples. He would remain with proud reserve in his Minnebiac woods; but his offspring should go and show forth his country for him. I found it out by noticing how his zeal to send us fluctuated with what was said over there about Canada. When certain people expressed their disparagements and their suspicions father's attitude would suggest that he would rather die than take a single step to change or disabuse them — let such a country stew in its own ignorance, choke over its own fatuity. But when any enthusiast made a speech he would almost insist upon packing our trunks. One day an invitation came for father, as a leading Canadian, to go over there and stump the country. I don't think he considered it for a moment.

"You can never tell those people anything," he said. "The more you tell them the more they think you are up to some dodge for getting the better of them."

His idea being, I think, that Canada should simply roll on to greatness until she rolls into sight, without making any demand upon imagination, or any tax upon faith. But the next day it was settled that Graham and I should go. We hadn't any mission; nobody had sent for us, yet father managed to impress upon us that we weren't going precisely and only to have a good time, or quite in the frivolous spirit of a visit to the United States, for instance.

"If you come across anybody who seems curious," father said, "you can explain that this continent grows something besides Americans."

That was as near as he got to definite instructions, but we felt as if he had handed us a banner, and I was glad that Graham, who would have to carry it most of the time, was better qualified than I.

CHAPTER II

We arrived in London with the vaguest ideas; but we decided almost at once to take a flat. We immediately felt the same feeling about London — we longed to be part of it.

And somehow from the beginning our flat had to be in Kensington. We looked everywhere, but came back to Kensington and lingered there; we seemed to know more about it than other places, and to guess more than we knew. It seemed an old address in the heart, with finger-posts pointing to it that did not guide us to other parts; and in sentiment at least we knew our way about it. We found it full of people with moderate incomes and kind faces, old ladies who would run and jump fearfully on an omnibus, with an elbow-lift from the conductor, rather than stop the horses, and young ladies with portfolios, who looked full of purpose. They had pleasant, interested faces, and we felt that they would be pleased to have us take a flat in their midst, if they knew we wanted one. It was the unpretentiousness of Kensington that most appealed to us, I think, after the swagger of some of the parts we

had felt it our duty to penetrate. Swagger depressed
us dreadfully, we were quite brow-beaten by it;
and it is one of the hard things to understand about
London, why such armies of people there should
be occupied in enjoying it and ministering to it,
and keeping it up. Perhaps if we had been accustomed to it we would have felt differently; but in
our country people still have to work very hard for
just a comfortable living. I am sorry to have to
refer so soon again to money matters, but it is exceptional there to be as fortunate as father is; and I
think most successful men with us who are vain of
their accumulations would be more flattered to have
them speculated about than pleased to make a dis-
play of them. There are, of course, financiers in
Montreal, and even one or two in Toronto, who give
eccentric dinners as they do in New York and seem
to enjoy being splendidly and noisily rich; but it
isn't yet characteristic. I suppose the average
wealthy person, if there are enough of them to make
an average, is too new to his wealth to be happy in
spending it with that kind of abandon; he has not
yet learned to play about with it. He still considers
his balances seriously, and perhaps makes economic
adventures with them that have a political side, like
father's railway in Guatemala which was so useful
to Government lately. Circumstances, of course,
make some difference, and I don't mean to say that

we haven't a carriage and coachman in Ottawa, though it comes from a livery, or that we do not live while Parliament is in Session in a suitable way; but when I speak of Canada I think of Minnebiac, where mother orders her own groceries, and father drives the team in the buggy himself. And it seemed to us that in Kensington people from Minnebiac might be almost as happy as they were at home.

It was Miss Game's flat that finally attracted us — Miss Henrietta Game's. The agent had told us he "thought" it was a third-floor flat, which prepared us to find it under the roof; but that did not matter, he might just as well have thought the truth; by this time we liked roofs. It was the fifth, the top one of the Court Flats, close to the Underground and all omnibuses.

We were very drawn to the person who let us in. She was broad and red, with an air of perceiving slowly and acting firmly. She looked like duty squared in a kitchen apron, under a rather smudgy cap, and she was exactly the right size for the passage. I mean she took it all up, so that until she turned round we were unable to get in. She looked at us with a spark of caution in her eye, as if she recognised in us the emergency she had always to be prepared for; and the civility about the lower part of her face was very reserved. She was bent in the honest way that does not impair usefulness, and she moved with more than middle-aged deliberation. Indeed, we could see that she was otherwise much more than middle-aged; she was the oldest kind of English servant, the kind we had expected to see everywhere, but this was the very first. We gazed at her with pleasure and interest, and as she manœuvred us in we saw over her shoulder Miss Henrietta Game, in hair-curlers and dressing-gown, fly across the hall from the drawing-room to the bedroom opposite. That is an embarrassing feature of many London flats. Once people are admitted there is no evading them except by the fire-escape.

We followed this good woman to the drawing-room, and wondered a little why she did not leave us there. She picked up the *Lady's Pictorial* where Miss Game had dropped it beside her chair, and looked vainly round the carpet for threads. That brought her to the end of her resources, and she took up a patient, respectful stand near the door, with the air of wishing she could think of something else to do. Involuntarily I glanced round to help her; but it was all fearfully tidy, there was nothing to suggest. Then I saw that Graham was looking at her deliberately, with gentle, calm, curious enquiry. It wasn't of the least use, she meant to stand her ground and *be* looked at, if necessary; but it was plain she was aware of his gaze and suffering; and I wished he wouldn't. She kept her own eyes steadily and with deference on the mantel ornaments; but she clasped and unclasped her hands upon her apron, and moved mechanically a little nearer to the door. I began to wonder whether she would really hold out, when Miss Game came in and she disappeared instantly. Then I realised what she had stayed for, and why Graham was indignant; and I looked round immediately to see what I could have taken if I had had the chance. My eye rested on the mantel ornaments, — there were a great many, — and when I saw Miss Game looking at them, too, I felt myself blush. There were quite fifty or sixty mantel ornaments, mostly animals, with painful expressions and elongated necks.

Miss Game wore eye-glasses, and that made her look perhaps even more suspicious. She hesitated at the door and decided to come in; she advanced to the middle of the room and decided to sit down. We could see her deciding everything, behind her eye-glasses, and hesitating first.

"We have come about your flat," I said, when I saw she was a little more decided.

"I *was* thinking of letting it," said Miss Game, looking at us intently.

"We heard you were," I replied, "from the agent. It seems a nice flat."

"I have had it for six years," said Miss Game, as if she were most unwilling to part with it.

"That speaks well for the flat," said Graham, and Miss Game answered, as if to make a reservation:

"It suits me. It has one drawback," she added hastily — "I ought to tell you at once. The bells."

"The bells?" we asked together.

"Of St. Mary Abbotts'. You see," she said, indicating the window, "how near we are. I do not object to the regular services; it's the peals. A great many people seem to marry at St. Mary Abbotts'; and they all think they must have peals. It's a drawback to these flats, and I always mention it."

"I wonder if one *would*, in London!" said Graham, more to me.

"I don't think so," I said. "*I* wouldn't."

"Would what?" asked Miss Game.

"Have one's wedding pealed in London," explained Graham. "Tell so many people who would not care. Annoy people in flats. Rejoice with nothing. Would you, yourself?"

"Oh! I," said Miss Game, as if she could not entertain the idea. But I thought she looked at Graham with a conciliated air. "You could, of course, keep the window shut," she said. "And that is better for the blacks, too."

"The blacks?" I repeated.

"From the chimneys. They come in worse in a top flat than anywhere. And ruin your chintzes,"

c

she continued, almost in a tone of confidence. "Should you require everything fresh calendered?"

Graham and I glanced at one another. We were not acquainted with the verb to calender.

"Perhaps we shouldn't," I said weakly, and Miss Game looked relieved.

"If I calendered for you coming in you would have to calender for me going out," she said.

"Then don't let us," I said at a venture, seeing that she didn't want to.

"Why should we?" said Graham, putting up a bluff; but at that Miss Game took alarm again. You must never go too fast in England.

"Then there's the Underground," she said dissuadingly.

"Yes," said Graham; "very convenient, I'm sure. The agent mentioned it."

"That man," said Miss Game severely, "is little short of dishonest. The Underground is much too convenient. It is almost beneath us. You can hear it and feel it."

"Not smell it?" I put in anxiously.

"Every quarter of an hour all day long. No, not smell it, so far as I have noticed," replied Miss Game. "There it is, now!"

We heard a distant friendly rumble, and two of the mantel ornaments shook. "It's much worse than that late at night or in the early morning,"

Miss Game told us. "As a matter of fact, I always get up by it."

"That would be a real good use to put it to," said Graham approvingly; and Miss Game considered him in silence.

"You are the third to apply," she said. "One was a lady who was separated from her husband and the other was a gentleman with dogs." We felt a glow of superiority.

"It is interesting in a way," Miss Game admitted; "letting, one sees a great deal of human nature."

I looked at Graham in the hope that he would find a suitable reply; but he was taken up with a wood-engraving on the wall, a kind of document, one of those things that are three or four hundred years old at a glance. Miss Game saw that his attention was attracted by it.

"Yes, I would leave that up," she said. "That is King Charles the First at the top, and a copy of verses supposed to have been written by him when he was lying in the Tower. An appeal to the Almighty. The language is very extravagant."

"Oh, well!" said Graham. "So were the circumstances, weren't they?"

"But it's of no consequence," Miss Game assured us, "because the King never wrote them at all. It was probably one of his bishops."

"It's exactly the sort of language," said Graham,

perusing it, "that would be used by a king in a tower, with curls like that. He may have plagiarised from some bishop, but I can't help thinking that he wrote it. Anyhow, he claimed it, for there's his signature."

"I have been told by a gentleman in the British Museum," said Miss Game uncompromisingly, "that it's a forgery. It may be a plagiarism, too, for all I know."

My brother looked grieved, but he did not, of course, dispute the British Museum. "I call that stretching veracity too far," he said simply, and Miss Game considered him further.

"Well," said Graham, getting impatient, which was foolish of him, for it wasn't nearly over yet, "if you wish to let your flat, madam, we are looking for one. Our references are pretty good; and we would make any arrangement that is customary about the rent. As we have never been married we have never been separated, and we own no dogs in this country. May we see the other rooms?"

Once more Miss Game hesitated.

"I have never let to Americans," she said.

"We are not Americans; we are Canadians," replied Graham quite calmly, as if it were of no importance. "I would have been proud to be an American if it had happened that way; but as it didn't happen to happen I am prouder to be what I am."

Miss Game looked as if she didn't see the necessity for pride in either case.

"Isn't it very much the same thing?" she asked.

"No, madam, it isn't," replied Graham firmly.

"Oh!" she said. "Well, I'm rather disappointed. I've always *wanted* to let to Americans."

I trembled for what Graham might say; but he only looked at her.

"They are first-rate people to do business with, madam," he informed her, and turned to me.

"Then perhaps we had better go," he said, taking up his hat.

"Oh, but you haven't seen it!" said Miss Game hastily. "It may suit you, you know, after all," and she led the way to the dining-room. In the dining-room there was an odd little sideboard carved with the Apostles, and Miss Game told us it was made of wood that came out of the Armada. By now, of course, we knew we could believe her; and as we followed her out of the room Graham pinched me, harder than was necessary, and said: "Don't make *any* fuss about terms."

I made no fuss, but Miss Game made a great deal. She went back to St. Mary Abbotts' and talked so much about that and other places of worship in the neighbourhood that I saw she would never let us have her flat until she knew what our denomination was. When I mentioned casually that we belonged to the English Church it made a difference at once. It was then that she directed my attention to the drawing-room carpet. It should be swept, she said, from the door to the window, and from the wall to the fireplace, on account of the nap, and she looked at me anxiously.

"If necessary," I said, "I will sweep it myself."

I think she thought this showed a proper spirit; but she did not take me to particularly mean it, so I added: "Often I have had to do it," at which, Graham declared, she bounded away from us again. However, she came back.

"You'll have to have the chimneys cleaned, you know, before you leave. It doesn't cost much. And the windows washed —that's two shillings. The porter does it. Maids are not allowed to, at this height, by law."

"That's something," I said to Graham, "to write to mother."

"About the bath-room tank," Miss Game continued. "I don't know. You will have to fight it out with the landlord. He maintains I ought to clean it, and I maintain he ought to clean it. I've done it once, and he has done it once. It's five-and-six. You will have to do the best you can."

We bowed submissively.

"I know you'll want to have the window open in

the kitchen, but if you put it up from the bottom I believe the oven won't heat."

"Thanks for telling us," I said. "I do hate a slow oven."

Miss Game stared. "The kitchen eight-day I should expect you to wind up every Wednesday night with your own hands. And if it stops there is a very good little man ——"

"Does it often stop?" I asked anxiously, and Graham said:

"There's no occasion for you to worry about the clock, madam. I'm rather fond of playing with clocks. It will be a pleasure to me to keep it in order."

It gave Miss Game a bad fright, but it was quite successful. She was silent with alarm for a moment.

"However," she said, "I'm not bound to leave you a kitchen clock, am I? I think we had better let it run down. It has been in my family since 1800."

Graham looked regretful, but consented.

"I should keep a closet," said Miss Game, and we said: "Why, of course," and she went on to particularise about the house-linen. She was far from open-handed in house-linen; and I had to ask her, diffidently, more than once, how we were to go to the wash. In spite of the most portentous signs from Graham I fought for four pairs of sheets, and got them

—she expected us to do, on some rotary principle, with three.

"Blankets," she said; "two to each bed is all I ought to give you; but I can't put them away on account of the moths, so I'll leave the rest between the mattresses."

"Implying," said Graham carefully, "that we may use them when necessary. We might give them a shake now and then."

"I shouldn't have any objection. Eight towels——"

"But we both *love* towels!" I said in despair.

"I was going to say 'are all I've got.' You see, I'm not——"

"A brother and sister. No," I said. "And, of course, if you haven't got them we can buy them."

"Brooms and brushes," said Miss Game, "I ought not by rights to leave out, but if you will promise to take care of them ——"

I really couldn't and wouldn't. I turned.

"No," I said firmly. "I will not promise to take care of your brooms and brushes. You can put them in the closet."

"There isn't room," said Miss Game calmly.

"Then would it be possible," contributed Graham innocently, "to take them with you?"

"To the South of France! No, I must stand my chance," said Miss Game. "One thing more — the fender. Do you use Home Glow polish?"

"I don't know what I use — in England," I said,
and I didn't care. I was getting quite worked up.
I could feel Graham's eye upon me, and saw the flat
disappearing, as it were, out of the window; but I
didn't care.

"We use no other," said Graham boldly.

"I am very particular about that. And, oh!
the most important thing of all; Towse — who let
you in. You would have to take Towse — she
knows about everything. I never let without
Towse."

"*Can* that be her beautiful name!" exclaimed
Graham, and was going to take Towse with out-
stretched arms; but I stepped in.

"I don't think there will be any difficulty about
Towse," I said coldly.

It was much the more proper way of dealing
with Miss Game. As I told Graham afterwards, she
would have produced an aged relation next, and we
should have had to take that, too — and take care
of it.

"In that case," said Miss Game, giving us a last
scrutiny, "I think I will let to you. I really want to
get to the South of France."

Graham, I have no doubt, would have fallen upon
her neck; but I kept my head, though it was exactly, oh, exactly, what we wanted.

"If we take it," I said, "you must arrange to put

all those things" — I indicated the menagerie on the mantelpiece.

"Where?" asked Miss Game breathlessly.

"In the closet," said I.

She said she would with such satisfaction that we always wondered under what circumstances she was robbed of a mantel animal, and which one it was.

"Old maids," remarked Graham, "will love anything," but he did not say that until Miss Game was safely in the South of France.

CHAPTER III

I NEVER shall forget the day we moved in, and the young man came from the agent. It was one of the first things we noticed, the number of young men in London who come on different errands and seem to have a legitimate excuse for ringing the bell and being taken into different parts of your flat. They are often quite smooth and sleek, with black coats and un-impeachable collars, like the young man from the agent, or they may wear respectable billy-cocks like the young man about the electric light, or billy-cocks on the back of the head like the young man about the gas cooking-stove, or merely cloth caps like the young man from Barker's by mistake; but they all have little narrow books sticking out of their coat-pockets; and they all come and ring, and worry Towse, who drats them behind their backs, though they treat her with the utmost respect. They seem to form a class by themselves, a kind of sub-profession so small to be so respectable, and so respect-able to be so small; and one wonders whether they stay in it always, and how much you can be when you get to the top. They look finished and accom-plished, as if their purpose in life was entirely achieved in becoming the young men from the agent; and they take themselves as seriously as possible. Very likely they marry, and bring up funny little respectable families in some funny little respectable suburb; and if so, what are *they* when they grow up? Perhaps they find an opening in sharpening pencils for their fathers.

The young man from the agent came when Graham was out. Towse showed him into the drawing-room, and didn't wait, as I was there; and he said in a cultivated voice that he had come in connection with the inventory. His manner was very grave, and thoughtful, and considerate. I asked him to sit down.

"I thought Miss Game made the inventory," I said. "She told me she would."

"She did, miss. At least, Mr. Mott made it for her, on her behalf, this morning. Here it is. Mr. Mott has sent me to go over it with you, on your behalf."

"I wish you would tell me what for?" I said. I was completely tired out after moving in, and when you feel like that, to have people coming making trouble on your behalf is ridiculous.

"For your protection, miss," said the young man from the agent.

"From Miss Game?" I asked. The idea of wanting protection from Miss Game seemed foolish. "She doesn't seem a person likely to inflict an injury."

The young man coughed and looked pained. "You see, miss, you have taken over from Miss Game, and Miss Game will have to take over from you, so it would be more satisfactory to both parties. You ought to know what you're responsible for, now, oughtn't you?"

"Miss Game's inventory will tell me that," I said; "and she knows what is here much better than I do. And I have confidence in Miss Game. She would never put down things that weren't there."

"My principal," said the young man with an air of strict integrity, "wouldn't do such a thing as that either, miss. But it's always considered more satisfactory ——"

"Tell me at once," I said. "Is it a custom of the country? If it is a custom of the country I have no desire to dispute it."

"It is, miss. Then shall I begin here?"

"Certainly," I replied. I was not going to have Graham say anything more about the good taste of not objecting to the customs of the country, whatever you may think of them; but I made up my mind that if this young man was so anxious to check the inventory, it was probably his business; and he could do it himself. So he began.

"Drawin'-room," he announced formally. "Brass handle to door, ditto lock."

"Well, of course," I couldn't help saying. "It

wouldn't open without one. You needn't put that down."

"Mr. Mott has put it down, miss, on the other party's behalf. Is it in good order?"

"You might just look."

"It would be more satisfactory ——"

"If I looked? Then it is in good order. No, it isn't — there's a screw out."

"Ah!" said the young man reflectively. "One screw out," and he put it down. "White lace curtains. Right. Spring roller blind. Does it work?"

"Try it," I said from the sofa; and it did.

"In perfect working order," he said, and wrote it down. "Cushions?"

"Nine," I counted.

"Nine. Six large, three small — one slightly soiled."

"I wouldn't call it soiled," I said. "Would you? A little gone in the colour."

"It's what *we* call soiled," he replied firmly, and put something down.

"Carpet on floor," he went on. "Three skins, various. Any holes in the carpet? Worn places?"

"I could only find that out by living with it," I said, "but it looks a pretty good carpet."

The young man walked abstractedly over it.

"In perfect order," he said, "except possibly under the sofa where you are sitting, miss, which I can't see. Perhaps ——"

"You must excuse me," I said. "I'm tired."

"Electric light fixtures," he tapped the globes with his pencil. "Cornice — chipped anywhere? Paper and paint?"

"If you look to the left of the mantelpiece," I said, closing my eyes, "immediately behind the scuttle, you will find a tear in the paper as big as a shilling. And I didn't do it."

"Quite right, miss; it's there. It's more satisfactory if you notice what you can." He seemed really relieved. "Gentleman's arm chair, lady's ditto."

"Not calendered," I said, remembering that we had settled it that way, but the young man put nothing down.

"Wouldn't you call them fairly fresh?" he asked, and I said:

"Oh, yes, fairly fresh."

"Forty-two mantel ornaments," he proceeded.

"Thirty in the closet!" I told him.

"Oh, she has locked them up this time!" the young man remarked. "On your behalf, miss, I should say a very good thing, too."

"I made her," I replied, with dignity. "All the animals but that pair of yellow cats which I thought looked cheerful.'

"But she has put forty-two down," he informed me gravely.

"Never mind. Write 'in the closet,'" I said.

"Claimed in the closet," repeated the young man, writing, but he looked doubtful. "It would be more satisfactory ——"

"No," I said, "we can't count them. She took the key, and she is in the South of France — I hope."

The young man looked at me with as much of a twinkle as his profession of young man from the agent would let him.

"She is a peculiar lady, miss," he admitted, "in some respects," and went hastily on to the furniture and fire-irons. He was very patient and persistent; and whenever I wanted him to look for himself he told me it would be more satisfactory; and whenever I wanted to skip or take things for granted he reminded me that he was there on my behalf. I can't say I gave him much help; but gradually he seemed to get interested; and it was he who got the blankets out from between the mattresses,— he would count them, and Towse was having her tea,— and he who found out that there were only five odd plates in the kitchen instead of six, and something funny about the carving fork. I left him at last; but from my own room where I had gone to lie down I heard him rustling in the linen closet; and he knocked at the door before he went, to say he hoped I would excuse him disturbing me, but I was "short" of one pillow-slip and a duster. He thought — as he was there on my behalf — it would be more satisfactory. Then he pushed the list under my door for me to sign, and I signed it; and then he went away, and never was I more thankful.

All the same, I thought it was quite an experience, and I related it to Graham, word for word; but he wasn't as amused as I thought he would be.

"You shouldn't go signing things," he said.

"Not when it's the custom of the country?" I asked, scoring off him badly, and left him to get my hat.

We had moved in, but Towse was the only person who had any provisions; which she must have inherited from Miss Game. So we went out to buy things, went out to meet the delightful necessities attached to being householders in London. It sounds a simple thing to be, but it was really complicated with emotion and excitement in a way I don't know whether I can describe. We went out into the general streets to take our share of the common supply of the wonderful city, to establish ourselves among the fundamentals of life in the very citadel of the imagination, to buy butter in Mecca. There is a housekeeping relish in life anywhere, but when you add to it the joys of the faithful who approach from Minnebiac ——!

Our first essential was a grocer, and we naturally chose one with a post office. Not all grocers have post offices in London, but nearly all post offices have grocers, so much so that I shall always associate the catching of the American mail with a smell of cheese and coffee. It gives the stranger a false idea of grocery custom. What he thinks is the grocer doing business is nine times out of ten only the King doing stamps or issuing money orders, or taking parcels at the very last minute for the country post. I don't know how the grocer's nerves stand it, never knowing whether he has a customer or whether she is only after post cards or the directory; but I suppose he is supported by British phlegm. When I think of Jim Jex, where we always deal at home — Jim would be out of his mind.

I am not able to say whether it is the grocery that takes in the post office or the post office that takes in the grocery, whether they go shares, on the understanding that they recommend each other, or whether the Government simply pre-empts the left side going in of any clean, respectable-looking grocery, and says: "Out with your sugar barrels; I am coming here!" in which case the right would probably date from Queen Elizabeth, and might apply to the city as a whole or, say, to the parish of Marylebone only. It is the sort of thing one would expect, somehow, in the parish of Marylebone only. Very few people would start in groceries on our side under those conditions; but in England I noticed they give in dreadfully to the Government; I suppose they always have. Why it is so generally a grocery is another thing I might have found out. One would think a book-shop more suitable for partnership with a post office; but no doubt there are not enough of them, and bakeries are here to-day and to-morrow cast into the oven; and public-houses of course they couldn't; and dry-goods would be unfair to gentlemen, especially during sales. But no district, however humble, could do without a grocery. Both men and women enter them freely, and the British constitution being founded upon bacon, and the world what it is as to condiments, they never vanish in the night. I think these are quite likely reasons, but anybody who wants to know definitely has only to ask at the counter.

There is nothing so obliging as a young man in a grocery shop in England, especially if you have newly come to live in the neighbourhood, no matter how little you want at a time. Graham and I ordered hardly more than half a pound of anything. Having heard so much of the corruption of British groceries we thought it better not to commit ourselves too far. But we were never so obliged in our lives as by that young man with his hair parted in the middle, all in his acceptance of the small favours that fell from us, for which he thanked us so unremittingly that we didn't know where to look. Whenever we spoke he said "Thank you," and whenever we paused. "Thank you" gladly when we said we would take it, and "Thank you" sadly when we said we wouldn't. His politeness was really beyond all bearing. He leaned toward us on the counter like one receiving a sacred trust; and before I could say whether the bottle I wanted was of oil or of vinegar he was out with his thank-you, and his pencil had it down. He offered us a choice of brands in everything with a deference one might have expected to be kept for the Royal Family. He hung upon our preference with a golden smile, and when we could think of nothing more and he had to take our address, he looked up insinuatingly and said: "*And what name would you like, miss?*" as if he had a selection to offer me there too. When I thought of Jim Jex —

"Fresh-ground, Miss Mary? Why, sure. Not quite so good as last time? You don't say so! Well now, that's too bad. I know the best ain't any too good for you — can't have *you* complainin'. I'll see it's all right this time. An' how's the folks?"

Thinking of Jim, I regularly despised the young man in Church Street, Kensington.

The behaviour of the fishmonger's assistant was much more independent. He let us wander about among his cod and crab for some time before he took any notice of us, and then his manner was rather short. It may have been because we asked the names of too many of the species he displayed — there may be a subtle affront to a fishmonger in this — or it may have been as Graham said, because of being obliged to repeat daily that his whole stock had come up from Grimsby that morning, as he told us. That, Graham thought, might have a bad effect upon the best disposition, and it may be so. But he seemed so ruffled when I asked him what a lemon-sole was and why it was so called — he said it was just the lemon kind of sole and generally so referred to because it came cheaper — that I thought I ought to explain.

"You see," I said, "we are from the other side of the Atlantic where there is a difference in fish. Nothing like this ever comes out of Lake Ontario."

His manner changed at once. People will always forgive you for mere ignorance.

"Would that be salt water or fresh?" he asked, a very intelligent question in the connection; and when I explained to him further that in Minnebiac, lake salmon came round with a bell in a wheelbarrow, and you got it for ten cents a pound, he smiled outright and said it must be a very desirable neighbourhood, though he could not have meant for himself. The great thing in England is to confess your deficiencies and divergences. They just love being kind to you then; and the fishmonger's assistant at once told us the names of almost everything that was lying down or hanging up about us, including ptarmigan and Bordeaux pigeons, which were, strictly speaking, beyond the bounds of our enquiry. In the end we bought the Bordeaux pigeons because they looked so neat and comfortable in a box with paper edging, and he said they were considered beautiful for lunch, and for breakfast chose plaice, under his prompting.

"I can't advise you better than plaice," said the fishmonger's assistant. "It eats very refined, plaice does."

Language in England is a great joy. The people themselves take pleasure in using it. I mean real language, like the fishmonger's, not mere words, such as are current with us. Graham says it is the result of Board Schools. If that is the case, Board Schools have diffused a great deal of happiness. It makes one feel as if one's own opportunities had been poor; but Graham says not to mind, we are a young country, making vigorous progress in every direction; and in the end we may talk, too, to some purpose.

We shopped up and down Church Street and up and down the High, we ordered our milk and our butter and our daily paper; and it was all as good as a play and better, because we were playing too. We were sorry Miss Game had left out so much; there were brooms and brushes I simply longed to buy; and to be obliged to pass a tinsmith's with indifference filled us with regret. They make small purchases very interesting for you in England by the importance they attach to them. In comparison our retail trade is about as interesting as a market report in a newspaper. Graham, who must find the moral of a thing if he dies for it, says the Kensington way is right; and that all the primitive transactions of life have the old forgotten sweetness of function yet, if one just has the luck to stumble on it as we did in Church Street. He is still enjoying his indignation at being asked fourpence for an apple. We carried our chrysanthemums with us from their corner shop because we wanted to go on smelling them, and finally we came in out of the rain because that also in the end is what you always have to do over there. We found the flat full of the comfort of the Bordeaux pigeons, which Towse had interpreted for supper, and a good fire which made us remember we had forgotten Miss Game's "Home Glow"; but it was not till the brown-paper parcels began to come tumbling up over one another in the lift that the delightful fact fully came home to me.

"Oh, Graham!" I exclaimed from the bottom of my heart as the boy arrived with the little bundles of kindling from the grocer's; "we *are* part of it!"

CHAPTER IV

I am longing to get to the really important things
that happened, but I am afraid if I do not mention
Towse now she may not come in at all. She never
would come in without knocking — I mean at the
drawing-room or the dining-room door, because she
began young as a scullery-maid and could not get
over the modesty that belongs to that rank in life.
It made one feel like a conspirator receiving friendly
warning; and I was glad to find that it wasn't a
custom of the country and that I could ask her not
to. But I might ask and ask, she would do it, entering with a smile of stolid apology which suggested,
nevertheless, that she was only doing her duty, and
conveyed at the same time the hopelessness, the
perfect hopelessness, of trying to change Towses
when they have once made up their minds what is
the proper way for them to behave. Then she would
cautiously back out, manœuvring a little to find the
door, like a liner leaving the dock, though there was
really plenty of space to turn in, except perhaps in
the dining-room. And I must treat of Towse, because I have been told by several people who saw her

that there are very few of her kind left, even in England. Everything that is almost extinct must be taken seriously for that reason alone, and preserved if possible; and, as far as I can, I will.

Towse lived out. There was a small division of the flat that would have enabled her to live in, but she had a husband as well as daughters by her first, and she felt it her duty to give him his bite in the morning. I don't remember her exact address, but it was rooms somewhere off the Earl's Court Road, wonderfully near and convenient to the early morning 'bus which passed the corner at exactly the right time to let her get her fire up. He worked at the London Docks — both the daughters by the first were married — and had to go by the Underground, starting ten minutes earlier; and often I used to wake when there was nothing in the room but the drab window-curtain, lighter and colder at the edges, of the London dawn, and think, "Now Towse is giving him his bite. Now he is getting off for his train. He doesn't kiss her, but she says: 'Don't forget your baccy,' which comes to the same thing. Now she is tying on her bonnet and locking up. Now I wonder if she has caught that 'bus!" And in exactly twenty minutes I would hear the latch-key in the door, and then I could sleep again in security if I liked, knowing that Towse was in possession.

Above all things you had that feeling with Towse,

that when she was in the kitchen you were perfectly safe. I would defy any undesirable person to get past her if she answered the door. She was a solid wall of defence, impregnable, immovable; the only chance would have been to blow her up. Errand-boys she held in aversion, with stray cats and organ-grinders and other irregularities of life; she would be curtly just to them, but she looked at them with a suspicious eye, especially if they delivered newspapers, and always had some advice ready for them beginning with "Mind." Telegraph messengers, or anything in uniform, stood a better chance with her; but she was very brief with them all, and I was thankful sometimes that Graham was grown up. She was delightful to him, fearfully respectful and self-obliterating and inclined to curtsey; but if he had been ten years younger she would have had quite a different eye on him. And no boy ever answered Towse back, or did anything but take good heed and warning and use the mat soberly, not even whistling, as a rule, before he was well out of hearing of her. The conviction that sparkled in each of her faithful eyes that a boy was a worthless, useless, troublesome, necessary piece of human furniture made a moral force of her, when she looked at him, that no boy could fail to recognise, or ever did. She knew how to put them in their place. Our Eliza, in Minnebiac, could not even keep her proper distance with them.

Towse had no great idea of men either; I never
could find out why, for both her married lives seemed
to have been quite satisfactory. She would talk with
a good deal of proper pride about her second, and
about her first very freely too. I always thought
that a first husband was buried beyond reference,
but Towse taught me better. She told me a great
many of his opinions, especially about the bringing
up of children, and them Irish; and I knew that
tomatoes was a thing he could not abide. He was an
under-gardener, and he often took more than was good
for him; but he would go to bed as quiet as a lamb
when it was in him, and never did anybody any
harm but himself. He was humble under anything
that might be said to him for his good, and he died as
peaceable as a baby. I know Towse thought a great
deal of him, because one day when I was opening a
box of Nephitos roses that came by post from the
country, I turned round and found her wiping her
eyes with her apron, and she explained that that was
the way her first always packed white roses to go by
post for the family; and it did take her back so. She
was extremely true to them both, but her fidelity
to her first had a sentiment and a sorrow which her
second had, of course, no right to share, at all events,
for the present.

But Towse's second had the advantage of being her
romance. She told me about it one day when we

were going over the things from the wash. She had known him ever since he was so high, and they had been sweet'earts, "if you will excuse me, miss," at school. Then he enlisted and went on foreign service, and she thought no more about him.

"Because, if you will excuse me, miss," she said in all modesty, "he never was as much to me as I was to 'im, miss."

So it gave her no trouble whatever to marry the under-gardener. Time passed and she buried him, and the daughters, being brought up very strict, got good places and good 'usbands, too, if I would excuse her. Towse never would speak to me of love or matrimony without apologising; I longed to tell her that I didn't really mind. And Towse herself was out at service again, when one day the regiment came back.

"Not as I knowed it, 'm — miss — though I daresay it was in the papers," said Towse.

"And you met him, Towse, walking in the Park in uniform of a Sunday afternoon, very sunburnt; I know you did!" I cried.

"No, 'm — no, miss. I might 'ave, but I didn't. 'E come with the milk," she replied, as if she had not yet got over the astonishment of it.

"And you recognised him!"

"No, miss. 'E reckonised me," said Towse, beaming. "'Why, Louiser, is that you?' he said,

Louiser being my maiden name, miss. Them was his very words. And I said pretty distant, I said: 'What if it is Louiser?' and he said: 'Don't you know Tom?'"

"Had he lost an arm?" I asked breathlessly. Somehow I thought to be delivering milk he must have lost something.

"''E stood there as sound as you or me, miss. And that very evenin' he ast me again, miss."

"And did you accept him at once, Towse?"

"No, 'm — no, miss; that I did not. 'Go along,' I said; 'you're old enough to know better.' But there it was, miss. 'E come twice a day with the milk, mornin' and evenin', and every time he'd 'ave his answer yes or no. It wore me out, miss, it did reely."

"But — but it has been satisfactory, I hope, Towse."

"Yes, miss, I've got nothing to complain of, not to compare with what many 'as. He's a quiet, respectable man, and as often as not when I go 'ome of an evening I find him comfortable in bed; and as fond of my married daughters, miss, as if they'd a-bin 'is own."

Sometimes in those early days when we had not so much to think about Graham and I would argue which husband Towse was most faithful to; and a little thing decided it, to our minds, in favour of the under-gardener. We were agreeing that we hated calling her Towse, like that, as if she were a man. Miss Game had handed her on to us under that name, and she herself seemed cheerful and contented to answer to it; but we didn't like it, and we couldn't get used to it.   I knew it was a custom of the country, and one was familiar with it of course in English novels, where it looks arrogant and nice, in a literary sense; but it is different in real life. In Canada we still manage to observe whether a servant is a man or a woman; we are not differentiated so far from them that we can't see that, and we thought it barbarous not to.

"'By the Ilyssus there was no Wragg, poor thing!'" said Graham, who often remarked that there was one great, hopeful and satisfying feature about the English — you could always quote their own authors against them. Graham thinks that to recognise a defect, even nationally, is the most interesting stage toward overcoming it, and that one reason why you enjoy life so much in England is because they are always walking round themselves there and suggesting improvements. But that has nothing to do with Towse.

"She is too old for Louiser," I said.

"Much," said Graham. "But why not 'Mrs.'? Ask her if she wouldn't prefer 'Mrs.' It's hers by law, twice over. Tell her she might as well go

without her apron as without her proper title. Say
that we find it indecent and illegal. Tell her it
hurts our feelings."

"I wish you would!" I said. "She may reply that
she doesn't like being called above herself. She would
never dare to answer you in that way."

"No," said Graham, "I can't. I'm beginning to
know my place, too. But if she does you might tell
her that in the East a cook is called 'Kalifa,' or the
skilled one. Ask her if she would object to being
called 'Kalifa, or the skilled one.' You may say I
have set my heart on it."

So one day when we were quite sympathetic and
I hadn't brought a dripping umbrella into the kitchen
for a long time, I said: "Towse, we can't bear to call
you Towse any longer."

She looked frightened, and replied: "Why, miss,
whatever is the objection?"

"There isn't any objection," I said, for in England
an objection is a very serious thing to have; "there's
a prejudice. We want to call you 'Kalifa, or the
skilled one,' as they do in the East. Do you mind?"

"Oh, miss!" she said, "it sounds like the name of
a cat."

"Does it?" I asked; "but it's really a compliment,
Towse. Think of it — 'Kalifa, or the skilled one.'"

She said nothing, but put some plates on the dresser
in order to turn her back on the suggestion.

"Compliments is more than I can expect at my age, miss; and to hear you say 'Kalifa, or the skilled one' I couldn't ever get used to think you was a-speakin' to me!"

"Well, never mind," I said hurriedly, because she was feeling for her apron. "What we really want is to call you Mrs. Towse. Towse is illegal and it hurts our feelings, and we don't think it's proper respect to — to you at your age, Towse."

Towse smiled broadly — it was like the sun coming out.

"That ain't the law, miss, if you'll excuse me; but how could you be expected to know the rights of it in England? Mrs. Towse I once was, but can't ever expect to be again, miss, not since I married my second. But nobody can say a word agin the Towse without the Mrs., miss, which I ain't denyin' don't rightly belong to it; and havin' charred all my first's lifetime, miss, I got used to it, and not bein' one to be fond of change I didn't make none, miss, when I married again, not so far as mistresses was concerned, if it's just the same to you, miss."

"Certainly," I said feebly. "All right, Towse. But what is the name of your second?"

"Bargus, miss."

Graham when I told him said it was a kind of bigamy backwards on Towse's part, and both of us found it difficult to remember whether it was her first or her second that was dead, until we had actually seen Bargus. Towse asked as a favour whether she might cook his dinner for him in the kitchen of a Sunday, that being the only day of the week on which he could get a hot one, and of course we said she could. And well do I remember the first Sunday he came and my embarrassment. She being up to her elbows in something I just went to the flat door myself.

"Oh, come in, Bargus!" I said; "Towse is in the kitchen."

He did not reproach me by so much as a look; but if he spoke to Towse afterwards it was no more than she deserved.

Oh, Towse was a dear comfort — and such an honest soul! In that matter of the Sunday dinner, for example, we always supposed, of course, that it came out of the pantry, that Bargus, in a quiet way, dined with us on Sundays. Until once just before he arrived, I went into the kitchen and found Towse lifting a savoury leg of pork out of its pot, which I knew could not be for us, and a hurried glance discovered other foreign items upon the kitchen table. It was a little humiliating; we had been thinking Towse so shrewd to dine her husband on Sundays at our expense; and Graham was indignant, and said Towse's private larder couldn't go on.

"What's good enough for us is good enough for Bargus," he said.

"Well," I said, "if you like to interfere with Towse's principles you can stop it."

Then there was the shilling a week I gave her for a special purpose. There is no use in concealing what it was — it was bath-money. Towse had been scrupulously brought up to wash her face, but she was a large person and the flat was a small flat, and, in short, I thought that a complete warm bath once a week would be good for us all, and that the shilling would put her in mind of it. I called it bath-money to save her feelings, as she was accustomed to speak of beer-money; and I am sure she used it once. But the second week she said it had given her the lumbago cruel, and if it was just the same to me she would leave off the practice. How many would have gone on taking the shilling and not taking the bath? It was not a thing you could point to.

CHAPTER V

We had no relatives at all in England, or even, as
is more likely with Canadians, in Scotland or Ireland.
Father came out with his whole family, including his
grandfather and two cousins; he was transplanted,
as he often said, root and branch, and mother's
great-grandfather had built his own log house on the
Bay of Quinté. We were strangers really, though we
knew the flag so well, and had sung "Rule Britannia"
since we could sing anything; such strangers that I
felt sometimes as if we had rifled the flag out of Westminster Abbey, and found the song in a book of
Runic rhymes. There was not a soul, except Towse,
upon whom we had any claim; but there were various
people we had known in Ottawa whom we hoped to
see again; and we had several letters of introduction,
one or two from Lord Coddis himself, our Governor-
General at home, who had more than once said what
a great respect he had for father. Certainly nobody
could have been more charming than the Coddises
were to us always. People often said it made a great
bond with the Throne, the Coddises' kindness of
heart. Of course, they were not without enemies;
certain Members' wives had their remarks to make;

but mother, who was devoted to Lady Coddis and had been in her bedroom on the simplest terms, declared she was as natural and unaffected as anyone she had ever met.　Lord Coddis was a soldier really — Brigadier-General Lord Coddis of Kafiristan, C.B., in full.　He had taken Kafiristan, which was thought to be impregnable, by direct assault, with great gallantry, for the British, but the Kafiristanese had impaired his efficiency by shooting him, so that he had to resign the army;　and as he had rank and wealth already, his country felt bound to provide him with an occupation, which was all he asked, and sent him to be our Governor-General.　No one could have shown greater gratitude.　He brought out a most beautiful Staff;　nothing like it had been seen for years.　He gave the most charming parties, spent twice as much as his pay came to, and did a great deal to revive the Canadian game of lacrosse.　We simply loved seeing him open and prorogue Parliament — the outriders alone, as Graham used to say, were worth the whole price of the entertainment — he did it so handsomely;　and I have often heard father remark that his head was as good as his heart; and there was no reason why he shouldn't be in the confidence of his Cabinet.

Well, Lord Coddis gave us one or two letters, and you will believe we took care of them;　and Mrs. Fullerton gave us another — she was the wife of

General Fullerton, the British officer commanding our Militia. Her great idea was to revive the hand-loom industries of Nova Scotia, but she was otherwise quite unassuming and sprightly and nice; and she said we simply *must* meet Mrs. Jerome Jarvis — she was such a character; and, of course, we were delighted. We knew she was a character, her picture was constantly in the London fashion weeklies, and I had even seen it in the Society Supplement of the New York Sunday papers. She was prominent in all sorts of ways, but chiefly as a character; novelists were supposed constantly to put her in. Mr. Jerome Jarvis's picture was never in the papers, though he was living, and important in the City. That was all that was generally said about him, though it was sometimes added that he was devoted to his fascinating wife. I remember mother saying when she read that: "Then I suppose the poor thing has *some* home life," and when we asked which poor thing, she answered darkly: "Oh, well, I daresay it cuts both ways!"

It promised delightfully to meet Mrs. Jerome Jarvis, a person widely renowned for no apparent reason, which was so much more subtle than being celebrated for any of the ordinary ones; and our letter to her was the first little chip we threw out on the great vague, friendly, impenetrable ocean of London.

We chose a wet day because we thought there would be a better chance of finding her in; though, as Graham said, if people in England made a practice of staying in on wet days! However, you never can tell, and we thought she might be, like mother, far from strong. Nobody, we speculated, could be such a character and be very robust; nobody ever was. Graham said she would be lying on a sofa with "Amiel's Journal," and one hand playing in the fur of a large Persian cat. I asked why Amiel, and why the cat, but, of course, he couldn't explain; he never can. We would have to excuse her getting up, but we would understand somehow that she never did, even when the Prime Minister came to tea; and she would immediately proceed to say several brilliant and remarkable things one after the other.

"We shall never remember them all," said Graham, "so you try to seize the first and I'll stick to the second and so on; and when we get home we'll write them down. Matthew Arnold praised her intellectual qualities as a child, Mrs. Fullerton told me, and Herbert Spencer frequently dined with her as a middle-aged women. It'll be a tax on two Canucks like us, Mary; but it'll be a treat. I only hope she'll be equal to seeing us."

It was pouring by the time our cab got to Rutland Gate, and we looked up more hopefully than ever at the windows behind which she was probably sitting, writing articles for the *Fortnightly*, or thinking of things to say. It was impossible that she should be out in such weather. We got quite wet paying the cabman.

"Are you sure you've brought the letter?" I said as Graham rang. To calm me he took it out of his pocket-book, and in a moment we were asking if Mrs. Jerome Jarvis was at home. It seemed to me that the man said "No, sir," almost before he had quite opened the door, so quickly that for an instant, while we dripped with disappointment, we stared at him.

"Well, when she comes in," said Graham, "you might give her this," and handed him the letter, while I produced cards.

"Yes, sir," said the man; "Mrs. Jarvis is 'unting in Leicestershire, sir," and the door closed.

We stood still while you might count three with the shock of it.

"Mrs. Jarvis is 'unting in Leicestershire," repeated Graham mechanically, and turned on me, the ideal shattered in his eyes. "Oh, come on, Mary!"

He put up his umbrella and gave me his arm, and we walked away together. There was no reason why a character shouldn't hunt in Leicestershire, but it couldn't be our character; and you might have felled us to the ground.

Next day I dashed to the door every time the postman came, but there never was anything from Mrs.

Jerome Jarvis, or the next day or the next, for nearly three weeks. We had almost stopped wondering about it when we heard from her — by telegram. It came in with the bacon in the morning; and as Graham was expecting one from a business man in Liverpool, we were in no hurry to open it. Then I read:

"Much regret bed fortnight bad neuritis do come my din.-party to-morrow for Roeboroughs' fancy ball hope see you my room after Jerome so much looking forward. — JANICE JARVIS."

"Read it again," said Graham, "and try to imagine the punctuation," which I did.

"Well," said Graham, "what do you think she means?"

"Why," I said, "she means to apologise for not having written before, and to ask us to dinner to-morrow night. It's quite clear."

"When her other guests," said Graham disapprovingly, "are going on to the Duchess of Roeborough's fancy dress ball?"

"Well?" I said.

"And she will be in her room and Jerome is so much looking forward. Why is Jerome so much looking forward?"

"Because she will be in her room," I said. "She can't say *she* is looking forward, you see, when she's in bed."

"Where she intends, apparently, to receive us afterwards."

"We've always heard she was a character. But she *can't* mean you," I deprecated.

"I don't see how I'm going to depend upon that."

"Well," I said, "it isn't anything so very dreadful. Some queen in history always did it."

"Contemporary queens don't," said Graham firmly; "and anyway ——"

"You didn't mind her on a sofa," I reminded him. "But of course, we can refuse."

"I think we'd better refuse," said Graham.

I was heart-broken to do it; but when Graham represented that he would be obliged either to sit by the bedside of a lady he had never seen before or to stay downstairs with the butler, I had no alternative. I myself was full of allowance for a character; I would have gone gladly; and so when a day or two later Mrs. Jerome Jarvis sent us an invitation to lunch I did not mention to Graham that it had come on a postcard. I thought "How nice and friendly"; but Graham will not always think what you want him to think.

We wondered very much, as we drove there, whom we should meet. Graham said he had no anticipations, but I noticed he had put on a becoming tie and was inclined to sit up straight and be absent-minded.

"Don't set your heart on the Archbishop of Canterbury," he said; and I said I wasn't, but there were a great many interesting and important people in England besides him.

"And it's exciting enough," I told Graham, "to know that we'll be the smallest toads in the puddle in any case."

He was not really indifferent; he pulled out his watch three times in a block in Knightsbridge and did not contradict me when I said it would be too fearful to be late. It was again a wet day; but the idea of keeping even the least distinguished of Mrs. Jerome Jarvis's friends waiting put us at last in such a fever that we abandoned our cab and walked out of the block to another. At last we arrived; and the same footman with the yellow-and-black striped waistcoat opened the door, as automatically as before, but wider; and we went in.

"Mrs. Jarvis isn't down yet," said the footman, which was a relief, for we were late — ten minutes, according to Mrs. Jarvis's clock. Nevertheless it did, as Graham said, make the perspiration dry up rather suddenly on the forehead. We were shown into a pleasant room with flowers in it, a large window, and a young man reading a newspaper. We have often wondered since who the young man was. He looked up from his newspaper as we came in, so we said "Good morning."

"Good morning," said he, and we saw that he had no wish to be uncivil. We were quite alone in the room and the clock was ticking. It was impossible to go on, with the young man reading a newspaper and the clock ticking like that, so I said: "It's raining."

"No — is it?" said he.

"Pouring," I said pleasantly. "The horse we had ——"

"I beg your pardon," said the young man. I glanced at Graham, but he had walked to the window and was standing like a post, looking out of it.

"The horse ——"

"Horse? Oh, yes, your horse ——"

"The horse in our cab slipped all over the street."

"Did he really!"

I don't know what made me think of a waiting-room except perhaps — well, that was what it was, wasn't it? And the way he fondled his newspaper. It seemed to me that it would be better manners to let him read and ignore the clock.

Presently he said of his own accord: "Here's Mrs. Jerome now!" but it wasn't Mrs. Jerome; it was a little girl and a little boy and the governess.

"Hullo, Patsy," said the young man. "Hullo, John!" And they both replied: "Hullo, Andy!" but came straight up to Graham and me and held out their hands.

"My proper name is Patricia," said the little girl; and the governess, who seemed to be dumb, smiled genially and nodded.

"Mother will be down in a minute," Patricia explained. "Will you come in to lunch?"

So we went in to lunch under the wing of Patricia; and thinking of all the interesting and important people there were in London besides the Archbishop of Canterbury I did not dare to meet Graham's eye.

"I think," said Patricia to me, "you'd better sit by mother — when she comes. I don't know where *you'd* better sit," she said to Graham. "Perhaps you'd like to sit by John."

"If you think we should get on," said Graham, "I should like to sit by you;" and Andy said dejectedly: "I don't suppose it matters where *I* sit." I am sure Andy was nice, though he did seem to think so little of himself; but we shall never know.

Then the door opened, and Mrs. Jerome Jarvis came in, like an exclamation. She was quite nice-looking and energetic and thin and young, and there is no word to describe her self-possession. I have thought since that she was exactly like mercury — if you cut her up into a million little bits each bit would continue to revolve upon itself. Whatever she did you saw she would never apologise, and whatever she said would just have to go on its merits. It did not seem to matter to her in the least that two strangers and Andy had come to lunch; but she did shake hands with us both, and gave us each a vivacious smile.

"In happy time!" she said to me; and "Don't get up, I pray!" to Graham, and "Morgen, Fräulein," to the governess, who was thus shown to be not dumb but German only, and "I'm famishing, William!" to the butler, and nodded to Andy. Then she stood up suddenly in her place and shut her eyes and said: "For what I am about to receive the Lord make me truly thankful. Did you say that to-day, duckies?"

"Must we ought to?" asked John. "When there's company?"

"But of *course!*" cried Mrs. Jarvis. "My life," she turned to me, "is simply ravaged; but I do like to see that they say their little graces."

"Never mind, mummie," said Patricia, "we will afterwards."

I could not think of anything to say, and neither, it seemed, could Graham, for he didn't say it; and as to Andy he was simply lunching, and went on with it.

"So you come from Canada," said Mrs. Jarvis. "John, son, do you know where Canada is?"

"No," said John, son.

"I know," said Patricia. "There are bears there. Are there bears there?"

"Beautiful bears!" said Graham.

"Ever get any?" asked Andy suddenly; but I

don't think Graham heard him, which was a pity, for Andy did not speak again, except to William.

"And you know the Fullertons?" continued Mrs. Jarvis.

"Yes," I said, "we do. Does —does Patricia know the Fullertons?"

"I do if John does," said Patricia.

"Nonsense!" said Mrs. Jarvis. "They're grown-ups. How can babies know grown-ups? Julia Fullerton is intelligent but superficial, and Alfred Fullerton deep but dull, don't you think?"

I said the stupidest possible thing. "I think they think you like them," I said.

"Oh, so I do!" but Mrs. Jarvis's eye wandered away from the subject, down the table to Patricia. I saw it soften as she looked at Patricia, and I do not agree with Graham, who said that she looked at Patricia in order that it should soften.

"Angel," she said, "what are you having? Have you got what you like?"

"No," replied Patricia. "I'd like some ham."

"Ham, sweetheart? So bad for the —for the — what is ham bad for? I'm sure it is bad for something. Just the tiniest scrap, then, William. And did you both have your sleeps, sweetmeats?"

"We didn't sleep a wink," said John, letting the milk-pudding run out of his suspended spoon, "and we both had the awfullest dreams."

"Oh, I say!" said Andy, so he did speak once again.

"How could you possibly have dreams if you didn't sleep?" asked Mrs. Jarvis, and winked delightedly at Graham. "Tell us your dreams."

"Well, p'raps we slept a little bit. I've forgot my dream, but it was about an efalun — no, that was my night-before-last dream. It was worse than an efalun, but I forget it."

"Your memory seems to be going early," said Mrs. Jarvis. "Who says motor for this afternoon?"

"I say motor. Can we take Bowser?" asked Patricia. "And you, too, darling?"

"Not Bowser, he makes you jump about too much. And not me, indeed. I'm going to pay visits in the carriage at a quarter-past three."

Our hostess said it very distinctly, looking at the flowers in the middle of the table.

"What are you pouting those pretty lips for, Muggins?" she asked Patricia. "She named herself Muggins, after a nurse she loved with all her little soul," Mrs. Jarvis said to me. "Nurse died."

"I want some soda-water," said Muggins.

"Oh, not soda-water! So lowering!"

"What's 'lowering,' darling?" asked John.

"Lowering is going down, down, down till you can't see yourself without a microscope," his mother told him. "Not a drop of soda-water, my heart. But you may have five drops of Malvern."

"Six," said Muggins; and Mrs. Jarvis looked at me with a smile of enjoyment, and said:

"Greedy girl!"

It seemed to me by that time that if nothing was done to prevent it Mrs. Jerome Jarvis would have an extraordinary recollection of our lunch with her, and I looked hopelessly over at Graham, who evidently felt the same thing, for he made a violent plunge into conversation by asking her what she thought of the new Imperialism.

"Mostly rot!" said Mrs. Jarvis. "I've no patience with the Colonies, wanting this, that, and the other thing, telling us what to do. Teaching their grandmothers to suck eggs! Andy, how *can* you let her have cheese?"

Andy said nothing, and we, too, recognised, though rather late, that it was not necessary for anybody to say anything. I saw the perception pass over Graham's face, and received it telepathically. All would have been over almost immediately then; but Andy unfortunately took an apple.

"Now, duckies," continued Mrs. Jarvis, who had not paused, "who do you think asked about you last night? Whoever, ever, ever do you think? Guess!"

They guessed happily for some time. John among other persons guessed Bowser, at which Mrs. Jarvis said to me: "He *is* going to be a genius, don't you think?"

"Quite wrong — wrong — wrong! The Queen! The sweet, gracious, beautiful Queen! And she remembered your name, Patricia — think of that!"

I hope Patricia thought of it; we did, certainly. It was charming, Graham afterwards admitted, to be lunching with a little girl whose name the Queen had remembered. It gave me a funny little thrill, as if one had stepped by accident quite near the Royal heart of England, which had always before beaten for us in a fairy tale far away. But it was impossible to tell Mrs. Jerome Jarvis such a thing as that; she might have said it was rot. So we sat as silent as before, and I am afraid our hostess must have thought Canada a country which produces very dull people.

Before Andy finished his apple Mrs. Jarvis mentioned the carriage again and a quarter-past three, so she must have thought them rather stupid, too. Yet she seemed quite surprised when we said good-bye as quickly as we could in the hall. "Aren't you coming up to have some coffee?" she said, "and see Patricia do her little dance?" but of course how could we? It was five minutes past three then. She really meant to be kind, however. When I thanked her for having us to lunch, she said: "Delighted! All in the day's work," most cordially; Graham could not deny it. And she accompanied us to the door herself, and said we could always catch her at lunch; we had only to drop her a postcard the day

F

before, and blew us a kiss as we went down the steps.

"That's something to remember," said Graham to me in the cab, "if ever we are in need of a meal."

We were silent for some time as we went along among the horses' heads past the Park, thinking about our experience, and whether — at least I was — whether it was common.

"What a lively person — Mrs. Jarvis," I ventured at last.

"Highly kinetic over a limited area," replied Graham absently. "Like things that dance over ponds. But what I am wondering is why ——."

"Matthew Arnold?" I divined.

"Exactly. And why ——?"

"Herbert Spencer ——?"

"Well, why?" said Graham.

"Oh, I don't know!" I replied, and indeed I did not. "Perhaps neither of them really did, or perhaps they didn't particularly mean it. But she *is* a character."

"Oh, yes!" said Graham.

"And I can perfectly understand her picture being in the papers," I went on — "especially, somehow, in the New York Sunday ones."

"I know what you mean," said Graham. "But —have we any more introductions, Mary, to characters?"

"I don't know," I said; "but if we have ——"

"Let's lose them," said Graham, which, of course, was the merest foolish impulse on his part; and nothing would have induced me to do it.

CHAPTER VI

THE moral of Mrs. Jerome Jarvis was, of course, that while introductions are as useful and delightful in England as anywhere else, it is better not to have them to people who are already too much engaged, or too prominent for any reason. Much better. Otherwise it gives one a last straw kind of feeling which there is no necessity, as one goes through life, Graham says, ever to have. There is a good deal of champagne in London, and people like Mrs. Jarvis seem to the observer the very bubbles of it. Nobody ought to burden a bubble; it was meant just to explode and begin again. One can drink it, of course, but there are better forms of appreciation and more important things to appreciate. I cannot stay among our introductions; the even more interesting things beckon me on so; but the fruit of them was very various. My brother Graham is a keen politician, and had carried Minnebiac for the Conservatives in a bye-election just two months before we started. He is Vice-President, too, of the Dominion Club, which pleases father fearfully, as it is

rather a compliment to so young a man. Nevertheless, it was rather astounding to be asked to dine
and meet very serious people indeed, like Professor
Byng, who wrote the standard book upon Off-Shoots
of the British Race, and Earl Watchett, the Colonial Under-Secretary, and be expected, as Graham
certainly was, to contribute something valuable to
the collections of facts these gentlemen were making. (He said afterwards that he found them pathetically anxious to be informed, and hated his own
incompetence, in view of the opportunity; but
anybody who knows Graham would be quite sure he
told them things after dinner that were useful for
them to learn, and did it nicely, too.) Against
that, in case we were inclined to think too well of
ourselves, we might put the attention paid us by some
people father had been able to be of use to in Ottawa,
and who had been quite charmed with Minnebiac.
We were unfortunate in meeting these people —
never, indeed, did meet them; they were always
just going out of town; but they very kindly sent us
tickets for Madame Tussaud's. We felt distantly
treated, but Graham insisted on going; he said it
was full of characters, and he wanted to compare
them with Mrs. Jarvis.

But it is along the ordinary ways of life and among
the people one would naturally know that the really
most interesting things happen to one; the others are

piquant and high-coloured, and their being hard to come by makes them seem wonderfully quotable when one gets home; but they are as adventitious and irrelevant as the circus used to be in Minnebiac, and soon fade away because one has no proper relation to them. We were having tea at Stewart's in Bond Street after a Winter Exhibition, I know, simply having tea, or rather paying for it, when we met Evelyn Dicey, whose father owns any number of the Thousand Islands (in the River St. Lawrence), and usually lived on one of them in the summer, though Mr. Dicey's home was in Troy, N.J.

Minnebiac is not far from those parts; and we used sometimes to talk about buying an island or two ourselves; but father said no, a small portion of the mainland on the right side, under the Crown, was good enough for him, and he never would. We used to exchange visits with the Diceys, which began in a business connection and ended in our thinking them a charming family, especially Evelyn. Still, she was not a person you wrote to or were able to keep track of; she just appeared and disappeared on our northern banks, like certain summer birds and flowers; and we were all immensely astonished to meet at Stewart's.

"What are *you* doing here?" we naturally exclaimed as we rushed together. I have noticed that people from our side always say that when they meet unexpectedly, as if nobody had any business to be in Great Britain but themselves. I had that feeling just for a minute unaccountably towards Evelyn. For us what could be more right or proper? — but there was she, and not in the least with the air of a foreigner.

"So you are having a look at the dear old Kingdom, too!" Miss Dicey went on, exactly as if she had shares in it.

"Yes," said Graham. "It's nice of them, isn't it, to let the public in?"

So Graham felt as I did. I don't think Evelyn missed it, but she only looked at him and smiled.

"It just does my heart good to hear you talk. I've been among these sweet British for two solid months now, and they are darlings; but they don't exactly catch on, do they?"

"Oh, I don't know!" said Graham. "Mary and I sometimes feel, in conversation over here, as if we belonged to the period of Alfred the Great. Don't we, Mary?"

"Oh, well! I don't know, of course, who you've been meeting. But now you are to come right back and have tea with me," said Evelyn.

We said we would come right back, but we couldn't have tea because we had already had it, and we sat down again with our American friend.

"The people of these islands," said Graham, "are

certainly degenerating, and no libel. They talk now with great fluency, whereas few and short were the words they used to say; they now indulge themselves in all sorts of jammy things like these, whereas at the noblest period of their history one is taught that they were content with a simple currant bun."

"Yes, isn't it heavenly!" said Evelyn, as her order, consisting mostly of coffee-icing, was placed before her. "We can't do a great deal more than this in New York; and then how much better the climate is over here for a tea appetite! I love the old climate myself, when I can see through it; and it does make you adore your tea. And really and truly I'm getting fond of the English. They have their qualities, you can take it from me."

"We have always thought so," said I.

"Well, this little one had to find it out. Oh, Mary! but didn't your American friend here land in a good old British bog! Wales, my ticket took me to — distant relatives in Wales. They lived in a castle with a moat; and it was only because Cromwell was careless that they didn't have a title; and I had just yearned over those relatives in Wales ever since I could understand. Well, the castle was there, and the moat was there all right — perfectly unnecessary. I used to look at the place sometimes and think, 'You poor old thing; aren't you ashamed of having a moat when nobody would take you as a gift?'

And the relations were there inside, too, all up to description in size and number; but, honey, I nearly died. There wasn't a thing to do in that place but learn to spell it and forget again; and the time came when you *couldn't* forget. No, my children, Wales is a romantic country, but if you haven't time to see it don't lie awake worrying. There was a little church three miles off, and the minister was the nearest neighbour. He preached against motoring, because, he said, the poor might often be in our way, but we had no right to destroy them. Oh, *dear!*"

"Good man," said Graham.

"The modern use of a moat round a place like that," continued Evelyn, "is to keep people from getting out of it. But I did get out, by the connivance of a Mr. Ap-Williams, who drove me to the station in his dogcart. I believe he thought I was going to elope with him, he looked so disappointed when I said good-bye out of the car-window; but all I wanted, of course, was to get over the ground. Most of the family, you see, had gone for the week-end to a kind of second cousin castle where there was a funeral, taking all the horses that could walk; and the Pollens from New York heard about my case that very day and telegraphed for me. And now I'm right in it, and the prospect brightens every hour. There is a lot of difference between many places and Wales. Now relate, please, exactly what you have been doing in this sweet old realm of Edward's. I won't say another word."

We were able to relate a good deal, by taking turns, and we poured it all out about Towse and the flat and the Crown Jewels and Thomas Carlyle's house in Chelsea, and the waxworks in Westminster Abbey, and how we had been admitted to go over the Admiralty's docks and Scotland Yard and Greenwich Observatory, and had heard Mr. A. Balfour speak the night before, and Evelyn listened with great patience and good humour.

"I'm keeping those things for my old age," she said. "I suppose you'll absolutely despise me, but I haven't done one of them yet — not so much as the Poets' Corner or the National Gallery. I don't see how you get time for them."

"But what are we here for?" I asked.

"Oh, for tons of other things! Haven't you been going anywhere — no society?"

"Why, yes," said Graham — "a little. We have met Mrs. Jerome Jarvis, and others; and we hope to see some of the others again."

"We had a delightful evening last week at the Colonial Institute," I said, "and we are asked to a conversazione of the Royal Geographical Society; and we've had three invitations to private views of picture exhibitions, sent by friends of the artists. We are enjoying ourselves very much indeed."

I didn't see why Evelyn shouldn't know.

"But, my dear lambs," cried Evelyn, "you ought to be having the time of your lives! Do you realise that you represent between you a good quarter of the mining interests of Nova Scotia, and enough New Brunswick timber to buy a county town with?"

"I expect we're having as good a time as that gives us any claim to," said Graham.

"Oh, you don't know this country! Of course you're not American," said Evelyn, considering us thoughtfully, "but you're next door to it."

"That's more of an advantage when we are at home, Miss Dicey," said Graham, but Evelyn was reflecting.

"We are hoping to get tickets for the House before long," he went on, "but it seems about the hardest show on earth to get admittance to. Were you thinking of going?"

"I went the day the King did," said Evelyn. "I thought it would be livelier; and it was. When Edward is really dressed, he's a dear. We've got nothing on our side like him, have we?"

"We've got *him!*" I protested, and Evelyn laughed.

"To be sure; I forgot. He's got you. But the House is easy enough — I can work that for you. Our Minister is always ready to oblige."

"Thanks, very much," said Graham; "we haven't a Minister, being more or less at home, but there's a fellow they call the High Commissioner for our part of the world, who has undertaken to see us through. He's pretty slow, but I expect we can depend on him."

"Well, if you have any difficulty, apply to me," said Evelyn; and we thanked her again.

"I can't get over it," she went on. "You and Towse and the flat, and your happy hours in crypts and places. It's ridiculous. Look at the time *we* have, and the — and the ——"

"And the duchesses you become," put in Graham gravely.

"Why, yes," said Evelyn. "The American duchess is a deservedly popular institution — good for the Duke and improving for the American. Do you know any?"

We both shook our heads.

"I expect Canadians are something new over here — that's what it is. Americans were new once, and frequented Bloomsbury boarding-houses and brought introductions from Emerson and Thoreau, and wrote their experiences afterwards in the magazines. Now you are."

"We were discovered by J. Cartier in 1535. One Wolfe planted firm Britannia's flag on us about two centuries and a quarter later," responded Graham. "I imagine we are known to their leading ethnologists, and perhaps to Lord Elgin."

"I just love to hear you talk," said Evelyn again, though he was chaffing her head off. "The fact is you haven't become foreigners yet — you still belong to them, so of course they think you're of no importance. Become foreigners, get Mr. Ambassador Bryce to come over and write you a Declaration of Independence, start a President, and take no further notice of them. They'll adore you. I don't mind giving you the tip."

"It's awfully good of you!" said Graham.

"Well, anyhow I'm going to introduce you in a minute to my very greatest friends here, Barbie Pavisay and her mother, Lady Doleford. Such a place they've got, poor darlings — pure Tudor — and not a penny. You remember Lord Doleford's death a couple of years ago, and how he had eight jockeys to bear him to the tomb, and nobody could prevent it?"

"I'm afraid I don't remember," said Graham.

"Oh, it was in all the New York papers — didn't you see it? Well, anyhow, the present Lord Doleford is in India with his regiment. He got a decoration of some sort the other day for something he did that had to do with plague; and they think he's a perfect angel because he won't let them send him any of the money they make by selling the ancestral cauliflowers. They get a house in town lent to them sometimes, but generally they live in about two rooms of Pavis Court to save fires — it's in Crosshire — and grow things for the market. It can't be sold, and it's too dilapidated to let; but the fruit there has a tremendous reputation, and it's pretty nearly all they've got to live on. I want to know if you ever heard of anything so sad?"

"Oh, yes! Lots of sadder things," I said. "I should love market-gardening."

"Not if you were a Countess," said Evelyn. "And a real one, mind. The best blood in England, as they used to say in novels. You'll see it's so, too, the minute they come into range — none of those cases you've got to take on trust over here. I'm not advertising the Earl, for I haven't seen him yet, though I thirst and long to. There's every sort of evidence that he's an absolute lamb, a dear and precious lamb. We are to meet at Christmas — he comes home then, and I don't get half my sleep wondering what he'll think of this American. Here they are!"

The shop door was darkened at that moment by two tall ladies. They looked about them with a kind of vague assurance, they were evidently unfamiliar with the place; but that, you saw at once, was its misfortune. Evelyn darted out and seized them, and the elder lady showed the same sort of relief that strangers do when you find the place for them in the Church Service. One would think Evelyn Dicey many degrees higher in rank than a mere Countess by the way Lady Doleford acted to her, instead of being just — well, just Evelyn Dicey. Lady Barbara took her more for granted; but you would think her mother was under every kind of obligation on earth to Evelyn. It seemed to me almost docile, the way they came along with her to the table where we were sitting, Lady Doleford talking and hesitating and explaining and excusing, her daughter following as if nothing in the course of nature *could* matter very much. They both looked a little pulled up when Evelyn introduced us.

"Two Northern friends of mine," she said, "that I've just encountered in the most wonderful way here in this shop. They stepped in here out of the past just as I did out of the future — I mean they had had tea and I was going to have it; and here we all are, aren't we, in the present, and what will *you* have, dearest Lady Doleford? I know you can't endure anything sticky."

Lady Barbara looked at us with more interest than her mother did. Lady Doleford accepted us graciously; but in her eye I thought I saw the recognition of us as attendant circumstances which she might well have been spared; and as to our consequence it was simply not decipherable.

"Oh, pray, dear Evelyn, no fresh tea for *us!*" she pleaded; "I am sure what you have there will be delightful. You know I like the merest water bewitched, and so does Barbara."

"No, mamma, really," said Barbara, "I like a cup of tea."

"Oh, very well, then," retreated Lady Doleford, "and a little bread-and-butter, dearest Evelyn, thank you," though if she could have asked for the bread without the butter I believe she would have preferred it.

"What, *nodings!*" cried Evelyn. "Nodings in all this variety? No chocolate cake, walnut cake, caramel cake—no éclairs, macaroons, petit fours! Do be a little more hospitable, Lady Doleford—more imaginative, Barbara."

"I'll have anything there is," said Barbara, "and mother will have a rusk, I know, Evelyn, if there are any. She adores rusks."

"Heaven send rusks," said Evelyn; and Heaven did send them, Lady Doleford subsiding after one more faint protest.

"It is really too good of you," she said, "to give us tea, after our proposing to have it elsewhere. But we found that my sister-in-law had been obliged to go out earlier than she expected, to see about getting her secretary, who has suddenly collapsed with nervous breakdown, into a rest cure. How dreadfully common these cases seem to have become."

My mind flew to Lady Doleford's sister-in-law; and I longed for the conversation to unfold why she had a secretary.

"You are Americanising too fast!" cried Evelyn. "It's what I complain of. Where are we to go for *our* rest cures, at this rate?"

"You must all come to Canada," remarked Graham. "We are doing very well; but there are still large areas in Canada that would be infallible for nervous disorders."

"Senator Trent might accommodate a few thousand of us," said Evelyn. "He might put us up, as they say over here, in one of those townships of his on the Restigouche, and never know we were there."

Lady Doleford looked at Graham with a little more attention.

"Are you Canadian?" she asked. "I thought Miss Dicey described you as fellow-Americans."

"I don't think I did mention Canada," said Evelyn, "but that was only my forgetfulness."

"They are so forgetful," I said. "It's what we keep trying to explain."

"But why should you mind?" asked Barbara.

"Why shouldn't you be flattered?" demanded Evelyn humorously.

Graham made a funny little stiff bow.

"We are," he said, "but our modesty shrinks from any category but our own."

"Well, do you know," said Barbara, looking at us thoughtfully, "I shouldn't have been quite sure that you were Americans."

G

"Alas!" said Graham, out of plain politeness to Evelyn; and he and Lady Barbara looked at one another kindly and laughed together. I am sure that was the beginning of it. He felt drawn to her for not being quite sure we were what we weren't, and she felt curious about him for wanting to be what he was. We went away almost immediately then; but Evelyn must have given a very good account of us when our backs were turned, for the very next day she wrote and said that Lady Doleford had made her promise to bring us to see them in Beaufort Gardens.

CHAPTER VII

I HAVE often wondered what Evelyn conveyed —
no, perhaps not that exactly, since about so frank
a person there couldn't be many guesses — but what
language and methods she found by which to convey to Lady Doleford that we might be, when all
was said and done, just worth looking at twice.

Lady Doleford didn't know us; she hadn't discovered our shining personal traits; she was as little
curious about strangers as anyone you could imagine,
and we had no earthly claim upon her. What grounds
remained, then, upon which we could possibly be
recommended to her except those that Evelyn had
so clearly in her eye when she suggested, if I may
put it so horridly, that we weren't quite getting our
money's-worth in London? Perhaps she felt them
solidly under her own feet; which may have made
it easier. All I can say is that if these *were* the
grounds of Evelyn's acceptance she danced about
on them with the most wonderful careless security.
She showed a confidence in them that we certainly
never could feel. Whatever the importance of
money may be, it seems a strange thing to make

one free of England. No, as soon as we had time to reflect we put away the unworthy thought, and decided that Evelyn was accepted because of the natural charm she possessed, and we invited because of the natural charm we might disclose. About my own share of that responsibility I was naturally nervous enough; but one could always depend upon Graham.

We began, of course, by going to tea.

"What do you expect?" I asked Graham in the hansom.

"What do you?" he replied; and we decided that we expected Lady Doleford, and Lady Barbara, and Evelyn, and perhaps Lady Doleford's sister-in-law, the one with the secretary, who probably, we decided, had some way of earning her own living, since she had a secretary. The cake would be rusks, and there wouldn't be much fire. We had already noticed that fire is the commonest economy in England — I suppose, because it can be carried out without any sacrifice of dignity. They put what they call cheeks into the grates. As Mr. Howells has explained, your back is seldom warm in England; and I would like to add never where there are cheeks. We thought Lady Doleford would revel in cheeks.

But in London you never can tell. The house in Beaufort Gardens was luxurious with that quality of luxury that nothing, oh! nothing can buy. The things in it were like books; one could stop before each of them, yet they had a subdued relationship that put them in the same type, allied them to the same standard of choice as the generations went on that had furnished the rooms. Mr. and Miss Trent were announced in a drawing-room that already held a quantity of people, people who sat about with opulent furs half-thrown off, and seemed to have known each other all their lives. Tea was being handed by a very old family servant indeed, and I never saw anything so overwhelmed with a sense of the importance of his function. He was as grave as a minister, at any rate as a pew-opener; and when you said milk and no sugar into the ear he bent toward you, there was a faithfulness in his bow of assent that made you feel that not for a king's ransom would he bring you sugar and no milk.

Lady Doleford welcomed us with the same permissive, acquiescent air she had at Stewart's, but very kindly. "What and who are these," she seemed to say, "that the tide of the time has washed to my feet?" but she quite saw it her duty to pick us up and make us comfortable. One gets so often, in London, that impression of being dreadfully adventitious; more adventitious, according to Graham, than one has any business to be. Graham said afterwards that one felt, with Lady Doleford. that one mattered so little, it was rather a shame one should matter at all. He had a moment, he said, of wishing just to relieve her of any effort she might feel called upon to make to take *him* in, just to efface himself, telling her ever so gently, "Don't bother! I'm gone." I had no such moment. I was delighted to be there, and so I told Evelyn. As we stood talking to her Graham's glance wandered round the room; and I, too, remembered that we hadn't seen Lady Barbara.

Evelyn at once took charge of us, which was right and kind of her, in view of Lady Doleford's apparent helplessness with anyone whom she had not known from infancy. She took it for granted that we would want to hear immediately and all about everybody in the room; and she proceeded to tell us. It was simply astonishing the amount of information Evelyn had concerning them, their ranks and their titles and the way nearly half of them were related to Lady Doleford, their aims and ambitions, and other things, too, that one couldn't have been supposed to know about them. She had been hardly longer in the country than we had, yet she had obtained the fluent biographical detail of a lifetime. And with a minuteness and show of accuracy that compelled respect, I must say. She must have tackled it with distinct purpose, and given it the most concentrated attention, made it simply her business, to have acquired so much; such thoroughness almost gave one the impression that that, really, was what she was there for. Graham said it was the virgin soil of the American mind, in which family trees would naturally take root and spread and flourish; but I couldn't help thinking there was more in it than that.

"The dark, good-looking man talking to Lady Doleford," said Evelyn, "is John Pontex."

"The man who wrote 'The Anglo-Saxon'?" asked Graham.

"That's right. It *has* sold, hasn't it — I mean, for anything that isn't a novel? And I hear he let the American rights go for a thousand dollars! He's a son of Lord Maberly of Derry. It's an Irish peerage, but carries a seat in the Lords. And the eldest son is distinctly wanting — isn't it odd?"

"Why, that's a great fellow!" said Graham. "That book of his is a searchlight right into the next century, and no funny fiction, either — cold probability."

"Well," said Evelyn, "his poor brother Guy's *really*, I believe, a confirmed epileptic, so he's quite likely to succeed. Money, too — through the mother. She was a Miss Zweitiger, the Vienna branch. That lovely thing on the sofa is the Countess of Garsings. You may believe just about half of what you've heard about her — she's really gone very straight since she brought her girl out."

"But we haven't heard anything," said I.

"Well, of course, you wouldn't — in the British Museum. And — don't look both at once — the little grey-headed man with his hands in his pockets on the hearth-rug is the Duke of Dulwich."

"Oh!" I said. "Graham, have you done looking?"

"Yes," said Graham. "Is he an interesting person?"

"Why, *Graham*, what a question!" I exclaimed, taking my turn.

"Well, sometimes they are," he defended himself.

"I guess pretty nearly always," said Evelyn; "even when they're as hard up as poor little Dulwich. They're so scarce. There aren't more than sixteen or seventeen in England, you know; eight in Scotland, and only two in Ireland. Not counting the Royal ones."

"Historically speaking," said Graham, "no doubt they are scarce; but I've always understood that there were circles, in this country, where you couldn't get away from them."

"I don't want to get away from them," I put in. "And I shall always love to remember, Evelyn, that I saw my Duke on a hearth-rug instead of in a procession."

"I should just think so!" said Evelyn. "The little woman he is talking to is Mrs. Jack Yilke. Doesn't she look as hard as nails? She's an M.F.H."

"First-rate!" said Graham admiringly; while I remembered, by a fearful effort, what an M.F.H. was.

"She hunts the Famine — has ever since her husband died. That's just about the *ne plus ultra*, you know. As far as I've observed the top thing to be over here is a Bishop, then comes a thing they call a Head Master,—they often turn into Bishops,—and then an M.F.H. And talk about dukes being scarce! Lady 'Masters' are a good deal scarcer."

We contemplated, feeling very much privileged indeed, the two exceptional persons on the hearth-rug. It was easy to clothe Mrs. Yilke in a safety-habit. She stood as if she were in one then, briskly talking to the Duke, with her best side, as it were, foremost, and tapped her leg with the fan Lady Doleford had given her to protect her from the fire, forgetting, I am sure, that it was not a hunting-crop.

"Why the 'Famine'?" asked Graham.

"Oh, I don't know. Some joke of the Duke of Wellington's, I believe. It's as cryptic by now as he is, but they cling to it. Now, there's somebody you are likely to see again — Margot Lippington."

"Why," I asked breathlessly, "are we likely to see her again?"

"Well, she's a cousin of Lady Doleford's and a great friend of mine, and her husband, if she can find out any way of doing it, is going to be your next Governor-General at Quebec."

"At Ottawa," corrected Graham. "One would suppose, Miss Dicey, that you had learned your Canada in England!"

"Well, anyhow," said Evelyn, "Margot Lippington's just dying to go there and put her weary little bore of a husband on the throne, or whatever you call it; and why she's so mad about it I can't imagine. They've got quite enough money to have the loveliest time right here in England; and he would rather hatch pheasants than do any other thing on earth. But, no, first she worried round till she got him the West Indies — don't ask me where — and then she worked the Antipodes — don't ask me what — and they're hardly back six months before she's worrying again to get him Canada. She's remarkably successful, you know; she just keeps *at* them; and she's a wonderful example of the value of leaving *no* stone unturned. I'll introduce you — she'd just love to meet anyone from Canada, especially when I tell her who you are."

"But we're nobody in particular," I protested. "It's our father."

"Oh, aren't you? Well, Margot will very soon make you think you are," said Evelyn, and a moment later we were being presented.

Lady Lippington received us with a grace and charm that had a curious general quality, suggested being part of a large reserve which she kept to meet

just such cases as ours. It was as impersonal as
light or heat, and she poured it over us in smiles,
though with a somewhat wandering eye, until Evelyn
mentioned that we came from Canada. Then it
was exactly as Evelyn said — she did show an interest. Her attention hovered much nearer to us;
I saw her perceive the kind of fur I was wearing.
She was one of those tall, thin women with mobile
lips and clear complexions and what Graham calls
the noble nose — and it *is* essentially the noble nose,
though, as he says, it is being grafted on to increas-
ing numbers of the mere gentry. Lady Lippington
lifted hers with an air of Imperial recollection at
the name of our country, seemed to stiffen, as Graham said, with a sense of approaching function.

"Canada," she said, "has the greatest fascination
for me. Its history thrill-lls me; its loyalty touches
me to the heart."

It seemed a good deal to say, in public like that;
still, I didn't see why it should have irritated Graham.
But it did always, any reference to Canadian loyalty
upon the lips of the aristocratic classes. He got so,
at last, that he preferred to hear them charge us
with selfishness and sedition.

"That would greatly gratify Canada," he replied,
"if she knew."

It sounded polite, though it was really temper;
and I was thankful to see that Lady Lippington

perceived only the sound. That was the worst of Graham in England; you never could depend upon his taking things as he was meant to take them. Luckily it was not often noticed that he didn't; so I suppose no harm was done.

"Well," said Evelyn, "if you're thirsting for information about those parts, Margot, and I know you always are, Mr. Trent is the very person for your extremity. What he doesn't know isn't worth knowing, and what he doesn't own isn't worth owning. He's a Member of their Congress——"

"Parliament, Evelyn!" I cried.

"Parliament — I keep forgetting — though so young. He runs the best fishing-club on the Saguenay. He's a kind of patriotic grandson of the Canadian High Commissioner — isn't that what you call him? — and his own legitimate parent, Senator Trent, is about the biggest berry on the bush over there. If you're interested in those maples they talk so much about on their side, why, here's the Maple Prince!"

"I've eaten maple sugar," cried Lady Lippington; "it's perfectly delicious! And do you know, I think Evelyn's title rather suits you."

She looked Graham up and down with a freedom, I must say. A freedom which I couldn't help thinking she kept in the same box with the charm I spoke of, for just such cases as ours. I expected signs of one of his ridiculous rages; but no, he didn't seem to mind the personal liberty. Or perhaps — you never can tell with men — it was because it was a lady, and at the bottom of his heart there was a little vanity that rather liked it. Anyway, he only smiled and said: "American titles are great. They carry no responsibility."

"But this is too delightful!" went on Lady Lippington. "I think I take naturally to Canadians — do you remember my Montreal friend, Evelyn — the magnate? The *magnet* we always called him, because he was so alive. Such good brains, and such a fine, unconventional nature! I was devoted to him — what was his name, Evelyn?"

"Sir John Ames," said Evelyn.

"Of course it was. Do you know him, Mr. Trent?"

"I've met him," said Graham.

"Then there's another bond! You must really — let me see — what can we arrange? You must come to tea with me at my club. It's a club with a real purpose — Daughters of the Rag — that's Daughters of the Flag, you know. In Brook Street. We have lectures — 'Outrollings of the Rag,' we call them among ourselves — 'Outrollings of the Flag,' of course, we ought to say. There's one on Tuesday afternoon — the very thing! — 'Canada at the Present Time,' with lantern slides, by such a clever man, who has been there twice. You will be interested in that."

"I should — immensely — thanks very much," said Graham, "and my sister, I am sure, will be delighted; but I am afraid I am engaged. Isn't that," he asked me, "the day Watchett mentioned?"

Lady Lippington did not seem to notice that I would be delighted. "Oh!" she exclaimed vividly, "do you know George Watchett?   Isn't he a dear?"

"Lives in his pocket," put in Evelyn.

Lady Lippington put up an inspired hand. "Could you lunch on Friday?" she asked. "And I wonder — Evelyn, do you think I could get Alfred Somerset? It would be invaluable for Mr. Trent to meet him; and I wouldn't hesitate, only you know what he is like about strangers — so ludicrously easily bored."

Alfred Somerset was the Colonial Secretary. "But, Graham," I put in, "on Friday you are lunching with Mr. Somerset."

"So I am," said Graham. "I seem to be desperately in demand. So sorry, Lady Lippington. But my sis——"

"No," said I. "Don't you remember, Graham, I was to go to Lady Selkirk."

"The High Commissioner for Canada — *those* Selkirks," said Lady Lippington. "Delightful people — I've been seeing a great deal of them lately. But we're not at the end of our resources — you must come and dine. Both of you."

"That is very kind of you, Lady Lippington," I said. "We should love to come and dine — both of us."

"And meet Lord Lippington," she added, with a little bow of deference which I felt she somehow accepted as coming from us. "You can testify, Evelyn, can't you, how glad Amherst always is to know Colonials, and how many of them we see. Of all kinds. That will be charming. And now, Mr. Trent, you must sit down here beside me and tell me what the climate is like in your part of Canada. A lovely summer you have everywhere, I know. I was so cross with Mr. Kipling for dubbing the country 'Our Lady of the Snows' — I told him so. These poets never know what mischief they may do."

It seemed clear that it was Graham she wanted to talk to, so I moved away with Evelyn toward Lady Doleford, who had just been accosted by a burly person with a commanding air, who wore an uncompromising bonnet with uncompromising strings, a cape of sables, and a coat and skirt of frieze well off the ground. There was rather a space round them; but Lady Doleford smiled at Evelyn, who seemed emboldened to approach, and I with her.

"How do you do?" said the large lady to Evelyn, with what I thought rather a grumpy nod, looking at me. "And is this another American friend?" she asked Lady Doleford, as much as to defy her to say it was.

"No," I said, "it's not." We had come to the briefest expressions of denial. We would refrain from affirming the truth when we thought people had rather we didn't; but let the matter pass quite we would not.

Evelyn, for a wonder, hadn't a word to say; and Lady Doleford, looking a little alarmed, hastened to explain.

"Oh, no!" she said; "this is a new Canadian friend, Agnes, Miss Trent, who lives by the beautiful lake of Ontario — I think you said," she murmured to me. "My sister-in-law, the Duchess of Dulwich, Miss Trent."

"Well, well — Canadian — that's better!" said the Duchess; and of course I loved her, frieze and bonnet-strings and all, then and there. But in the hurry of the moment I could think of nothing else, so I said:

"How is your secretary?"

"Dear me!" said the Duchess of Dulwich. "And how came you to know about my secretary?"

"The one that had to go to the rest-cure," I explained, dreadfully frightened.

"I'm afraid I mentioned it, Agnes," pleaded Lady Doleford, and established that it wasn't my fault.

The Duchess laughed, as if at some exquisitely humorous perception that was going on within her. We all waited, quite perceptibly, to know what it was.

"Upon my word," said Her Grace, "I thought it not impossible she had read it in one of the papers. I saw with my own eyes the other day that the Portmores had lost their butler, who had been with them twenty-five years, 'and the family were plunged in grief.' They had got hold of it! Well, if they put in the death of the Portmores' butler why shouldn't they put in the illness of my secretary — which plunges me in confusion, I assure you. But I'm glad to say she's better — I'm glad to say she's better."

"How tiresome for you, Agnes," said Lady Doleford. "Just in the midst of your Royal Commission, too. Have you been able to replace her?"

"Oh, yes! I've got another, rather more woolly-headed than the last. Love-sick, half of these young women are, I believe. One eye on your Blue Book and the other — well, where shall we say the other is?" and the Duchess looked at me in the way that used to be described as quizzical. I mean she distinctly implied that at my age my other eye might be wandering too.

"What is your Royal Commission about, Duchess?" asked Evelyn respectfully.

"The Assimilation of Aliens. The quickest and most effective methods of turning them into loyal

H

British subjects," said the Duchess. "How best to understand them, and deal with them without damage to their national, political or religious prejudices. How most permanently to bind them to us, to win their affections, to educate them in British standards and traditions. We have been given the widest scope. It was, no doubt, my well-known interest in the repatriation of the Jews," she went on, "that induced them to put me on it. Personally I am not very fond of aliens. I would repatriate them all."

She looked severely as she spoke, not at Evelyn, but at Lady Doleford, who cast down her eyes.

CHAPTER VIII

I KNEW exactly how it would be. As soon as I let myself begin to tell about the people we came to know and the things that happened to us, all the wonderful daily romance that London has for the stranger, from the hour when "'Ulk" sounds with a clatter of tins through the cold grey dawn, to the last irresponsible beat of a hansom in the abysmal streets, would simply swim and melt away and refuse to compete, as it were, in one's memory, with such centres of interest as the Lippingtons and Lady Barbara. It is as if all the dear, homely details knew their place, in the national way, too well to let me say another word about them when once more important matters had engaged my attention. They all humbly escape, as I knew they would, out of the back-door of my mind; and Towse, alas! Towse is the very first to go. So that while I long to linger and dwell, and relate all the small commerce and adventure by which London really opens its heart to you, it is the Lippingtons' dinner-party that I find myself "at," as we say, in the historical sense, and the Lippingtons themselves who walk in, without any special invitation, and take possession of this page. I am sorry to see them;

I meant to devote it to Towse's views of Out-Door Relief, but that is for ever impossible; they are already there.

It was not much of a dinner-party in the party sense, only eight altogether. We were the first to arrive; and Lady Lippington said at once that she hoped we wouldn't mind its not being "a function." The only thing we minded, of course, was that she should think we could; and even that, I am afraid, we were too much interested to mind much. (Do not cast up Mrs. Jerome Jarvis: if we minded there it was for altogether a different reason.) Lady Lippington went on to explain that she thought it would be so nice to begin with a little glimpse of them quite intimately, a little impression of what they were like in family life. That is, I'm afraid, a confused way of putting it. What she actually said was that they wanted a little glimpse of us quite intimately; but clever people often unconsciously convey themselves so much more clearly than stupid, literal ones do, though using exactly the same words. Anyway, she was quite right — we were delighted; and it was fascinating to hear her call Lord Lippington Amherst, and reveal her affection for him openly, and think that in a few months one might be curtseying to them both while the band played "God Save the King!"

I couldn't help wondering, in those first few instants, why Evelyn had called Lord Lippington a weary little bore. He had a droop of the eyelids that certainly was weary, and perhaps his moustache carried it out. He had, too, a pathetic look of having done for a long time whatever was suggested to him to do, flinching at nothing, and simply seeing it no part of his duty to enquire whether nature had equipped him for the task. His eyes followed Lady Lippington now and then with a fidelity that seemed to say — or was it my imagination? — that somehow or other he knew she would see him through; he had only to do his best, and she might rely on him for that. This wasn't boring at all, but interesting and touching; and so were his perfect manners — the way he took up his stand, nevertheless, upon his own hearth, and the inalienable rights of a British nobleman, his gentle agreeable little commonplaces, which would have compelled attention quite rightly just by the way they were said.

"The Tanners are coming, Amherst," said Lady Lippington. "You remember the Tanners, who so thoughtfully put their stables at our disposal when ours were burnt at Christchurch? They very kindly called over a fortnight ago, and I was beginning to be afraid we couldn't manage anything at all, but luckily, in spite, I'm afraid, of very short notice, they were free to-night. You people from abroad," Lady Lippington charged me humorously, "are always so desperately engaged when you come to London. You will like meeting Sir Thomas and Lady Tanner. They represent, like yourselves, if you don't mind my saying so, quite the best type of Colonials."

It made one feel very silly; but I don't go so far as Graham, who declared afterwards that it was a flagrant thing to say. He stood provokingly dumb under it, however, and Lord Lippington said hastily that Tanner was a very good sort indeed.

"And so able," added Lady Lippington. "A Member of Lord Lippington's Government when we were there, Mr. Trent. It gave you so *much* pleasure to recommend him for his knighthood, didn't it, Amherst? Did I understand that your father was a member of the present Canadian Government, Mr. Trent? No? What a pity ——"

"Sir Thomas and Lady Tanner!" declared the footman.

The stout gentleman who came quickly in had the air of being able to meet any emergency, but seemed in a hurry, and wiped his face, already very red and polished, with a beautifully fresh pocket-handkerchief. His wife moved, on the contrary, most languidly, so they made rather a disjointed approach. She was dressed very elegantly indeed, and wore a tiara, that seemed, when she sat down in the blaze of the fire, a fairy addition to the electric lights. I saw Lady Lippington just glance at it, but not at all enviously.

The Lippingtons welcomed them very pleasantly, but were almost unable to reassure them about being punctual.

"I know we must be outrageously late?" said Lady Tanner, clinging to the hand of our hostess as if for absolution. "Do you know — I am afraid I must confess it — I lost your note!"

"I saw it on your dressing-table — stuck in the looking-glass — just before we started," Sir Thomas put in.

"Oh, did you? Why didn't you tell me? And then the three hotel clocks all told a different story, and Tom won't alter his watch from Australian time."

"I ask you," said Tom; "a watch I've had twenty-five years, and never touched a hand of it!"

"And on the top of all our wretched hired motor broke down in Bond Street! Positively it made me wish we had brought one of ours with us. Tom gave the man such a setting-out, and that didn't mend matters —— "

"But you're not the last," Lord Lippington got in.

"What a relief! But I said to Tom: 'Never mind; they'll forgive us — for old acquaintance' sake.'"

"Yes, indeed," said Lady Lippington almost as cordially; and there was a slight pause, broken by the footman, who announced, almost with a smile of satisfaction, the last comers.

"Lord Doleford, and Lady Barbara Pavisay, m'lady."

"So here you are, Peter!" cried Lady Lippington, kissing Barbara, as it were, by the way, but directing all her welcome with both hands, to the young man who came in with her, looking modestly pleased to see everybody, and as modestly expectant that everybody would be pleased to see him.

"Here I am!" he replied; and there he was. Apparently there wasn't much more to be said about it, but one might feel a good deal. What was most obviously to be felt was just the feeling of family. It at once took possession of the occasion, almost of the room; it was big and happy, and simple and serious; and it was nice to see other things in Lady Lippington quenched in it, and everything in Lord Lippington expand and sun itself. The Tanners and ourselves, incidents and accidents, were duly introduced; but the fact of the evening, of which nobody, when all was conceded to politeness, could question the importance, was that Captain Lord Doleford, a cousin of the house, had returned on leave from India after an absence of three years.

He sat next to me at dinner.

Of course the pleasant enthusiasm of it wasn't allowed to remain among us long, especially as there was so much that Lady Tanner wanted to ask Lord Lippington if he remembered — picnics and race meetings — but it lasted till the end of the soup.

"And I see," said Lord Lippington to him by way of congratulation, "they've given you a fairing."

"His beautiful medal!" exclaimed Lady Lippington. "What is it like, Peter? I've not seen any of the Victorian Order decorations."

"Oh, it's solid, I believe!" replied Lord Doleford; "I've been told I could raise ten bob on it — but not by a dealer."

"What a shame, Peter!" cried our hostess; and Lady Tanner exclaimed: "Quite shocking!"

"It's more becoming, really, to Barbara," said Lord Doleford. "She has tried it on several times already — I think she has her eye on it."

"Barbara mustn't," said Lord Lippington. "A lady went to some Royal function lately wearing her husband's order — fancied it, I suppose — and the King wasn't at all pleased. Had her attention called to it. The case, I assure you."

"There you are, Barb!" said her brother; but Lady Barbara and Graham were already getting on very well together, and did not allow themselves to be interrupted.

"I understand perfectly why one should like to wear one's brother's medal," I said to Lord Doleford. "It isn't because it's becoming — it's because it's his. Besides, it's so seldom that you can wear them yourselves."

"That is the most valuable point about them," he said. "If they were worn every day they would have about as much importance as bacon for breakfast. But seeing them once in a blue moon, they have a better chance, somehow, of standing for something. If your brother had a medal, would you like to wear it?" he added casually, and not in the least because he wanted to know.

"No —not after what you've said," I told him. "I'd rather feel that it was put away in a drawer, getting ready to mean something. He has got one, by the way —my brother. The D.S.O."

"Really? That's ten times better than the thing my cousin was talking about. But I thought he was an Amer —— "

"For heaven's sake, don't!" I said warmly. "Don't get it all out. In that connection, you see, I'm afraid I couldn't bear it."

"In that connection? Yes, I see. It is rather rough. But —he's not a civilian, then?"

"Well, just now he is," I explained, "and most of the time when he is at home." And I unfolded what there was to unfold about South Africa and the Minnebiac Rifles.

"And please go on about the D.S.O.," he said. "I'm horribly jealous —they give my thing, you

know, to head-cooks and people; but never mind —
go on."

"I'm not so very anxious to tell you," I informed
him, "though I am his sister. I can see what you
think of sisters."

"Oh, I think they're quite sound — sisters!"

"I don't want you to uphold us," I said. "Well,
it was for a forced march, with just a company, to
relieve Colonel Smiley at Pietsdorp."

"Old Smiley of the Second Lincolns! We knew
him well — he took the regiment out from India.
Poor old chap — they potted him afterwards, didn't
they? He was too fat, much too fat, the old boy.
I remember, we heard about that Pietsdorp business; he wrote to one of our fellows. He was in an
awfully tight place, and when the Canadians showed
the enemy took them for the advance of an Army
Corps at least, and cleared out."

"Well, it was only Graham," I said, "and eighty
men."

"You see," Lord Doleford explained to me carefully, "the Boers were right enough in thinking it
was the main body of troops from Volkstaadt, because they were the only ones they thought could
possibly get there."

"But they weren't!" I said; and he laughed and
said "No — sister!" and I naturally laughed also.

He was no better-looking than Graham, but in a.

much simpler way, a way that made you think first of his looks and how good they were, while with Graham you remembered afterwards that he was handsome — I mean it was not the thing that did strike you first. Lord Doleford's features at once suggested a race and then a type and then an order, and a kind of direct correspondence of character — he was written beautifully plain. I don't know why he made me think of a Crusader — it was certainly nothing that he said — unless it was that sign of purpose and intention, which would be, one felt, as simple and as high as modern circumstances permitted. I thought immediately that I would like to see him in a coat of mail. It would look as if it had been riveted for him by his own armourer. Any one, a Hairy Aino, would have admired him — and I was no Hairy Aino.

I looked at Graham, and longed to hear what he was saying. Lady Barbara was giving him all of her attention. In her face one could clearly see two apprehensions going on, one of Graham and the other of his conversation. She was considering him as if he were something quite new to her; and if most of the men of her acquaintance were like her brother, of course he was. I heard just a scrap.

"Why do you say 'run' for Parliament?" she asked.

"Because," he said, "in our part of the world it's

thought the quickest way of getting there. If we stood, as you do, we might, perhaps, be left standing."

So they were only talking, after all, of national idioms. Lady Barbara's profile was bent towards Graham, and I could see its likeness to her brother's —where it came up and where it fell short. There was a good deal of falling short; but the design, one could see, had the original nobility. It had the same look, too, of being part of a simple, necessitated scheme, as indisputable as the Catechism, but the aim and purpose finished there, as if, being a woman, she did not need them further. I glanced back and saw that their presence made the life of Lord Doleford's face — he was talking to Lady Lippington — as their absence made a kind of death in his sister's. But she sat there, a very distinguished expensive product of nature, very much aware, I thought, of what ought to happen to her, as such a distinguished expensive product, and the reflection visited me, "How absurd it would be if Graham fell in love with Lady Barbara!" I got no further than that; it just seemed to me, at a glance, absurd, as if he should offer himself, as it were, in exchange for a Gainsborough out of the National Gallery — and where would he put it in Minnebiac! But with Graham you never could tell. It was not safe to assume that he would be put off any view because it was ridiculous.

"New Zealand mutton!" said Sir Thomas Tanner at his first mouthful of the joint. "And very good mutton, too."

"Is it really!" exclaimed Lady Lippington, with dismay. "How dread — I mean, well — of course, when we were in New Zealand we loved it, but ——"

"And I daresay you paid the price of the best Scotch for it," Sir Thomas conceded handsomely. "But you never could deceive me. That mutton left Auckland two months ago. It's been properly thawed, and a better slice of mutton I should never ask to see on my plate. It's all prejudice, you know, the notion that prevails over here about cold storage mutton — all prejudice."

"Is it New Zealand mutton?" exclaimed Lady Tanner, throwing herself, so to speak, into the awful breach. "I should never have guessed! So you have imposed upon me, Lady Lippington. But, Tom — of course, how stupid of you! — they had it out of compliment to us!"

"The cook must have known you were coming," said Lord Lippington with a laugh, in which Lady Lippington promptly joined.

"I hope," she cried humorously, "that she will remember to send up something from Canada, too! Please recognise the apples, Mr. Trent, in the meantime."

"If she discloses no form of chutney," said Lord

Doleford, "I shall be deeply hurt!" And Lady Lippington, looking round with an air of gratification, cried:

"What an Imperial little party we are! I don't see how we can finish without the King's health. Amherst — what do you say?"

"By all means," said Lord Lippington, "if you can produce musical honours."

"We must sing them," Lady Lippington returned; "I am sure we all would. I used to detest port," she told Sir Thomas Tanner, "but having to drink it so constantly of late years when Lord Lippington proposed the Royal toast, I have almost come to like it. The true Imperial feeling will make one like anything, I believe."

"Oh, my wife is quite a connoisseur!" jested Lord Lippington; and Sir Thomas Tanner assured him that since he left Government House it was impossible to get anything there that was fit to drink.

"I'm not hard to please, myself," said he; "but when it comes to giving champagne at the Birthday Ball out of bottles with no labels on 'em! Well," he said, scratching the portion of his neck just behind his ear and above his collar, "it does create a certain amount of bad feeling; and complaints are bound to arise. Bound to. When all's said and done, the Colony pays that very considerable salary — which was never, I may say, sir, paid more ungrudgingly

than when it was handed over to you — and people
feel that it's only getting a little bit of their own back.
At least, I suppose that's the way they feel," added
Sir Thomas, at a fearful eye-beam from his wife. "I
never take anything on those occasions myself.
Much too old a bird."

"But in your time, dear Lady Lippington," darted
in Lady Tanner, "every one said how much too
prodigal the entertaining was. One could feel absolute confidence in the wines; and the men used
simply to rave about the cheroots. You did far more
than you need!"

"That's so. Must have been out of pocket by it, I
often said," her husband supported her.

Lady Lippington did not blench. It seemed to me
almost as if she saw an opportunity of taking the advice of the ancients and rejecting nothing for her
fire that could be thrown into it, as if the testimony
came rather pat to the occasion.

"I'm so glad!" she said, bending forward quite
appreciatively. "It used to give me such anxious
hours, sometimes. But when one has the interests
of the Empire really at heart ——"

The rest was lost in an enforced decision about
mushroom mousse.

"It's a terrible topic, isn't it, Imperialism?" said
Lady Barbara to Graham.

"In itself?" he asked.

"No, perhaps not.   But people have got so dreadfully tired of it."

"I know," said Graham.   "As a subject it makes them yawn, one might say, before they open their mouths."

"Does it really interest you?" she added; and he laughed and said, "I wouldn't admit it for the world."

"Why not?" she asked; and at that it seemed to me that, after all, Graham was fairly safe.   Anybody that at such a point could ask "Why not?" — well ——

I was quite sure that her brother Peter would not. He would know, infallibly, whether one were joking. He would never have had the reputation, as Evelyn said he had, of being a lamb, a dear and precious lamb, without a sense of those things.

"I think," I said to him, "you know our friend, Evelyn Dicey?"

"I met her," he replied, "the day after I arrived."

His tone implied — or was it again my imagination? — that it was rather soon.

"She seems to be a great friend of my mother's," he went on.

"We have known her for years," I observed.

"My mother hasn't.   It was only the other day that she picked — I mean it's quite a recent acquaintance."

"Evelyn seems devoted to Lady Doleford," I said.

I

"Yes," he admitted, "she does seem to have wakened them up a bit."   But he spoke with gloom. "She's very American," he added.

"I think Americans like being very," I said, "and I don't believe they can help it."

"Well, yes — I suppose they couldn't be just rather," said Lord Doleford, "but it might be nicer of them somehow."

"You see it's so radical," I said.   "But Evelyn is charming. She's such fun!"

"Yes, she is charming. And she is fun."

"You will find her so," I assured him; and at that he gave me a look with a curious little tinge of resentment, which I hope, however, he saw at once that I did not deserve.

When the men came up after dinner Lord Doleford and Graham came in together, with the air of having talked all the way upstairs. They were afterwards separated with difficulty by Lady Lippington, who wished to converse herself with my brother upon a sofa. That was always the way with Graham. People who would not look at me twice —— However, it was only proper that Lord Doleford should go and sit down beside Lady Tanner; and besides, at that time it did not make the slightest difference where he sat.

"You are going on somewhere, I suppose," said our hostess, with the slightest perceptible glance

at the tiara, as Lady Tanner said good-night; and
Lady Tanner, with just an instant's hesitation, said:
"Yes."

"Where?" asked Sir Thomas; and the question
did not seem impertinent, but his wife took no notice
of it.

"And you?" asked Lady Lippington.

"Only to bed," I replied, at which dear Lord Lippington laughed so heartily that I felt I had made
quite a consummate jest.

CHAPTER IX

We had long supposed — and wouldn't you? — that we had seen the very last of Mrs. Jerome Jarvis. But, no; one day, in sweeping out her conscience, she found us there in a cobwebby corner. I am sure conscience must be turned out in London like rooms, periodically, if people are to live upon any terms with their obligations. The air is as full of distractions, of endless, delightful, hurrying interests as it is of "blacks"; and one could perfectly imagine Mrs. Jarvis finding things in a fearful state and dashing at the task. Or perhaps somebody reminded her of us — she knew Evelyn and Earl Watchett. At all events, we received from her during one week a perfect torrent of propositions, all friendly, all casual, and never extending more, by any chance, than twenty-four hours' notice. Our own little plans had begun to multiply so fast that we could never do the things she suggested, without consideration of whether we wanted to or not; but at last she sent an invitation which found us free. Mrs. Jerome asked us to dine with her — no party — the following Wednesday, and go on to a dance at her sister's

— Mrs. Jack Yilke — in Gros. Street: "Do squeeze it in somehow," she wrote. "I've been mis. at seeing nothing of you."

"Oh, Graham," I said, "we must go! Mrs. Jack Yilke is an M.F.H."

"Didn't we come across her somewhere?"

"Yes," I said, "at Lady Doleford's. She was the one that talked most of the time to the Duke — on the hearthrug."

"At Lady Doleford's?" said Graham, and appeared to consider. "Nevertheless," he continued, "another meal at Mrs. Jerome Jarvis's is more food than I think we need accept for nothing, Sis."

"I don't think you ought to cherish that luncheon," I told him; "it just didn't happen to agree with us, and we ought to forget it."

"Well, if you think going to dinner will help you to forget going to lunch ——"

"It always does!" I exclaimed triumphantly, "in everyday life! How can a lunch survive a dinner? You know quite well."

My brother consulted a pocket-diary, and his brow cleared.

"Wednesday," he said, "is one of the possible days Watchett mentioned for the Decentralisation debate in the House. I couldn't miss that, Sis. Suppose you go this time by your lonesome? There's nothing in it for me — and life, you know, is short."

"Yes, it is. And you spent three quarters of an hour of it yesterday looking at that old Venetian sideboard while I waited in the cab," I reminded him. "And it's 'you Mrs. Jerome Jarvis wants, you know, Graham. She hasn't been mis. at seeing nothing of me.

"However," I continued — seeing that I could persuade him if I really tried — "I might go alone. If she doesn't like it she won't mind telling me — that's one comfort."

"Well, if you could," said Graham. "You see I would be no manner of use at a dance, would I — with my leg?"

He knew quite well that no argument could withstand a reference to his leg, though to do him justice he very seldom made one. I would always bow to his leg.

So I went to dinner with the Jerome Jarvises alone. I half-expected to find Andy, but he was not there. John and Patricia, of course, were in bed, and Mr. Jerome, to my disappointment, was attending a City dinner. I had been counting on observing this time the other side of Mrs. Jerome's character. I was longing to see whether her eye would soften when it rested upon Mr. Jarvis. Graham, when he put me in the cab, had asked me to notice if it did.

Instead of Mr. Jarvis there were two young men,

one of whom was very solemn and bowed with a look of gratification every time he replied to Mrs. Jarvis, who called him Guy. I thought, perhaps, he explained to some extent, the fascination she was supposed to have exerted over the great philosophers of the past — and I looked at him with much attention; but he was like Andy in having very little to say on his own account, so one could only guess.

The other young man was a Mr. Milliken, and to my astonishment he called Mrs. Jerome Jarvis "mummy." So Mr. Jerome Jarvis had had a predecessor! I could not help wondering whether she had been as successful a character as Mrs. Milliken, or whether it had taken the two J's to bring her out.

"I'm sorry you didn't bring your nice tall brother," she told me. "It would be much better for him to be seeing London than sitting in the Strangers' Gallery in the House. He could have read the debate in to-morrow's *Times*. I always do, when any of my friends speak; and the House is full of my friends. It's a great mistake to take things too seriously; I take the *Times* with my coffee, and get it over for the day. What do you do?"

"I see that Graham gets it," I said. "He says it's compressed England. I read a smaller paper — just compressed news."

"What do **you** do, Billy Milliken?" asked Mrs. Jarvis.

"Never see any of 'em, practically," said Mr. Milliken. "They get to Oxford too late in the mornin'. There's an afternoon rag published there I generally look at. An' the *Sportin' and Dramatic*, as a rule."

"You can say the 'Pink Un,' if you like. It won't hurt my feelings, Billy," said Mrs. Jarvis. "I believe in calling a spade a spade, and the 'Pink Un's' the very ace of spades, isn't it?"

"Now you're trying to get at me, mummy. As usual. I don't bring it home, do I? It's ripping good literature, the 'Pink Un.'"

Mr. Milliken was small and fair and ruddy, with a yellow moustache, and looked very knowing.

"Are you studying at Oxford?" I asked him.

"I'm up — yes," he said.

"Isn't it thrilling, being at Oxford?" I asked. "My brother says it's the greatest temptation of England — Oxford."

"I don't know what he means by the greatest temptation. It's a damp hole. What does he mean?"

"I think he means that Oxford would tempt him to be an Englishman more than anything else over here. If a person could choose, of course. He isn't an Englishman — no, he's not an American either. He's a Canadian, so, of course, it's settled for him. But if he could choose. Do you know any of the Rhodes Scholars at Oxford?"

"Can't say I actually know any of 'em. I've seen them about, of course. They're not hard to pick out, by any means. But they're getting broken in a bit now —they're not so woolly as they were, really."

"Aren't they?"

"They're chaps with such extr'ordinary ideas, you know, and such remarkable clothes. I think myself it was a rippin' good idea of old Rhodes's — it only wants one thing to make it a success. The men ought to be forbidden to bring Colonial outfits — see? Then they'd get their kit in Oxford, an' any tailor could put them on to what was worn in term. Pity he didn't think of that, isn't it?"

"It is a pity. Great men are so often careless about clothes, aren't they?"

"That's right. Of course it would take them longer to get into what might be called manners an' customs. This is the sort of thing those chaps do. A lot of us were dining in Hall one night at the beginning of term, when in walked one of 'em, very raw. He took his seat, looked round, and 'My name's Goodge,' says he, sort of bluff, you know, and hearty. Well, nobody says a word — what was there to say, you know? Nobody'd asked him what his silly name was. But after a minute the fellow opposite him — I forget who it was — looked him all over, and said: '*Aow!*' Well, what else was there to say, you know?"

"Poor Goodge!" I said.

"Personally, I don't mind them," conceded Mr. Milliken. "I have no prejudices in the matter whatever. They simply haven't happened to come my way."

"Is Billy telling you about Oxford?" asked Mrs. Jarvis. "Ask him, please, from me, if he sees any prospect of his degree this term. He finds Oxford so fascinating — nothing will induce him to leave it."

"Getting at me again," responded Mr. Milliken calmly. "Fearful thing, the modern mother. Always getting at you. You're fearfully modern, mummy. And it's old-fashioned this year — quite out of date. Ain't it, Pontex?"

"I don't know. You must ask my brother," said Mr. Pontex. "Whenever I don't know I always ask my brother."

"That's his brother John," said Mrs. Jarvis to me, "who wrote 'The Anglo-Saxon,' you know. A very clever man."

"Yes, John is a clever man," said Mr. Guy Pontex; "a great deal cleverer than I am, as anybody can see. But he wrote a stupid book. I can't read his stupid book, though my brother John wrote it."

"Cheer up, old man!" said Billy Milliken. "Neither can I."

"And I've only read about so much," said Mrs. Jarvis reassuringly, measuring it off on her finger. "It's much too clever for me, Guy."

"It's too stupid for me," said Guy, with a grave inclination.

I remembered what Evelyn had said about his being "wanting," and wondered why Mrs. Jarvis had asked him to dinner. However, it was not very noticeable so long as he only bowed after he had said something. But he sometimes did it in the pauses of the conversation, as if to contribute what little he could, and then one could only try not to see.

"I hope you will tell Billy all about Canada," said Mrs. Jerome to me. "You may take him back with you if you like. I have absolutely no further use for him."

Mrs. Jarvis did not explain what use she thought I could have for Billy, so I said: "Could he milk cows?"

"What a practical question!" exclaimed Mrs. Jerome. "Say 'Yes!' Billy, at once. Miss Trent won't look at you if you can't milk cows!"

"Can you milk cows, Guy, old man?" asked Billy; and poor Guy replied — it was agonising for me:

"I don't know. You must ask my brother John."

"Well, there is one thing Mr. Pontex can do,"

Mrs. Jarvis assured me. "He can dance divinely —
can't you, Guy? And he is going on with us to-night
when you will see, my little new friend from Canada,
how well he dances."

"Am I bagged, too," said Billy Milliken, "for a
dance of Aunt Joan's?"

"Yes, Billy," said his mother firmly. "I promised
her faithfully. And I look to you, Miss Trent, to
see that he fulfils his obligations. I leave him to
you."

It was Billy's opportunity to say something grace-
ful; but he postponed it. He tried to look lugu-
brious, but his moustache was so yellow and his face
so round that it was impossible. We finished dinner
while I was still wondering why I should be given
such insistent charge of Billy. However, it was
better than being made responsible for Mr. Pontex.
That I should have managed, I think, to decline;
but Billy was too absurd to object to.

Mrs. Jarvis and I drove in her electric brougham,
Mr. Pontex and Billy following in a cab. Mrs. Jarvis
looked out once or twice to see whether they really
were following.

"It is coming behind, all right, the cab," she said.
"They won't shake us off now."

"Don't they want to come to the dance?" I asked
in some surprise.

"Oh, my dear, innocent child, what is a dance to

young men in London? Just a great big bore; and as they don't even pretend that it isn't, why should we? I like being perfectly simple and candid, don't you? I must say I sympathise with them to some extent. They know perfectly well what they are brought there for. I suppose in your beautiful Arcadian Canada you have no such thing as designing mammas?"

"I don't think there are many," I said.

"Oh, well, London swarms with them, and nobody is too young to be caught. Poor Billy himself was once well hooked, but luckily by a relation, so I could insist on his being put back."

"Put back where?" I asked.

"In the pond," said Mrs. Jarvis. "That is a little simile of mine. Do you know what a simile is? He was only twenty-one — too absurd. I do thank my Heavenly Father for having sent me in addition only Patricia. Not that I wouldn't love a grown-up daughter, but in the meantime I must look to Billy for that. What do you think of my Billy?"

"I found him very entertaining indeed," I said.

"I'm *so* glad! Not clever, you know, in the sense of the word nowadays, but a heart of gold, dear old Billy. And so frank and straightforward — he takes after me there. No special prospects, you know. Never more, I'm afraid, than four or five hundred a year of his own — just a well-groomed, well-mannered young English gentleman. And there's nothing like it in the world, is there? I mean, whatever you do, be on your guard against foreigners. What you may call the marrying foreigner is usually perfectly unscrupulous. I could tell you tales!"

It is the kind of thing one is ashamed to write, but I must confess that I drew from Mrs. Jarvis at this moment the definite thrill of a new perception, something captivating and delicious. Suddenly, without Graham, without anybody, moving through the lovely, thronged, wet, lamplit London streets in Mrs. Jarvis's electric brougham, I felt myself realised — realised in London, not only by the person who happened to be near me, but in a vague, delightful, potential sense by London. Realised, not a bit for what I was — that wouldn't, I am afraid, have carried me very far — nor exactly for what I represented, but for something else, for what I might, under favourable circumstances, be made to represent. The odd part was that seeing it on this lower level made no difference to the thrill, which had its wonderful source in the fact that London should take one into account at all. It was even part of the thrill to know that one would be obliged, in a way, to hand oneself over. It was even a happier excitement to see that nothing in the matter was to be taken for granted, that I was only a possibility, a raw product, to be melted or hammered or woven into London, by my leave. And that was superb to experience, the solicitation, even tacit and involved, of London, the knowledge that one was taken as important enough, one was coloured by what one had or what one's father had, as being important enough, to make suggestions to. I suppose it was a practical lesson in the consequence of having; but what I drew from it immediately, besides the joy itself, was a point of view. It was a point of view from which one could feel, looking out at the endless luxurious whirl of it, a kind of divine disdain of London, as if one had suddenly got behind the scenes with her, and no longer felt so prodigiously impressed. And that in itself was a sensation intensely worth having; but all this time Mrs. Jerome Jarvis was talking, talking.

"I have quite fallen in love with your brother, you know," she was saying. "Hopelessly in love with him."

"People nearly always do like Graham," I replied calmly.

"I think his nickname suits him beautifully."

"Has he got a nickname?" I asked.

"Didn't you know he was called 'the Maple Prince'? Why, it was in the *World of Society* last week; didn't you see the paragraph?"

"Evelyn Dicey," I reflected aloud, "must have started that."

"Oh, it was a charming paragraph! — a little

about you, too — and it made you out the most enviable young people imaginable. And there was a little joke in it, too, about the Maple Prince being the only one in London at present who could point to his principality — a place called New Brunswick, isn't it ?"

"Not the whole of it," I remonstrated.

"You must show me on the map. Well, I've always been in favour of drawing Colonial ties closer. You, of course, are a charming little person, with a very pretty style of your own — you don't mind my speaking straight from the heart like this? — but I am one of those who think that he is perfectly possible, too."

"Perfectly possible !" I repeated. "Do you mean my brother ?"

"What I mean is this. You must have noticed that American men are very seldom absorbed in this country. American women, of course, go down like anything — we can't swallow them fast enough; but the men, somehow — no. But with your nice brother it's different. Colonial he certainly is, but only to the extent of a few mannerisms, which he would soon lose. Try to think of him as a country gentleman in England, and he's quite in the picture, isn't he? You and he together," said Mrs. Jarvis impressively, "might do a great deal for Canada in this country."

"How?" I enquired.

"Popularise it socially.   Drag it out of history and geography," said Mrs. Jarvis.   "Nobody cares about history and geography, but plenty of people will care about the Maple Prince — and Princess."

"Well, if it involves Graham's turning into an English country gentleman," I said emphatically, "I'm afraid it won't come off."

"Why not? I am sure he could do it. Very creditably after a bit."

"Because nothing," I said, "would induce him to."

"Ah! We'll see," said Mrs. Jarvis. "He could turn into something much worse, you know. Here we are at Joan's. And Billy and Guy, the angels, here they are, too!"

K

CHAPTER X

THE first person we saw when at last we got through
to Mrs. Yilke's ballroom was the Earl of Doleford
dancing with Evelyn Dicey. Evelyn danced perfectly always; she got the last possible vibration of
grace out of the movement and the music, and her
partner suited her. They looked there in the twin-
kling perspective of Mrs. Yilke's ballroom like two
people doing something together, something more or
less dictated that they should do together, and doing
it rather well. The glimpse of it made me obscurely
feel London again, or the great English world that
flowers so supremely in London, the great auto-com-
pulsive English world of London, suggesting that
Lord Doleford should dance with Evelyn, and Evelyn
with Lord Doleford, as the sum of all the proprieties
and expediencies, the quickest, surest way of earning
her indispensable blessing.

"Are they engaged yet?" asked Mrs. Jarvis, as the
two waltzed past us.

"I don't know. I don't think so," I said.

"The Countess and Barbara are simply dying for
it. An American for Peter has been their only hope
for years; but poor dear Lady Doleford has always

wanted to pick her American. As if it mattered two straws! Now she has picked her American and *la voila!* Not so prodigiously rich as some of them, but with the right ideas about religious teaching in the schools; and that, with the dear Countess, was of the first importance. She was desperately afraid of what you might call a secular American."

"But how could Evelyn know what to think about the schools?" I exclaimed.

"I don't know; but she got hold of the right views somehow. Americans are so assimilating, I always think. It's part of their success. Lady Doleford had her to stay for a week at Beaufort Gardens, and sounded her, I imagine, before she took her to her bosom; but now she is always there, and it all hangs on Peter."

"I see," I said, as Billy came up for his dance.

It was at once quite plain, Mrs. Jarvis's wisdom in bringing Billy, who, to do him justice, did dance, very energetically, when once he was resigned to it. Mr. Pontex, too, in his stately way, took me round the room once or twice; but I did not find those perfections which Mrs. Jarvis had advertised. It was a little like dancing with a clock-tower, which kept the most accurate time, and bowed instead of striking the quarters. I preferred to bound like the antelope with Billy. But these two did dance, as I say; and Mrs. Jarvis had known they would. One was a schoolboy and the other very nearly an imbecile; but they did dance; and the room was black with young men who didn't. I looked at them with great interest to try and discover what they were there for; it was certainly no form of exercise. The most active thing many of them did was to stand about and wear their clothes and caress their moustaches. They looked tolerant, well-disposed, inclined to be pleased if it was not too much trouble, and, above all things, beautifully taken care of, perfectly produced. They seemed in a way the achievements as well as the hopes of the women who sat about admiring them, and pathetically waiting for some attention from them. Other persons of course must have contributed — all sorts of trainers and tailors, and one was sorry for them that they couldn't be there to take their humble part in the splendid result. Impassive in appearance, they were conscious in fact, like prime creatures upon exhibition, and they had a tendency to move toward one another, with furtive glances, from which they seemed to derive mutual support. Speaking as a stranger, I was very pleased with them; but it was impossible not to wish that they wore their awards. Most of them, I think, would have obtained at least a "Highly Commended." It seemed to me that they treated one another with a certain deference, as if each recognised in each something very special and supreme; and beside their lofty freedom poor Billy had all the air of a terrier on a string.

As a rule I noticed that the younger ones had very little to say. The briefest exchange over folded arms seemed enough to indicate their acquiescence, as it were, in the occasion; and smiles were freely used as substitutes for anything more laborious. This was particularly true of those, in the very pink of conscious desirability, who were there upon their own divine bachelor sufferance, and a little oppressed, one could see, with the idea that it was weak of them to come. It was less and less characteristic as the bloom rubbed off, and fostering conditions perhaps began to be withdrawn; and among those with the look of being quite thrown upon their own resources were the few industrious dancers. I thought myself fairly certain of a dance when Billy introduced a bald gentleman, a Mr. Lane-Gwithers; but I was disappointed. He explained at once that it would be impossible; he could only ask me to sit out. He took the matter very seriously, and enlarged upon it.

"It's a curious thing, you know," said Mr. Lane-Gwithers, "but as a matter of fact, I should be absolutely precluded from dancing with you to-night."

"Not lumbago, I hope," I said.

"Not lumbago. Oh, no! Something even more binding."

"What can it be?" I said. Whatever it was I could see it was very much on his mind.

"Well," said Mr. Lane-Gwithers, "it's something in the nature of a public disavowal. Do you see the *London Daily?*"

"Generally I do," I said.

"If you look up the *London Daily* for last Wednesday, you will find in it the statement that at a certain ball in Belgrave Square a number of dancing men were present, including Mr. Ambrose Lane-Gwithers. That's me. Those were their exact words. 'A number of dancing men,' et cetera. Well," said Mr. Lane-Gwithers, slapping his knee in a desultory, accustomed manner with his gloved hand, "what was I to do?"

"And weren't you there?" I asked breathlessly.

"What was I to do?" repeated Mr. Lane-Gwithers. "It was a serious matter for me, you see, bein' published like that as a dancing man. These editor-fellows, in their anxiety to fill up their papers, don't stop to realise what they're doing half the time. I don't particularly blame them — I daresay it isn't so easy — but what was I to do? I'll tell you what I did do. I wrote to the paper — a regular letter to the editor, you know."

"Did you tell him what you thought of him?"

"Not I! He wouldn't have put it in — and that was my object, you see, to get it in. I began by quoting his statement in full, just as I have to you.

Then I said: 'Now, sir, I can prove to your satisfaction that there is only one Ambrose Lane-Gwithers in London society; and I will ask you to accept my personal statement that I have never been to a ball in Belgrave Square in my life. Further,' I said, 'I am afraid I cannot claim to be a dancing man, being of the opinion that the spectacle of a bright and shining pate circulating round in the gay and giddy waltz is simply ridiculous. Apologising,' I said, 'for trespassing at such length on your valuable space, I am, yours, &c., A. Lane-Gwithers.'"

"And did he put it in?"

"Rather! The very next day. I daresay he saw the humour of it."

"I wonder if he did?" I said pensively.

"Of course I've been roasted over it ever since, but I expected that. And I consider I've saved my reputation."

"Taking into account the number of people who read the *London Daily*, I should think you had made it," I replied.

It was so interesting that I quite regretted, after that, any invitation which was not to sit out. I wanted so much to discover the precise point at which each of them would have felt compelled to explain about himself in the papers. Which of them, for instance, being reported by a journal to have appeared in the Park with a red tie, would have assured the

public that he never wore a red tie in his life, at all
events since he had chosen his own ties, that red was
peculiarly obnoxious to him and particularly impossible, he being of opinion that the spectacle of this
colour combined with a fair complexion and a yellow moustache was an outrage upon society. I did
not elicit as much as that; but I made careful ex-
plorations and was very well rewarded. Profound,
profound it was; one hesitated at the brink of such
a sense of personal importance. Graham, when I
told him about it, said that probably none of them
had ever earned a penny in their lives, and that
nothing so contributed to swelled head as a false
relation to the economic basis of society. But I am
sure it needs more than that to explain the solemn
phenomena of those young men. There must be
climatic, moral, philosophical reasons to account for
them, probably something very creditable. It is
impossible that they could come to such perfection
anywhere but in the captial of the most serious
country in the world.

Lord Doleford asked me for Number Seven, and
whether I cared about it. I said not particularly. I
thought he looked disappointed, and was immediately
sorry, suddenly remembering that he was just back
from India and perhaps would have liked to. So I
said as awkwardly as possible: "I'll dance if you
like."

"Suppose we take just one turn," he said; and we went round two or three times.

"But," I said, as we paused, "you seem to like it!"

"Of course I like it," he replied; "that's not surprising, is it? Did you think I was too infirm?"

"Not at all," I said, "but the others don't, do they?" It seems a bald and foolish reply, and that was what I felt it to be.

"The others?" he said, and looked at a knot of them, standing near. "Oh, those fellows! They don't know what's good for them. They've been allowed to stay too long in England. I'd like to see every one of them planted out for three or four years in Dera Ismail Khan. When they came back they would dance, and be uncommon pleased to get the chance."

"Would you like to go on?" I said.

"Not if you're tired. No? Then — it's awfully good of you!"

We finished it so vigorously that for a moment or two, when it was over and we found chairs, we simply panted in unison. I was more or less glad I had to pant, for I now saw clearly that I would never be able to talk at all intelligently to Lord Doleford. I don't wish to say that I found him antipathetic — not in the least. I am afraid I can't account for it by anything in him, unless I might have suspected him of being somewhat critical of people from our side of the Atlantic — had he not been rather severe upon Evelyn? Now that I come to think of it, that had, I daresay, a good deal to do with it. There must be some way of explaining it when a person properly brought up, and quite well, is as nervous as I was whenever a pause in the conversation seemed to suggest that I should go on with it. I had positively to remember that I had been properly brought up, and that I wasn't likely to make any mistakes that mattered, even in this conventional England, where, I had already noticed, one may say a hundred things that are not at all correct so long as they are of the kind that it is correct to say incorrectly. I felt very angry with my paralysed tongue. To confess all my silly fears, I was afraid the Earl of Doleford might think — how little I knew him ! — that I was stupidly impressed with his exalted rank and his so beautifully matching it in appearance; which, of course, I was in a way, but not in that way. I was not, as a rule, awkward and silent with people; and their being earls, when they were earls, had made no difference so far. Having been brought up with Graham helped, I suppose, to account for it; it wasn't as if I had nothing to fall back on.

Fortunately, Lord Doleford had himself a good deal to say, and seemed extraordinarily interested, too, in saying it — extraordinarily, that is, for a young man in London. He was like a person who has had his conversation dammed up for a long time, and he poured it out delightfully, not noticing, or not seeming to notice in the least, that I was falling from abyss to abyss of sheer imbecility. What will be thought of me when I say that he was finally obliged to ask my opinion of English weather?

"I like it," I said; "it's always clearing up."

"So it is," he agreed. "Always improving — or getting worse. Like life. There's variety in our old English weather. I like it too. You can't count on the infernal sun, day in an' day out. I imagine there's variety in the Canadian weather, too, isn't there? Pretty violent variety."

"I know," I said, "you think we're constantly either having our noses frozen or getting the skin burned off them. But it isn't like that always, or even for much of the time."

"I daresay we get hold of wrong notions," he said. "The old tales, you know, of the Elizabethan explorers — they stick in our heads. You might make your climate over again before we realised there had been any change in it. It must be a good country — Canada. I'd like to see it."

"Why didn't you go there, instead of to India?" I asked.

"One can't always choose," said he. (Mightn't I have known that?) "My people have generally found their job in India, somehow. Besides, they run their own show out there. They wouldn't have any use for a chap like me."

"We do run our own show," I told him. "But there are lots of other things to do, you know, besides running the show."

"I know. I suspect it's the mistake we make, we English, that we must always be in the management, wherever we go. The Colonies teach us better, but we're slow at seeing things. And there's always India to keep up the idea. I thought once of ranching — I'm not such a duffer at horses — but that takes capital, doesn't it?"

"Graham could tell you," I assured him.

"I'm afraid it's too late in the day!" he laughed. "And I don't regret India, you know. It's a fine thing, India — and great luck for us, that we've got it to do. Either for soldiering or civil work — I've had a little of both — there's a day's work to be found in India that asks a fellow for all he's got. And it's a country a man can stretch himself in, you know — not like this."

"England isn't quite big enough to be a country, is it? In the geographical sense, I mean. But it's a heavenly place," I said — "especially London. Don't you think so?"

"I grant you this," said Lord Doleford — "it's a good place to come back to. And when you're in harness anywhere in the open it's out-and-out good to know it's always there. But it's a bad place to find work in, if you want anything better than a secretaryship to a charitable organisation. You suffer so from the competition of cleverer chaps. It's full of infernally clever chaps. Unless you're one of them I don't think it's much of a place to spend a lifetime in. And the air's thick with money. To me it would be a kind of penal servitude," he said gloomily, and as if it were an argument he often had occasion to use.

"Have you got to face it?"

"Oh, well! sooner or later it will have to be considered, I suppose. Personally, I should like to get into the permanent civil line in India — enter the Foreign Office, you know, and work up. If you're any good they may give you a little kingdom to run before you've done. There are lots of them going."

"Little kingdoms?"

"Yes; belonging to Maharajahs, you know. You take the Maharajah on as well, of course. But my mother is dead against it, and my uncle, and everyone belonging to me."

Lord Doleford stared into space with real dejection, and I felt very sorry for him. I looked all round my mind for some way of saying so, but there was nothing to be found, so I could only try to make my silence as sympathetic as possible. His case seemed another illustration, amazing and a little absurd, of that curious authority by which the simple social structure and scheme of things in England could interfere with a person born in it, at all events if he happened to be born at all importantly.

"I call it great luck to belong to a place like Canada," he said; "no bother in seeing your way, out there. No impedimenta."

"I was just thinking so," I said.

"Look at your brother. There's a fellow to be envied. See what he can do, and help to bring about, in a country like that."

"I know," I said; "and he's going to." There was something very exhilarating in hearing Graham envied by Lord Doleford.

"They offer me politics, too, you know," he went on; "or what they call politics. A seat nobody can take away from me, and the opportunity of making speeches nobody is interested enough to interrupt. Bah — birth's a rotten borough!"

"My father is a member of our Upper House," I said, "and he was appointed, not elected, and it's for life; and they don't interrupt him a great deal; but he doesn't feel like that about it."

"If he was appointed it was because he jolly well deserved it, I imagine. It's a very different thing, making your own place and finding it ready-made."

I had, at the time, a confused feeling that this was unreasonable, and the argument of a person on his defence against doing something that he didn't want to do; and afterwards in the night, I saw quite clearly that Lord Doleford's real place couldn't be made for him by anybody but himself, and that it didn't really matter much whether his starting-point was in the Lords or the Commons, or just in the street. But at the moment none of these useful ideas came.

"Yes, it would be nicer!" I said out of my vacuity. It seemed to me we were in desperate regions for discussion, and that I must drag myself out of them somehow if I was to look back upon a single intelligent remark on my part in the humiliating course of the evening. We were sitting near a half-opened window, and a sharp sound struck through the street. I grasped at it desperately.

"There!" I said. "That's the only thing I don't like in London."

"The hansoms?"

"No, the whistles for them. The poor nervous horses trying to catch a passenger, and getting lashed and tearing up, knocking their poor hoofs against the cobble-stones, and not knowing why in the world, but just blindly competing in the dark under the whip. I get horrid thrills of sympathy for the horse, especially for the disappointed horse."

I saw by Lord Doleford's smile that he understood exactly.

"There is no disappointment this time," he said.

"Is there? Only one came up. Poor brutes, yes.
One sees it in their eyes sometimes, that single frightened spark that says 'I've got to get there, whatever
happens.' You like them, then — horses?"

"I adore them!" I said, and presently we were
both, metaphorically, mounted. I do not wonder
that horses played such an important part in ancient
mythology — they will save any situation. As a
subject they appeal so, in their simple, serious, noble
way, that there is not room left in the mind for a
shred of self-consciousness or any of the meaner
things. Anybody who can claim acquaintance with
a horse is on masonic terms with anybody else who
can; and after that, thanks to the fact that I could
tell him from personal experience something about
bronchos, I was pleased to feel that Lord Doleford
did not consider my conversation quite negligible.

"I hope you will come in for some hunting," he
said.

"I don't hunt," I told him, "but I hope to see it
done."

"'See it done!'" he repeated, as if it amused him.
"Well, at this time of year there ought to be no
difficulty about that. Which Hunt are you going to
honour by inspecting it?"

"I don't know," I said, "but we are to stay with
the Lippingtons in the country in January, and Lady
Lippington mentioned that there would be a Meet

while we were there.   It was the very thing I most longed for."

"Oh, but that's the Famine!" exclaimed Lord Doleford. "The South Crosshires. Capital! We must find you a mount."

The music had begun again some moments before, and he suddenly consulted his programme.

"Can that be Number Ten?   The dev — I mean I'm afraid I must leave you, Miss Trent.   Or can I take you anywhere?"

"Please don't mind," I said.   "Here is Mr. Milliken, and I think it's his dance."

Billy Milliken thought, however, that an interval should be allowed for refreshments.   There was rather a jam near the supper-room; and while we waited our chance to penetrate, I glanced back and saw Lord Doleford once more engaging Evelyn Dicey in the waltz.

CHAPTER XI

By this time it had grown quite clear to me that
Graham was seriously in love. Not with any lady —
with England. It might be thought from what I
put down earlier that it was always he who supplied
the critical note in our experiences, and I who blindly
admired and gratefully seized. But that had regard
only to things of the surface, little matters of taste
and custom, and especially to the national attitude
toward other Anglo-Saxons. Wherever we pene-
trated deeper it was Graham who really cared most;
and I think his sensitiveness to the little things was
exactly because he did care so much about the big
ones. I was always amused in London; Graham
was always occupied; where I found spectacle, he
found drama and the matter of life. I was in love
with England, too, but not seriously; mine was an
attachment I could take home and talk about. I
wanted to take other things, too — clothes and ideas
and old china, anything portable. I had distinctly,
now that I come to analyse it, a plundering feeling
toward the mother country. One couldn't remove
St. Martin's-le-Grand, or a blue distance out of
Hyde Park, or a wet omnibus with the sun on it, or

the Cockney character, but I thanked Heaven that there was a good deal that one could remove, and I wanted to fly back with it, like a bird of prey, and enjoy it with my family in Minnebiac. Graham, on the contrary, seemed hardly to have a rapacious thought. What he seemed rather to bemoan was the impossibility of contributing anything.

"Look at that!" he would say of Westminster Abbey, or the hall in the Temple where Shakespeare played to Elizabeth. "Confound them, they've finished it! Where do *we* come in?"

That was his trouble always, that everything fine and supreme was finished, consummated, left standing, and that the Further Briton, however eager his heart, could only "come in" like a wave of the Atlantic, and break upon the shore. One or two little things he did find to do, concerned with a certain sacred folio and a small Jacobite collection, for which the local authorities were outbid by gentlemen from New York and Chicago. Graham saw it in the paper and was just in time in each case — it was only a matter of a few hundred pounds, from Heaven or anywhere, according to the *Times*. They were very nice to him about it, the local authorities; he said when he came back that he had been given the moral freedom of Oxford, and that the old gentleman in charge of the folio very nearly wept upon his shoulder. He took a high line that evening about the treasures of the race that had been carried off by the Americans, and talked of a crusade from the Imperial North at some future day, to rescue and restore them. I think he saw himself, with satisfaction, riding over the border in some time of inter-American war, at the head of a chosen predatory band, or navigating some majestic ship as far as possible up the Thames, laden with spoils recaptured for the National Gallery.

Graham was so desperately serious about everything that I could not help thinking of his growing attachment to England with a little anxiety lest something should come of it. I could see exactly how it was affecting him. It was with a kind of passion to realise his right of identification with the people, their ideas and their standards and their history, their ways of doing things and the things they had done. He wanted his moral birthright, in some kind of recognisable way.

He didn't thirst at all to assist in their immediate problems. He was, indeed, unsympathetic to Colonial members of the English Parliament; he called them geographical anomalies. For his own energy and muscle his own country was the field; but there was a part of him that longed for dedication and share in the common wealth of æsthetics that is so much richer and more rewarding where the Empire began.

"Don't you see, Sis," he said to me, "the dear old

show is far more our priceless inheritance than it is that of the freeborn Briton who pays the taxes, and thinks he comes in for it. He doesn't inherit it at all — how can he? He's always had it. He doesn't know how beautiful and appreciable and humorous it all is — how can he? It's what he has been brought up to."

"He sees funny little things in us, I daresay," I observed.

"Yes," said Graham, "but they don't amount to a fortune. Now, we with our empty country and our simple record, we've got a point of view, if you like. It's inestimable. Life isn't long enough to look in, if you want to get anything else done."

He would get quite feverish about that. And the worst of it was, we hadn't to be near any great national monument to produce such ardours in him. A street contact would be enough, a paragraph in a newspaper. Towse would do it; Lady Doleford, in particular, had this effect upon him.

"She's like some dear old abbey," he said. "She doesn't belong at all to the present; she has no modern improvements. She looks as if she would much rather be dead and buried and razed to the ground; but she won't be, you'll see, until Peter the Earl marries Evelyn, and she sees things the way she wants them. Till then she'll totter, the way she does now, but she won't fall; her traditions will hold

her together. The day after the wedding we will
hear she has collapsed in the night."

"What about Barbara?" I asked.

"Won't Evelyn take care of her?"

"I suppose she would," I replied; "I didn't think
of that."

"She's a nice girl—Barbara," said Graham
thoughtfully. "I take an interest in Barbara. I would
protect Barbara myself if she were alone in the world.
But with a brother the size of Doleford, and relatives
like the sands of the sea ——"

"You won't be wanted," I completed. "Evelyn
says the relatives are all badly off, though. They
haven't sixpence among them, except the Lippingtons, and they're not very near. There seems to be
a kind of English relation that can lend you a house
in town and mount you in the country, and present
you at Court, but her usefulness stops there."

"Then it all depends—for Barbara—upon brother
Peter," said Graham.

"I'm afraid it does," I said.

Graham flung himself down in an armchair and
thrust his hands into his pockets. We were in the flat.

"How do you think Lady Barbara compares with
Ethel Carter?" he enquired.

"Ethel Carter of Montreal? Why, I don't think
there is any comparison!" I exclaimed. "They're
so different."

"There's always a comparison," he insisted, "between one girl and another. They're both tall, and they've got the same coloured hair."

"Yes," I said, "and the same number of fingers, and probably of toes. But as to type —— "

"I don't see," said Graham, "that there's such an extraordinary difference in type. Ethel hasn't the bearing, quite, of Lady Barbie, but she's much better read."

"The daughter of a hundred earls, or even fifty, ought to hold herself well," I said. "I suppose it doesn't matter so much what she reads."

"Perhaps, on the whole," pursued Graham, "she is more like Kitty Curtis."

"Kitty Curtis of Toronto!" I exclaimed.

"I don't know any other. And I don't know why you say 'of Toronto' in that tone precisely. It doesn't convey — to me — any local disability."

"Not in the least — when you're there," I hastened to agree.

"When you're anywhere. I think Kitty's manner is quite as good as Lady Barbara's. Where she, Kitty, loses by comparison is in simplicity of nature," pursued Graham. "What impresses you so much as dignity in Barbara Pavisay is just —— "

"Having nothing to fall back upon."

"Not at all. I was going to say just directness. She is absolutely devoid of self-consciousness,"

Graham mused. "It's very attractive. One likes comparing a girl like that with one's own country-women. I must say she holds her own very well."

"That's handsome of you," I remarked ironically, but inwardly I was quite well pleased. If my brother could calmly adjudicate in this way upon the merits of Lady Barbara it seemed pretty clear that there was no need to fear a hopeless entanglement for him in that direction. Why I should have considered it so hopeless I can't quite say; but even then I did. I don't wish to seem exacting for Graham; but it seemed, without knowing more than the outside of Barbara, queer, unlikely, and ridiculous to the last degree, the kind of thing you instinctively dismissed from your mind without stopping to consider why.

Under this impression I encouraged Graham in his tendency to compare Lady Barbara with the girls at home, which he seemed rather to like to do about that time. He was constantly placing her among them, as if to see how she would look; any discussion of her had a way of leading to that. He would never agree with her superiorities where I found them; and where she came short, he would admit it somewhat grudgingly. What he apparently wanted was to establish to his own satisfaction that she occupied much the same level, was in all essentials very much the same sort of girl. That was inconsistent of him, for anyone could see that it was just as part of something very different that he admired her, part of the fine old scheme of things from which we were cut off by exactly that point of view which he valued so much. There was, of course, her beautiful figure, as there was her lovely hair, and one might go on enumerating, but the result would only be so many items and such an aggregate; I could almost see him turn from it with a sigh. It was as if he wanted, even then, for the interest of it, to take a simply human view of her, but invariably she would retreat before his efforts into the impressive architecture of her order; to all his invitations she remained obstinately æsthetic.

We were seeing a good deal of her, of everybody. We were in the midst of a period of dances and dinners and At Homes which made us feel like conjurers' balls, with such wonderful nimbleness we went from one hand to another. One had always thought of London as a place of the austerest conventions, where it was very improbable that any stranger would quite know how to behave; but it was not easy, in the absence of almost all convention and behaviour, to recognise difficulties of that kind. I mean, of course, convention and behaviour of the sort one expected. These seemed to lurk only in an occasional grey citadel like Lady Doleford, which had an apologetic air of begging to remain, though consciously useless against modern weapons. I wouldn't imply that there were not plenty of delightful standards, but they were certainly not exacting of time and circumstance; they made for ease and fluidity and forgetting — a word, a smile, an address scratched down, and there you were, breathless and enchanted, until you were somewhere else. We sometimes wondered how there could ever be time in it all for a friendship to be born, or even a reliable acquaintance; and I asked Mrs. Jerome Jarvis once, who told me that for her part she made a point of keeping her friendships for the country.

"You'll see," she said, "how they grow in the country — how they blossom in our lovely old halls. Has Margot Lippington told you that Billy and I are to be fellow-guests with you at Knowes on the 15th? I am devoted to Margot, you know, and she to me; there is nothing that we can't and won't perform for one another. I must say for Margot she's a staunch friend."

Then I began to wonder whether, for all its appearance of whirl and scramble and superficiality, the whole great organism wasn't very much knit together indeed, by ties of mutual loyalty and obligation — wasn't one fabric, down below, that was thoroughly warranted to wear. One heard so openly of efforts made on behalf of this or that desirable plan, of things done avowedly to help the Lippingtons to get the Canadian Viceroyalty, to fall in with Lady

Doleford's idea of an American for Peter, even to dispose suitably for his own good and in the general interest of Mr. Guy Pontex. These schemes and plans were never very practical or effective; they wore all the restraints of morality; but they were full of benevolent intention, and inspired, above all, with a sense of praiseworthy expediency. It must be very interesting, I fancied, to be fitted into them in any important way, as Evelyn was, and as I began to think Graham some day might be. (It was only that he was more and more about this time at the Colonial Office, and Lord Selkirk chaffed him openly about the probability that he would one day fill the official shoes of the High Commissioner.) Even my own small allotment in the general disposition, represented, as it was impossible by then not to see, by Billy Milliken, brought me an amusement that I won't attempt to justify. I felt like a mouse in the paws of Mrs. Jarvis, her own small Colonial trophy, which she would presently drop at the feet of Society, like rather a fraudulent mouse, perhaps, that really felt no great alarm, and listened with fascination to the purrings of conquest.

Besides, Billy wasn't so inconsiderable, after all; at least, in the eyes of the world, judging by the flattering attention paid him. It couldn't have been entirely because he would dance. His income, though small, was definite; and he had chosen the

Bar as a profession, though this, he confided to me, was nominal, and merely masked, for the moment, his intention of going into politics.

"The country's got into the hands of such a lot of bounders lately," he told me. "A fellow feels more or less expected to do what he can to get it back again."

He had, therefore, lofty ideals; he was ready with any reasonable personal sacrifice for his native land. I say any reasonable sacrifice because there was, I understood, a limit. It had to do with an amendment of the Rules of Procedure about adjournments, which threatened week-ends and the dinner-hour.

"Of course they may make the House impossible for gentlemen altogether," said Billy. "And if they do ——"

If they did, one was obliged to contemplate the contingency that Billy would withdraw. He had not hitherto paid much attention to political matters; he would have to mug them up fresh in any case, he said, at the approach of his candidature, so there was no special point in worrying about it beforehand.

"Besides," he said, "there's always some Cabinet Johnny to speak for you, you know — it isn't as if you had to do it all off your own bat."

"He has great confidence in his mother, too. Haven't you, Billy?" said Mrs. Jerome Jarvis, who was party to this conversation.

"I don't wish to boast, but it would be .idle to deny that my Panhard and I made our Member — last year, in the Redbury bye. How I slaved for that man! I took statistics to bed with me, and spoke three times a day to get them off my mind. Much the best way — otherwise you muddle them. I consider statistics the worst feature of English elections. But Billy shall be returned, Miss Trent — you have his mother's pledge."

It was to Billy's political influence — or possibly his mother's — that I owed the tea-party in the House, the day I was at last sent an order to view. Graham had often been; but there is very little room for us, and I had to wait such a long time before Lord Selkirk could arrange for my admission that Mrs. Jarvis took it into her own hands. It seems a little ungrateful, if many Members owe their seats to a lady and a motor, not to provide more accommodation; and Evelyn, who was also of the party, said that such a thing as the grille couldn't live in Washington for ten minutes.

"The American woman," she remarked, "may not be such a power in politics as they are over here; but the men know better than to invite her to appear in public in a cage for any reason whatever."

We were in charge, very naturally, of the Member for Redbury, to whom Mrs. Jarvis had been such a successful godmother. His name was Tally —

Mr. Albert Tally. He presently came for us, and took us down to the Lobby, where among groups of living legislators in silk hats and effigies of dead ones in stone, we were joined by Billy Milliken, who had been in the Distinguished Strangers' Gallery. Mr. Tally also introduced a Mr. Popplewell, who was even a greater surprise, as a Member of Parliament, than Mr. Tally had been. I had thought Mr. Tally as young as it was possible to be, and be elected; but Mr. Popplewell was younger still, younger in appearance, at all events, even than Billy Milliken. However, it was all very cheerful, and when we were presently further joined by two cousins and a youthful aunt of Mr. Popplewell's it became even more so. We went along the corridors in a body, corridors lined with shelves, weighted with Acts of the serious Parliaments of old days, and finally found a little Gothic room with a window on the river and a table spread.

"Nursery tea — how perfectly sweet !" exclaimed Mr. Popplewell's youthful aunt, and one of Mr. Popplewell's cousins at once removed the seed-cake from his reach, because, she declared, this was a party and he mustn't have all the cake. Mr. Tally at once retorted by seizing the bread and butter, and Mr. Popplewell's aunt, who had been asked to pour out tea, held the teapot aloft and threatened to withhold it until they should behave more properly.

"I call it a nice alimentary tea," said Mrs. Jerome Jarvis, and it was. Honest bread and butter and plenty of it, buns of the most corpulent, good thick slices of seed-cake.

"I'm afraid they've forgotten the jam," said Mr. Tally, and this made everybody laugh very much. Mr. Tally was very lively, very talkative, and his mouth had a disused air when he wasn't laughing. Mr. Popplewell, though less mature, was graver in appearance. He suggested, to have arrived at his present dignity, having done something remarkable at the University. I asked Billy if this wasn't so, and he corroborated it.

"Double First," he murmured; "but Tally was stroke for Magdalen the year they went up three places on the river."

"What's going on?" asked Mr. Tally. "I've been in the reading-room. I've only occupied a seat for a quarter of an hour myself this Session, and then I was turned out."

"Federated Employers again. Whangworth was up when I came out. Rotten subject and a rotter to talk about it," said Mr. Popplewell.

"Why were you turned out?" I asked Mr. Tally.

"Well, there isn't anything like room enough for us all, you know, and the new lot's so beastly keen on places — they seem to enjoy sittin' in 'em. Can't imagine why, unless it's because of the cushions. I find it rather stuffy myself. I'm sorry you came in for Whangworth — he's about our most colossal bore."

"Queer thing, you know," said Mr. Popplewell, "a bore like Whangworth can always catch the Speaker's eye. I suppose he knows he's got to see them in the end — they get up like india-rubber till he does. At all events they're most successful in getting the floor. And then, in the classic phrase of the newspapers, 'the House empties.'"

Billy was entirely occupied with the aunt and two cousins of Mr. Popplewell — they were ardently discussing different kinds of buns, Billy stoutly maintaining against all attacks that there was nothing to be said for any kind of bun. Mr. Tally listened longingly to the debate, but he was too far away to join.

"It's a pity," he said to me instead, "you didn't happen to hear Sammy Simmons instead. Awfully amusing speeches he makes. The House always fills up when it's known Sammy Simmons is on his legs. I go in myself."

"Rather.   Simmons is as good as a musical comedy," said Mr. Popplewell.

"How can we hear anything behind that absurd grating?" asked Mrs. Jerome Jarvis. "I feel like something in the Zoo — I do really — and not the politest animal either. Yet you allow us to call you civilised men!"

"It's your own fault, I'm afraid," said Mr. Popplewell; and we all exclaimed: "How?"

"You used to be allowed in, you know, but you didn't behave at all nicely on a certain occasion."

"When?" asked Evelyn.

"Oh, not very lately!"

"What did we do?" I enquired.

"Cheeky to the Sergeant-at-Arms, I believe. Wouldn't go out pleasantly when he told you to. Sat tight, and no opera-hat was ever in it with your head-dresses."

"I don't believe a word of it!" said Mrs. Jarvis.

"Solemn fact, I assure you. You were technically recognised as strangers then, and when somebody moved that the House be cleared of strangers not one of you would budge. It took two hours to get rid of you."

"When?" asked Evelyn again.

"I'm not absolutely certain, but I think about 1778," said Mr. Popplewell.

"Two hundred and fifty odd years," remarked Evelyn. "You know how to take notice of a thing, don't you? About when do you usually begin to forgive and forget a matter like that?"

"It really is your own fault, though," repeated Mr. Popplewell. "For a hundred years before that we let you in freely — as strangers."

M

"And now we're not even strangers!" exclaimed Mrs. Jarvis.

Just then a bell sounded in the distance, and Mr. Tally and Mr. Popplewell leapt to their feet. "Division!" they cried, and sped with flying coat-tails out of the room, abandoning their tea.

"Take care of my party, Milliken," Mr. Tally put his head in to say. "I'll be back in ten minutes or so," and continued his high-spirited course to the lobbies. It was a very sporting exit.

They did come back to finish the honours of the afternoon, and Billy carefully corrected me for asking who won.

Evelyn and I drove home together. "I never thought," she exclaimed, "that the Westminster House of Commons could be so cheerful."

"Nor I," I said.

"Of course we were lucky in our Members," she said. "Most of them are at least ninety-five and in the habit of sitting there all night."

"I hope a few of them are ninety-five," I said, "for the sake of the country."

"I have sometimes wondered," continued Evelyn, "whether your brother Graham won't some day sit on one of those green benches. He could do it quite as well, you know, as Mr. Tally or that funny little Popplewell. And there are some Canadian Members already, aren't there?"

"Yes, I think he could," I said with hideous irony, "and there are some Canadian Members. But I don't think he will. For one thing, he has lately been elected to the Ottawa House."

" Oh, the Ottawa House — "

"The Ottawa House," I repeated firmly. "And I've heard him rather rude about Colonial M.P.'s over here. He calls them geographical anomalies."

"I think he ought to identify himself with this country," said Evelyn, "and so does everybody."

"I wish father could hear you," I told her.

"He ought to make a brilliant social connection by marriage," Evelyn went on. "He could if he liked. Go into politics, and finish, easily, a peer of the realm. Why don't you put him up to it, Mary?"

I just laughed, but with misgivings. Evelyn never talked absolute nonsense.

"He has made a fearfully good impression, you know. Lady Doleford and all that lot think him charming, and she, anyway, isn't so easily pleased. I think Barbara likes him, too."

"I'm so glad!" I said guardedly.

"The poor dears are all most fearfully depressed just now. It seems Pavis Court must be sold this spring. They would go barefoot to keep it, but going barefoot won't keep it. Nothing will. The banks and lawyers and people have been very decent,

I believe, but nobody can postpone it any longer. Old Lord Doleford and his father broke the entail, and it's twenty years since the last possible penny was put on it in mortgages. Isn't it wicked? One of the loveliest places in England!"

"Can nothing be done to save it?" I asked.

"I have heard of nothing yet," said Evelyn.

CHAPTER XII

ALL this time the flat was our constant joy, the basis and background for the whole pageant, solidly our own for retreat and reflection, always invitingly there. It made a kind of stronghold for us, against feeling too much as London wanted us, wanted everybody to feel — I mean impressed and intoxicated and carried away just by London, and inclined to deliver ourselves over with rapture to let her play upon us any tune she liked. The flat stood for us, just for Graham and me. It meant the identity we clung to. Here, we could say, we are; here is our wandering tent. We are not swept away and lost among the grandeurs we might purchase if we liked. This is just the size and importance we choose to connect ourselves with, at all events, for the present. A historical proportion, Graham said, was better than a contemporary misfit; and it was somehow good for our self-respect to drive home from marble halls and talk it over in front of Miss Game's twelve remaining mantel ornaments, when Graham had made up the fire in the grate. And if it was a retreat when London was too alluring, it was also a refuge when she set us at naught, and made us more or less conscious of lapses and blunders and country manners. It said for us in a comforting way that we made no particular pretensions, that nobody could be more honest, and that Towse, at all events, thought us very well. We were sorry for all Colonials without flats, exposed as they must be; and if there were times when I could have wept in Towse's apron, it was at least fortifying to know that Towse and her apron were there.

Evelyn Dicey thought it ridiculous, our flat. She said there was no use in placing ourselves in an absolutely false position, and suggested that we should at least have our tea-parties at the Carlton instead. We would have liked to oblige Evelyn, to whom we owed so much, in any way we could; but that we didn't find possible — hospitality was hospitality, and a hotel was a hotel. We asked everybody to tea at the flat, everybody who asked us, and most of them came. Not the Duchess. We didn't actually ask the Duchess, though she had been very kind; but Graham declared it was a shame that she should be left out — invidious — and upon Evelyn's advice we asked her if she would like us to. She said not on any account — she made a point of always being at home herself at tea-time, and we could come to her instead, which we felt to be quite as it should be.

"Thank you all the same," she said handsomely;

and it was much pleasanter than being worried by
the idea that she might have thought we had inten-
tionally left her out.

Evelyn, naturally, often came; and it was our best
way of seeing Lady Barbara (our best even after
Graham began those elaborate theatre parties which
did of necessity lead to the Carlton, since Towse
couldn't possibly cope with them). Lady Doleford
came, too, more than once, but it was the once, the
first time, that seemed, I remember, to mean so
much. She wasn't at all precipitate about coming;
our little interior appeared to be the last thing she
wished to know about us. She found out, in one
way or another, almost everything else first, from
Evelyn, and I heard afterward, from Lord Selkirk,
and by the discreetest questions, from ourselves.
For a long time we had been pale and ineffectual
ghosts among the concrete figures, mostly of relations,
that filled her drawing-room and the ante-chambers
of her heart; but in a day — I don't know what happened, what was said or surmised — we turned into
realities, suddenly found ourselves in focus and re-
sponding to the laws of gravity as they operated for
Lady Doleford. It was then that she came to tea.

She came alone and early; I was just finishing the
azaleas.

"Ah, how pretty you are!" she said, looking about
her for a minute with graciousness as gentle and as

sadly faded as anything about her. "What a dear, tiny nest !"

"It isn't us, you know," I said hastily, seeing her eye rest upon the mantel ornaments. "It's Miss Game. There were a great many more. We locked them up."

But in England about æsthetics you never can tell.

"Locked up dear funny pussies like those !" exclaimed Lady Doleford. "There is, of course, the danger of breaking them, and I daresay you are quite wise, but I am afraid I should have left them to look at. Aren't they quaint and amusing, with their different expressions ?"

"There were numbers of dogs, too," I said, "and pigs. The dogs were as lean as the cats, but the pigs were fat."

I had the same fatuous feeling with Lady Doleford as with her son; why, I cannot say, unless possibly because she was his mother. A whole family will sometimes have this effect. I was not quite at my best even with Barbara.

Lady Doleford cowered — it is the only word — into an armchair by the fire and glanced about her.

"You are quite right to keep it small," she said, "and Evelyn is wrong, I am sure, in wanting to install you more in accordance with — with her ideas. I think Americans are often too much impressed with the importance of mere size in arrangements. But

you are so *manageable* here!" and Lady Doleford
sighed.

"We aren't so manageable as we were before Graham began to buy old oak furniture," I replied.
"Tables with melon legs seem to take up more room
than modern ones; and I am sure Elizabethan settles
were never designed for flats. I think it would be
so much better to have them shipped direct; but
Graham won't. He says he likes staying with them
for a while in England first — just letting them serve
him here, where they 'belong.' Graham is funny
in some ways."

Lady Doleford listened very attentively. "He is
fond of old things, then — your brother? Of old
English things?"

"He lives in museums," I told her, "or in the House,
which is itself a kind of — very distinguished collection, isn't it? And his dearest friend is a dealer in
the Hammersmith Road. At least, almost his dearest friend."

There was a slight pause, filled with anguish on my
part; for had I not tried to be clever, and not very
successfully? I am sure it is always better, when you
feel stupid, just to be stupid, and let Providence take
care of you. But when Lady Doleford spoke I saw
that she had not observed it at all. That is often the
case, too.

"Then," she said, rather diffidently, "when you

come to Pavis Court we shall perhaps be able to show him a few pieces that may interest him. Has he seen any joint-stools? We have a couple with medallions, so odd, dating from the time of Henry the Eighth, and a Carolean chest with a very funny old inscription, and some other things."

"I am sure he would love to see them," I said, rather puzzled, for I had no idea that we were going to Pavis Court.

"You will be quite near us — within easy driving distance — at Knowes, you know. My cousin Margot Lippington tells me she is to have the pleasure of a visit from you there."

"We are very much looking forward to it," I murmured.

Lady Doleford's next question was still more surprising.

"And when," she said, "do your people think of coming home to England to settle?"

"But they are at home now, Lady Doleford!" I exclaimed.

"Can one be at home out of England?" she protested gently.

"I know what you mean," I told her. "But, oh, yes! — one can. Father would never consent to leave Canada now, and mother, of course, was born there."

"That must naturally make a great difference,"

Lady Doleford conceded, alluding to mother. "But we are so accustomed, you know, to people coming home — from South Africa, and India, and even Australia. They seem to prefer it," she added modestly, "when they have — when they are able to."

"But Canada is different," I said. "Nobody prefers to leave Canada."

"I think it must be. One of my forebears was in Canada, when we fought the French there. He was a staff officer of General Wolfe's. Do you live in Upper Canada or Lower Canada?"

I had to think for a minute. "Upper," I said, "or what used to be. But the division has ceased to exist, Lady Doleford."

"Has it? Indeed!" she replied doubtfully. "I always used to hear my father speak of it in that way. How very interesting! And when did that happen? Some years ago, perhaps."

"Yes," I said. "Not very lately."

"Ah, well, things change very rapidly nowadays. But your brother — I understand he has ideas of settling in England."

"I am afraid not," I said. "He loves and adores it, but he is quite devoted to his own country."

Lady Doleford looked, for an instant, almost taken aback and inclined to question, as she did about Upper and Lower Canada. "Oh, really?" she said. "I had quite a different impression — I wonder how

I got it! I am sure he has a career before him —
anywhere," she added, looking at me as if she wanted
support and assurance for what she said, "and perhaps, if, as you say, he loves England, he will like to
spend a great deal of his time here."

"I think that is very likely," I said —"later on."

"I suppose where you are it is all quite civilised
and nice by now?" pursued Lady Doleford with a
trace of anxiety. "I am afraid my ideas are almost
entirely coloured by my great-grandfather's letters
from Quebec. They were privately published. But
I daresay there are comparatively few Iroquois about
nowadays. And perhaps no hostile ones."

"We aren't often disturbed by war-whoops at
night," I said, laughing, and Lady Doleford smiled
apologetically.

"And of course communication is so much easier
than it was," she continued. "People seem to think
nothing of crossing the Atlantic, or even of spending
long periods in America. I myself have a nephew
in California, and, as you know, Amherst and Margot
Lippington are wild to go out to Canada. And that
would be for four or five years."

"It seems more intrepid than it actually is," I
assured her. "They would encounter hardly any
hardships, really. The kettle boils at last. I am
so glad. It's always said to be dull, watching a
kettle boil, but I think it's rather interesting. So

much seems to be going on in its mind, and then at last it speaks, doesn't it?"

"Perhaps the people who think it dull are those who are impatient for their tea," said she, accepting a cup. "If I may, I think I will take off my glove."

"Oh, do!" I said hospitably. "Why not take them both off?"

But Lady Doleford removed the right glove only. It somehow vaguely suggested that one hand was all that she was prepared in her scrupulous way, for the moment, to offer. I looked at the glove as it lay, black and kid and shiny in her lap, and at the thin, nervous, rather knuckly hand with its two or three loose old-fashioned rings, the hand that had held Peter as a baby. And Barbara, too, of course.

"I am wondering so much," she said earnestly, "how they are feeling in the Colonies about this sad Romish marriage of our dear Princess. Have you heard whether it has been taken up at all in Canada?"

"I'm trying to remember," I said, "but I can't. I don't think they mind very much."

"Ah!" said Lady Doleford; "no doubt because it is so largely a French, and therefore Roman Catholic country."

"But it isn't," I interposed.

"I can understand — perfectly — your not wishing to admit it," said Lady Doleford kindly, "but I am afraid the fact is there, isn't it? We must make the best of it. Well, it would of course account for a difference in the popular feeling."

"You think that French Roman Catholics might perhaps not be very pleased?" I asked. It struck me afterwards as being a tactless thing to say.

"Dear me, no — why shouldn't they? Don't they get her, body and soul?" demanded Lady Doleford, with something very like warmth. "But for Protestant England — is it not a terrible concession and a sad example? Many of us hope that it is not yet too late. My sister-in-law has written to the *Times* only this morning."

"The Duchess?"

"Yes; suggesting that if the whole nation would unite in fervent prayer for say a week, the marriage might still be averted."

"Poor Princess!" I exclaimed. "To be at the mercy of a nation's prayers! But here," I added hastily as Towse loomed in the doorway, "is the tea-cake, and here — that's splendid — is Graham!"

Lady Doleford turned quickly in her chair, and I recognised in the movement the fact, to which I was now quite happily accustomed, that it was Graham she had really come to see.

CHAPTER XIII

WHAT I hated about it I may simply say was this,
that Barbara and Lady Doleford were taking Graham
into account on exactly the principles which they
applied to Evelyn; and while I didn't mind for
Evelyn, it is the short fact that I did mind for Graham.
With regard to Evelyn — well, one saw that the
situation was perfectly simple, and allowed no inter-
pretation that might be foolish or misleading.   Evelyn
was one of those Americans who are plainly born to
emigrate into the Very Most Desirable state of existence, even though it should entail great pains and a
long voyage.   The clearness of perception and directness of purpose with which they are equipped to carry
this out can only be called a miracle of nature; it is
arrow-like.   One is so filled with admiration of the
straightness and sureness that one can't be very
sorry for them because of the various matters that in
such haste they must pass by.   Especially need one
not pity when, as in Evelyn's instance, the necessary
nobleman is a lamb, a dear and precious lamb.   But
with Graham the case was quite different — now
wasn't it?   Anyone could see, I think, that his

vision of what he wanted was very imperfect; and
even if he quite knew, there would have been fifty
considerations before which he would pause and
ponder. Those various matters which Evelyn could
so well afford to neglect would have been his whole
life's fortune; he was, in fact, badly handicapped for
Very Most Desirable transactions, by his heart.

Then I considered, too, that while Evelyn could be
taken simply, for intrinsic reasons, Graham couldn't
be taken quite so simply. After all, when one pur-
sues it, what was Evelyn? A set of attractive
features in rather slight American connective tissue,
a good temper, a sense of humour, and ten thousand
pounds a year. Graham was a great deal more than
that, though I say it who am his sister, and perhaps have not made it plain — more than that even,
if I must add it, to the figure. The figure, however,
is absolutely out of my argument, which is concerned
with Graham himself. It was himself, the actual
self of him, that I couldn't bear to see left out of consideration the way, it seemed to me, that Barbara and
Lady Doleford left it out. I need not try to put
what they did seem to consider in its proper order of
importance; but they clearly weighed his manners
and his appearance, his education and his morals,
his future and his fortune — everything that you
could put in a list and nothing that could not be
catalogued. These were the matters that went into

their serious summing up of him, and rightly enough, I suppose. Only they left out so much which seemed to me quite as valuable that their leaving it out annoyed me beyond words. Everything that was most really Graham. It may have been unreasonable to be annoyed; but I couldn't stand their ignoring just that, with the ridiculous implication that it was of no consequence, that he was in the balance against other considerations altogether. So much so that when in talk now and then, a little essential bit of him would shine out, they would exchange glances in which I could read wonder and a little apprehension.

"You noticed that," Barbara's eyes would convey; and Lady Doleford's in return would suggest, "It is one of the things for which, after all, it would be quite possible to make allowance."

I now see that I did them injustice, poor dears, and that it was only a kind of density in them which isn't any less opaque for being very well-bred; but I am revealing my impressions as they came to me. And at the moment I could not help thinking it the more unfair in Barbara, as my view of her brother, which was naturally being formed at the same time, gave him credit for so little more than what he was.

I had always thought it would be so very easy to fall in love with Graham. I had even, there is no harm in saying, seen it happen, with dreadful facility —more than once I could remember having to look

N

discreetly the other way. There was his natural
charm, and his character, and his leg; it could not
be considered surprising. And at home it had happened, without so to speak, any incentive, just
because, I suppose, it was a pleasant thing to do.
Now it was constantly borne in upon me that Lady
Barbara was trying to do it and finding it difficult.
Nobody in my position could think that nice of her.
I don't know which I was inclined to blame her most
for, trying or failing. It all comes back to her point
of view. With the right point of view it would have
been, I insist, not only easy but hard not to. But if
you wish to become attached to a set of desirable
facts, slightly qualified by circumstances not so
desirable, it is not wonderful that you have trouble
with your heart.

I do not mean to say that Barbara regarded my
brother Graham with aversion; but it simply did not
make any difference to her if he came into the room.
She would look at him as calmly as she would look
at me — Lady Doleford was much more agitated.
To Barbara I think he represented a necessary part
of the scheme by which she might be perpetuated,
or at least continued, as she was; but Lady Doleford
was aware of responsibility. Barbara had been
brought up to a great exigency, and it naturally filled
all of her mind. Lady Doleford dated further back,
to a time which admitted more argument, a time which

was only anxious and not despairing, when it was still
to be expected, by a mind naturally devout, that
Providence would step in. Morally, therefore, Barbara's was much the strongest, most unvexed position;
she felt none of poor Lady Doleford's quavers and
hesitations. On the other hand, Barbara had a
warmer nature than her mother, whose faint flame
kindled only, I imagine, in church — Barbara was a
Pavisay. The old Earl had loved horses better than
his place in the world, and there might be something
his daughter would love better too; it was just a
possibility. Barbara wasn't very clever; the principal thing about her was her heart, when you came
to think. That was why she seemed to me to be
making a real effort, with no encouragement from
herself, to care about Graham, an idea suggested to
her, I was perfectly certain, by Evelyn Dicey, who
had begun to point out symptoms of inclination in
Graham long, I am sure, before Barbara or anyone
else could have noticed them.

"I know he admires her immensely," I admitted
to Evelyn, "as a little bit of the beautiful old fabric
over her, chosen and cherished and yet so situated
that it can be admired, rather freely; but I don't see
why that should take us so very far."

"It isn't only his admiration," said Evelyn, "but
it's all so suitable."

"I don't see that it's so suitable," I said.

"Well, why should all these — affairs — be arranged with Americans?" demanded Evelyn. "Why should we come in for everything?"

It was a fine, large, generous way of putting it; very like Evelyn, but I could think of no form of acknowledgment.

"I don't know," I said. "Unless — well — you're supposed to have more enterprise, aren't you?"

"It's quite time you cut in," she said good-humouredly. "And you ought to remember it isn't only desirable for itself. As Mrs. Jerry says, there's politics in it."

"Colonial politics?" I enquired.

"Why, yes."

"Then it won't come off, in this country."

Evelyn laughed. "I see what you mean," she said. "But, my dear Marykin, better not be too sure. You don't know the English as well as I do, when they have anything to dispose of."

"Evelyn," I said, "I think you're horrid!" but Evelyn cared no whit.

"The only reason they haven't thought much of the Colonial market so far," she went on cheerfully, "is because it's been so small. Maple princes and princesses ——"

"Oh, maple syrup, Evelyn! Don't be odious!"

"Have only lately been quoted in the share lists. But prices are firm, Marykin — and rising. And

Mrs. Jerry — she's a great old operator, isn't she? — declares that it's a Heaven-sent way of drawing the ties of Empire closer without tinkering ——"

"I know," I said, "with the tariff. One isn't supposed to mention it, is one, over here? They've got tired of it. But between you and me, of course, it doesn't matter."

"But Mrs. Jerome's red-hot again, and sparing nobody," said Evelyn. "Hadn't you heard? She's a fearful Let-Things-Aloner, and they've got hold of Billy!"

"Who have?"

"The other side — what do you call 'em — Imperialists. And now, when Billy runs for Parliament ——"

"Stands," I said.

"Stands — he'll go to the polls all done up in the flag, and sweet he'll look, that nice little Billy. And this innocence is all very well, Marykin, but I can tell you that it's very generally put down to you. Mrs. Jerome says that you are the only consideration that offers the least excuse for Billy."

"Oh, dear!" I said, when we had partly recovered; "I'm afraid I can't offer Billy even an excuse! But I'm just as glad, on the Empire's account. It's safe now. But, Evelyn, Billy is one thing—Graham is another. I mean, don't you — well, worry about Graham — since you don't want to marry him yourself."

"Not I," Evelyn assured me. "There's one solid advantage about being my type — money is absolutely no object. I value money," she continued thoughtfully, "about as much as I value — punk. No, Marykin, when it comes to the gold attraction, I'm not taking any."

"Well, that's nice and clear," I said.

"And this is the place," she went on with conviction, "to make you thankful to be able to say so. It's simply disgusting, the importance of money over here — just the dead importance of it. They don't like talking about it any more than they do — or half so much as they do — about the food they are digesting; but it's just as necessary to keep them morally healthy and socially alive. They've never had to earn it; it's always been there, like the air, to exist by, and they've got to have it — it's a matter of self-preservation. When they absolutely haven't got it and finally can't get it, there's no sort of way for them to live — they become extinguished."

"What you say, so far as it's true," I observed, "makes one feel awfully sorry for them. It's a horrid position for them, poor things; and one wishes something could be done, but one must stop short of wanting them to marry one's relations to get out of it."

Evelyn looked at me a little ambiguously, as if she did not quite want to say what she thought she ought to say, and was rather amused at the necessity of saying it.

"Graham is a darling, honey," she said, "but ——"

"He's a lamb," I said. "A dear and precious lamb, just as much as anybody, and in some ways more."

"Of course he is. But, you know, my chicken — he's just a simple Canuck."

"Don't you suppose I see that too?" I demanded. "He is just a simple Canuck — and he can't be too simple or too Canuck; and I wish they would let him alone."

I could say things, of course, to Evelyn, that I could not say to anyone else, and say them more strongly. She understood in a hundred ways better than anyone in England could understand. She understood now, foolish as she thought the text I offered her; and she gave me in return a very tactful consolation.

"I think it's quite as much on his side," she said.

Then came the rescue in the fog.

It was for us the luckiest fog possible; there had not been one like it for years. It did not arrive or descend; it transpired, took place, suddenly, like a whim, obliterating all the Christmas shopping. It was more yellow and thick and sulphurous than I can describe; it extravagantly realised all the descriptions I could remember, and it had the effect upon London of a blanket over a particularly noisy parrot in a cage.   London huddled on its perch and was dumb, but underneath one knew it to be alert and ready, on the smallest gleam and the shortest notice, with all its outcries.

I watched it from the flat, though it had only the variety of a very yellow night.   I sat down in it, under the electric light, and poked the fire, and thought: "Now I am in the middle of a real traditional London fog — I know exactly what it looks, and tastes, and feels, and smells like;" and I wished very much that Graham would come home so that we could enjoy it together.   He had gone out intending to be back soon after lunch; and though I quite realised that under the circumstances nobody's intentions could run to time, by five o'clock I was quite certain that he had stepped over the Embankment. I sat with that conviction until half-past six, and there was nothing you could do.   The only resource was constantly to tell Towse to bring tea again in half-an-hour's time; but at last I was having it, when I heard out in the despairing depths of the streets a cart, going very slowly, but going.   It was the first signal.   From the window I saw with thankfulness a blob of lighter yellow where the nearest street lamp stood, and heard in other streets the single cautious adventures of other carts, and shouts, with a distinct note of optimism.   After that it seemed less likely that Graham had wandered into the Thames; and I was enjoying a second slice of Substitute in the relief of thinking so, when I heard the key of the door, steps and voices along the passage, and out of mystery and nowhere appeared my brother and Barbara Pavisay.

"We *are* grateful to you for being here — with tea," declared Barbara. "Mr. Trent was quite sure you would be."

She was looking extraordinarily pleased with herself, and had a lovely colour. "We have had such adventures!" she exclaimed.

"I am very grateful to you for bringing him home," I told her. "Did you bring him home, or did he bring you?"

"A four-wheeler brought us both," said Graham. "About how far is it from Kensington High Street station?"

"Perhaps a quarter of a mile," I said.

"Well, we have been just one hour and three-quarters doing it," said my brother. "I think Lady Barbara will have a cup of tea, if you don't mind, Mary."

"I beg your pardon!" I exclaimed. "But you're such ghosts, I forgot."

"The man walked by the horse's head the whole way," explained Barbara. "Yes, please — two lumps. And, oh — muffin! How too luxurious! Your brother found me on a bench under a lamp in

High Street station. I thought it was Victoria!
And then I knew it wasn't, and I was simply in
despair. And suddenly he appeared out of the fog,
coming up to the lamp to look at his watch. I assure
you I simply clutched him. And how he induced
the four-wheeler to start I don't know; but he did,
and here we are. And is there anything in the world
so good as muffin!"

"It's lucky for you both," I told them, "that I
trusted in Providence and kept tea waiting. I was
certain Graham had walked over the Embankment,
or been in a collision in the Underground. It must
be too dreadful in the Underground in a fog. I
wonder either of you got out alive."

"It was the only place to-day where one could see
two yards in front of one," remarked Graham.

"We have been walking round and round Kensington Square," Barbara went on. "And, oh! we kept
meeting a funeral. It was lost too, and so forlorn."

"I think it was the funeral of Kensington Square,"
said Graham. "It hasn't been what it was, you
know, for some time; it's just been pining away after
Thackeray."

"But we met it first coming into the Square,"
objected Barbara.

"Let me get you another cup," said Graham.
"How thirsty they must be by now, the people in
charge of that poor corpse! Which of the Louises

was it that said about a lady of his Court they were burying in the rain, that she had chosen a *mauvais temps pour s'en aller?* I'm afraid I felt about as cynical towards our corpse, didn't you?"

"I don't know which it was," said Barbara. "I didn't think about the corpse — what would be the use? But I was sorry for the mourners."

"It's shocking to confess," meditated Graham, "but I believe I enjoyed that funeral. There was something queer and drifting and Dantesque about it, always turning up in that fatal way at one's elbow out of the fog. There must be a moral synonym for it somewhere, if we weren't so fearfully dense."

I tried to think of a moral synonym, but failed.

"Don't let us talk any more about funerals," said Barbara. "I didn't enjoy it; it gave me the creeps. I wonder what the fog is doing now?"

I went to the window and pulled up the blind.

"It's worse," I announced. "The lamp at the corner has gone out again, and there isn't a sound. You can't possibly get home — you must spend the night. If you don't mind sharing my room," I said. "We would love to keep you, wouldn't we, Graham?"

"If I may, I'll go out at once and telegraph to Lady Doleford — or are you on the telephone?" said Graham.

"We're not, but Aunt Agnes is," said Barbara. "And I'm supposed to be with Aunt Agnes till

to-morrow.   If you could telephone Aunt Agnes ——
But it may lift in an hour or two.   May I stay and
dine, and see afterwards?"

"I don't see how it can lift," said Graham, inspecting it.   "By itself, that is.   It is more likely to sink
and settle in deposit on the pavements.   I suppose
you have fog ploughs for such a contingency, or do
the citizens turn out with shovels?   May I telephone
that if it isn't penetrable by ten o'clock, you will
stay till to-morrow — or till it is?"

"Thank you very much!" said Barbara, and
presently from the passage came my brother's voice,
enquiring, "Is that Two Three Seven Five, Victoria
— the Duke of Dulwich?"

"Your aunt," he said, coming back a few minutes
later, "came to the telephone herself.   She said she
had ascertained that you had not arrived at an address, which I could not hear, in Hill Street, and was
wondering whether it would do any good to send out
the town crier."

"Aunt Agnes always has a sense of humour," said
Barbara, "but I'm afraid she was really anxious."

"She clearly was.   But the telephone enabled me
to wring her consent to your staying the night," said
Graham.   "It gave me a kind of wringing leverage
on the situation.   I couldn't hear any of the Duchess's objections.   But I was obliged to make out
that if it lifted by ten, she is to send Broad for you

with the electric brougham. If not, not. It won't lift, I'm happy to prophesy."

"I don't think she'll send Broad," said Barbara. "Broad had a cold this morning, and she was dosing him with eucalyptus; I'm afraid she'll take you at your word."

It was quite clear and simple. Barbara wanted to stay; she liked the adventure of it — and Graham wanted to have her; he liked the part of Knight Hospitaller. My business was merely to go and tell Towse.

CHAPTER XIV

Dᴜʀɪɴɢ the next twenty-four hours I made a discovery that complicated my feelings enormously. I discovered that I liked Barbara. Outside, the fog stood like a solid wall till the next afternoon at five o'clock. Till the next afternoon, therefore, Barbara stayed, till five o'clock; and in that time I became attached to her. It seemed then as if the fog crept into the situation as I saw it, blotting out everything except the fact that Barbara was a dear.

Perhaps you come to know a person better when she is fog-bound in your flat, with nothing but the things she arrived in. The mere chance that your slippers happen to fit her seems to do a great deal, and she has various opportunities of being more charming than a regular visitor. Barbara took them all. She was sensible, she was considerate, she was merry. At every moment, at every angle the time presented, she was unfailingly exactly right and something over, something you could only reckon as the delightful benefit of having always been exactly right.

"It's instinctive," Graham said when we discussed

it. "She does it on a principle that has become subliminal. We see only the results."

Graham appreciated it, enjoyed it, just as much as I did — even more, with his inveterate eye for the beautiful. And Towse, I can only say that Towse grovelled, beamingly and at once, before Lady Barbara. Merely ministering to her at breakfast, hovering, in so far as Towse could hover, with the sanctioned bacon and the traditional marmalade, was a gratification to Towse, I could see, after our uncanny trans-Atlantic habits of raw fruit and wheat biscuits. There was an immediate kinship or clanship; Towse belonged to the scullery end of the family edifice, but she belonged to it out and out; and Barbara called Towse a darling.

As a matter of fact, up in our little lighthouse, Barbara was literally out of her element and profited by it. London was drowned outside, and London was the element that defined her by pointing out her necessities. There with us she had no necessities; at least they were not in sight; she was just a very nice girl, enjoying an absurd little accident. It seemed to me more and more odd that so nice a girl could admit London's limitations — could allow the importance of her life to be placed in the chance that some thousands of pounds a year should arrive and be at her disposition. It was pleasant, even for that little while, to forget it.

I suppose the fact of one's own appearance being rather insignificant made one enjoy it more, seeing Barbara sitting after dinner in the Tudor chair with the panelled back that Graham had proved only the day before not to be an imposture. He had insisted, as a matter partly of principle, partly of discipline, upon burning every "fake" that he was deceived into buying; and though we had some lovely fires, I was oppressed by the waste of money. It was very pleasant to see Barbara with her head against the warm brown panels of this, just under the bar of jewel-carving. Her hair was almost reflected in it.

"You are very becoming to that chair," I told her.

"I'm so glad. But it would be nicer of you to say that it is becoming to me," said Barbara.

"Do you think it would? But not so gratifying for us," I laughed, "because the chair is ours to keep, you see."

I had a perfectly terrified instant, for Barbara looked at the fire and burned redder and redder and redder. A sudden suspicion seized me of what might have been said in an hour and three-quarters in a four-wheeler. But Graham himself dispelled it.

"And Lady Barbara, alas! is only ours to lose," he said cheerfully in the door.

"Do you mind his cigarette?" I asked her. "Or shall we order him back into the dining-room?"

"I love it!" said Barbara. "Peter smokes everywhere. Mother and I sometimes wish we smoked ourselves, just to be on terms with him."

I looked at her with amazement. "Your mother!" I cried.

Barbara laughed. "Dear me, yes. Mother often says things one wouldn't expect her to. You don't know mother."

"I couldn't conceive it — could you, Graham?"

"Lady Doleford smoking? No," said Graham.

"Nor me?" Barbara asked him.

"Nor you," he told her.

"Well, I have no old-fashioned prejudices," she said; and as Graham to this made no response, the silence threatened to be a little awkward. Unnecessarily so, seeing that we were only considering the idea of such a thing. I filled it up by telling Barbara about what he insisted on doing with the sham antiques.

"There was an octagonal table of the time of Charles the First," I said. "At least, there was the drawer of an octagonal table of the times of Charles the First. That was the only part that was genuine. He let me keep that; I've got it still. But it isn't much use without the table."

"Do let me see it," said Barbara; and I went into the kitchen and got it from Towse, who had been keeping receipted bills in it. Any drawer is rather a forlorn object, divorced from its surroundings, and

o

this one was pathetically small and black and worm-eaten as well. Barbara looked at it gravely for a moment, and then went off into a peal of laughter.

"Was this really all that was left of the original table?" she asked.

"I suppose so. It was all that was original of the table that was left," said Graham; at which we all laughed. It was a ridiculous object.

"But what — but what are you going to do with it?" demanded Barbara.

"I don't know," I said disconsolately; "but I did like it so, with those funny little Gothic windows running across the front of it. I had to save it."

"And you burned all the rest of it?" she asked Graham.

"What else could I do?" he replied. "It was a forgery."

"One word was genuine," I complained.

"That made it worse," said he — "much worse! Without the drawer it would have been a fraud. With the drawer it was a criminal fraud."

"Why didn't you make the dealer take it back?" asked Barbara.

"I preferred to buy my experience," said Graham. "Besides, I can't imagine that he would. I had paid for the thing."

"Then I should have got rid of it," said Barbara practically.

"No, you wouldn't really — when you thought about it," said Graham.

"One would sell it for what it was, of course," said Barbara, flushing a little.

"That wouldn't prevent its getting into circulation again."

"Like bad money. And, of course, that can't be even given away," reflected Barbara.

"It's a question," said Graham, "whether one wouldn't rather cheat a man commercially than æsthetically — he would mind it less, don't you think?"

"Oh, but there's a law against passing counterfeit money!" said Barbara. "One might be put in gaol. So it would be worse. Have you burned many things?" she asked curiously.

"Oh, no — only two or three. It's my rage at being taken in," he said.

"It's nothing of the kind; it's his tribute to sincerity!" I protested. "He thinks sincerity's about the biggest thing there is, and he loves sacrificing to it. Don't you, Graham?"

"I think it's a pretty big thing," said Graham, with a half-tone of boredom, "of course. And I'm not original in that view. There's a moral efficacy as well as a moral charm about the real thing, isn't there?" he asked Barbara. "And one comes in for such a lot of it over here. It's what one likes so in England."

Barbara said nothing, and I picked up the little black drawer.

"Suppose we burn this too," I said. "It's absurd not to!" but she seized my hand.

"No, please!" she said. "Give it to me — I'll find a use for it. It will be like a text," she added simply, "to remind me of sincerity. And I can keep my bird-seed in it."

So Barbara was not at all devoid of sentiment. I already knew that she wished to do right, and loved her birds. She had been taught to do very right indeed, and to love all animals. She had been taught everything, in the primary moral sense, that could, I think, be imparted. There was just perhaps room for the suspicion that with Barbara the primary morals were the only ones that counted; but that was immediately qualified by the assurance that the secondary ones had only to be perceived. How much she did perceive was just the problem of Barbara. She certainly, even then, perceived my brother Graham, but how far and how fully, it was difficult to make up one's mind.

"Oh, please do tell me," she said presently, "what are the chances of Margot and Amherst Lippington getting that Canadian post? We are all dying to know. Do you think it is likely?"

"Quite likely, I should imagine," said Graham.

"I am so glad. And if you can say any little word

to help, you will, won't you? I know you will. We're asking everyone we know who is at all likely to have influence. Margot has simply set her heart on it, you see."

"I'm afraid I am the last person whose views would carry weight," said Graham, smiling.

"Oh, we don't think so! We think it might do a great deal if you just mentioned to Lord Watchett that you thought they were the right sort of people," said Barbara. "That is, of course, if you do think so. We hear they are so anxious this time to make an appointment that will be agreeable to the Canadians. They would do beautifully for it, wouldn't they?"

"Beautifully!" assented Graham.

"And now that odious Lord Hemingwall is mentioned everywhere as quite in the running for it!" Barbara went on. "And he is a bachelor. How can a bachelor do the social part?"

"Lady Lippington is certainly one of her husband's most obvious qualifications," said Graham.

"Oh, that is nice of you! Margot will love to hear that. She just slaves for Amherst, you know. And he's a dear in himself, don't you think?"

"A regular dear!" said Graham.

"You see, Margot comes of a family who have always done such things," continued Barbara, "and Amherst's father was Governor of two or three different places. Margot would be simply lost without anything to govern. And you couldn't have anyone more conscientious."

"I'm sure we couldn't," said Graham.

"In little things as well as in big ones. She's one of the busiest people, and yet do you know she is putting in two hours at Prince's every morning improving her skating, because she saw in the *Times* the other day that Lady Coddis's proficiency in the national pastime won the Canadian heart. Did it?"

Graham laughed. "I saw that in the *Times* too," he said.

"We did think it rather nice of Lady Coddis to skate so well," I put in. "You see she learned in Canada."

"Oh, I must tell Margot that!" said Barbara intelligently. "She has learned already, unfortunately; but she could easily put off improving till she got there, if that would do any good."

"I'm sure it would appeal," said Graham.

I asked him afterwards whether there was any likelihood of an opportunity for the little word Barbara requested, and found it had already been spoken, as far as it went; which could only, Graham insisted, be the shortest possible distance.

"Watchett did ask me," he said. "In the vaguest way, of course. I gathered he was collecting hints for Somerset upon the subject."

"What did you say?" I asked.

"I said I thought the Lippingtons would be very popular indeed. So they would. She knows a lot about 'Colonials' as they call us, and would be very keen on making it a success; and he's as nice a chap as ever stepped, and no silly initiative. He wouldn't want to come nosing into things he didn't understand, and things he did understand he'd show us like a gentleman. Oh, yes, I backed up Lippington! I hope we may get him. We might go further and fare a lot worse."

"Why didn't you tell Barbara?" I said.

"I didn't think it was any of dear Barbara's business," he replied equably.

But everything, we soon found, was Barbara's business that had to do with friends and relations. Friends and relations were her warp and woof of life. She lived solidly among them, entrenched on every hand. It would be impossible, I thought, to be very sorry for a person so secured, whatever might otherwise befall her or not befall her. Her own existence was filled and complicated with what they had done, were doing, were going to do; the world turned round for that. And the important thing was that everybody's plans should be carried out. The idea of Lord Lippington's appointment having a public significance to the Empire which ought to obscure its private one to Barbara was absurd; and so I told Graham. His little word, his little friendly word, was a matter of course to her. Everybody, in her experience, who had little friendly words to say, said them, and why not he? It was nice to think that he had said one, as it were, in spite of himself.

We had naturally, she and I, a long talk in my room that night, when among other things it was settled that I should call her Barbara and she should call me Mary.

"I never can bear the other thing for ever and ever," she said. "Can you? I've gone on with it with you much longer than with most people. I don't know why."

"When I'm affectionate I'm always shy," I said. "I've been affectionate to you, and wanted to call you Barbara, ever since dinner-time. But I'm afraid if you hadn't I never would have."

"Then I'm very glad I did," said she heartily, and approached her lovely cool cheek for me to kiss. I kissed it, thinking, "Now after this, whatever happens, I can never be altogether against Barbara."

"It is nice, isn't it?" said she, taking down her hair.

"What is?"

"Our liking each other."

"It's always nice to like anybody," I said cautiously.

"Yes, isn't it? I like a fearful lot of people, I'm thankful to say. And in such different ways. You and Evelyn, for example. I like you quite differently."

"Do tell me how," I said, "and why? I should like particularly to know, because — well, because Evelyn is an American, you know." I stopped, wondering whether that was entirely why.

"What has that to do with it?" asked Barbara.

"Well, I don't know that I can explain exactly, but Americans do seem to come in on rather special terms, don't they, over here? Under a sort of most-favoured-nation clause, as they say. And one would so much rather be liked for one's — I mean for not being an American, I suppose. It's because we do get so mixed up with them," I apologised.

"Now that I know you apart," said Barbara, "I should never mix you up again. And do you know, I sometimes think I should like Evelyn better if she were not an American."

"How nice of you," I said, not meaning anything whatever.

"And I'm sure Peter would."

"Would he?" I said. "But I thought —— "

"Yes, I know; everybody thinks that. But it isn't so — at all events, not yet. And I think it's just because she's an American. She's awfully nice, you know, otherwise."

"But I thought —in such cases —it was almost essential?" I ventured.

"So it is. And I believe that's why Peter dislikes it so —because it is essential," said Barbara luminously. "Just as if somebody said to one 'You shall wear only velvet and diamonds,' one would at once be inclined to pick holes in velvet and diamonds. Peter does nothing but pick holes in Americans."

"It does seem such a pity," I murmured, 'when Evelyn is such a charming one!"

"Yes, isn't she? An awfully good sort! Oh, I'm very fond of old Evelyn. And, you know, Mary, it would be such a —such a useful marriage."

"I know," I said.

"Mother's dreadfully harassed about it. You know, mother is funny in some ways, and she has a way of thinking that the thing that's —well, that's usual and proper, is bound to come off. And she's always perfectly certain that Providence will be on her side. When Evelyn turned up —we don't know many Americans —mother thought she came straight from Providence, and was awfully grateful, and just about adopted her —took her as a gift from above. Which makes it more awkward than ever."

"Poor Lady Doleford!" I said.

"The worst of it is we believe Aunt Agnes is backing Peter up," Barbara went on. "There's just a chance, you see, that he'll succeed to my uncle's title some day, and Aunt Agnes has horrid nightmares of being made a dowager of by an American. She behaves as if Peter ought to live on the possibility — I don't know how she thinks things are to be managed in the meantime. It's extremely unreasonable of Aunt Agnes, for there's a very good life between."

"Who is it?" I asked.

"Scansby, our Uncle Christopher. He's a queer old thing and has never married, but of course he will; they always do, don't they? He will be with us in February; you will probably meet him. I'm sure you'll think him a character — I say he ought to be put in a book," said Barbara, with a vast yawn. "But isn't. Peter an old silly — about Evelyn? I wonder — if you could say any little word to him; I wish you would."

"I'm afraid I have kept you awake talking," I said. "It's too bad of me. Good-night, dear Barbara."

CHAPTER XV

EVELYN was now staying at the American Ambassador's, and from that point of flight was exploring London more thoroughly than ever. Nothing seemed to interfere with her power to do that — nothing, I mean, that one could think of as a check, or a state of suspense. We thought ourselves most happy and most lucky, in the way of social experience; but Evelyn, if happiness and luck can be so multiplied, was twice as happy and three times as lucky. Of course they can't; but one must have some figure of speech to express the houses at which Evelyn arrived, the circles in which she managed so gaily to float. There is a shibboleth of London; it resides in an expression, in a manner, in things taken for granted as possible and things tacitly acknowledged as impossible, in the lift of an eye-lid, in the angle of salutation, in I don't know what, but Evelyn did, and demonstrated it to perfection. It was the flower of the thing she seized, so securely yet so deftly, with one hand, as it were, holding up her skirts with the other, the thing she was born to seize. Graham and I could point it out, dwell on it, enjoy it, but adorn ourselves with it, never. Evelyn wore it, of course, with a difference, but she did wear it, and it was infinitely becoming to her.

I think there was something of the true spirit of adventure about Evelyn; she was really one of the old Elizabethans cruising back again, with this difference, that she knew precisely where the treasure was, and her voyage was all charted. And she took possession of vast tracts, in the name of her Republic. Her own name was constantly in those chatty little paragraphs that are so prominent a feature of the *London Daily*, as being one of the most effectively "gowned" or most happily amused guests at some smart party at the Ritz or the Carlton, discerned as the charming right hand of some Duchess in her stall at a charitable bazaar, as being "brought" to some notable gathering by some notable lady, when she was alluded to, as if she were one of the public's oldest acquaintances, as "that delightful American, Miss Evelyn Dicey." She could not even take a walk in the Park, after a time, without being distinguished there.

"That delightful American, Miss Evelyn Dicey, who was saying that she would not have believed such weather possible in England, was among the most hardy."

When Mrs. Willie Walker included her in a house-party to meet Royalty, I read it aloud to Graham, as a final proof of our friend's extraordinary cleverness.

"They just love her, don't they?" I demanded.

"Oh, she amuses them!" said Graham; "and presently they are going to gobble her up. It's only decent of them to give her an innings first."

"Well," I said, "she gets it all back again, we may be sure. They amuse her."

"Very differently," said Graham. "They are her Chief Good. You're not amused with your chief good. No — Evelyn gets it back, if she does get it back, in another way, I think."

"What way?"

"Oh, in getting round them the way she does, in being so much cleverer, and just bagging the dear innocents, for all the things that are so valuable in them, that they don't see themselves. Do I make myself clear?"

"Not particularly," I said.

"Well, in the gentlest and most honeyed sense, I see them her prey."

"But you said just now they were going to gobble her up! And now you say —— "

"And so they are, in one sense. In one sense, of course, Evelyn's their prey. But it's a much more bodily, ingenuous sense. It's a great deal worse to be a prey in your temperamental parts," Graham insisted. "And it makes a more poignant spectacle."

"That is one of the things which I don't know what you mean," I said. One can't always wait to be grammatical in talking with one's brother. "And I think they know very well, the English, how fine they are."

"No," said Graham; "they only know how fine they want to be. It's what we love them for. And the more you see how fine you want to be the less you can possibly see how fine you are, and the more likely you are to be the quarry of those who — well, who appreciate you. Is it clear now, Marykin?"

"No," I said; "it isn't. Though I'm not quite sure that I don't see what you think you mean. It's to Evelyn's credit, anyhow, that she does appreciate them. And I'd just as soon you didn't call me 'Marykin.'"

"Why not, Sis?"

"Because Evelyn does," I said.

"Well, as long as she doesn't want to gobble *you* up!" Graham laughed.

"We are on the best of terms," I said indignantly, and so we were. I saw far more to admire in Evelyn than Graham did, at all events, far less not to admire, and in her present position, applauded as it might seem, I saw reasons to be exceedingly sorry for her. Evelyn wasn't a reticent person; and one could not imagine that her legion of friends had been kept quite in ignorance — given no hint at all — of the delightful arrangement that Lady Doleford, in her closet, had been putting up with Providence. Lady Doleford wasn't reticent, either, when she could trace heavenly origin and depend on heavenly support; one could quite see her taking Evelyn into her arms and indicating, by all the signs of the zodiac, the direction in which hope and promise and fulfilment lay — could imagine her letting dear Evelyn, as far as was consistent with delicacy, into her wonderful scheme before Peter had even sailed. Evelyn would, no doubt, be able to give some sign that she understood, would even find some way of conveying that, barring a hump back or a cloven foot she hadn't been told about, she assented. One could see it end in an embrace which poor Lady Doleford would try to make as little contingent as she could. Barbara would be even less discreet — Barbara would be one exclamation mark of joy and hope. And with all this one had to count Evelyn's own unblinking expectation, so clear and so complete that non-fulfilment seemed almost impossible to it. It was the historic view, backed by numberless precedents; it was the personal view, based on a justified self-confidence; it was, above all, the practical view, with every circumstance to endorse it. It seemed an anomalous and a distressing thing that one might find oneself before the eyes of a world all ready to applaud commercial sagacity, the victim of one's business instinct; and that fate, as things happened and happened and didn't happen, seemed really to threaten Evelyn. It was excellent to see her spirits, under the shadow of it, so unflaggingly advertised in the *London Daily*.

I don't know that these reflections would have occurred to me so vividly but for the fact of Evelyn's visit to Pavis Court being postponed, at rather short notice and for no very convincing reason, from Christmas to the middle of January. Somehow we had all been looking forward to that Christmas visit as marking the limit of our suspense. Things that hadn't happened, under one excuse or another, up to now, were surely bound to happen then, when the intimate occasion — there was to be nobody else — would combine with the happy festival to abolish all excuse. Why one thought of it in terms of excuse it is impossible, so long afterward, to say; but one did. One even considered different excuses, and speculated about other ladies.

Christmas is a time in England when everybody supposes you will be going to more intimate friends. For Graham and me that resulted quite satisfactorily, as we certainly were our most intimate friends and had only to stay at home; but Evelyn deplored it. The withdrawal of Pavis Court, as it were, for further consideration, deprived her, she declared, of a festive board of any shape or kind. Her friends at Dor-

P

chester House were going to Paris for the week; and she had joined some people from New York at their hotel, who were also deeply engaged upon Christmas Day. The *London Daily* was full of the names of her town acquaintances, and particulars of their flight to their various country-houses; she declared herself alone in London. It seemed the natural and the only thing that she should come to us; and she did.

I shall always remember her appearance in the frame of the door as Towse ushered her in; it was one of those things that bring an impression one doesn't lose. She was all slender and lovely in one of her unapproachable dresses, with the grace and the complexion of a flower, if you could imagine a flower in pearls that had nothing to do with dew, with its hair done in a manner before which any zephyr would sink away abashed. She had very little connection, in her beautiful effect, with the flat or with the occasion; she had plainly had the generous idea of not dressing down to us, of taking just as much pains with her appearance as if it were to be described in the next morning's *London Daily;* and after the first gasp we did of course appreciate it. But it made her look a little like some strayed reveller, some star that had wandered from a galaxy that had gone on without it, and dropped through space to light us, in this temporary, accidental way. Detachment, that was the note she struck, for an instant only, in the door; it was soon lost in talk. The moment we opened our lips we all became trans-Atlantic together.

"What a darling turkey!" she exclaimed, as we sat down. "And — am I in Kensington or in Connecticut? Cranberries! Oh, I have done nothing to deserve this — it's too lovely!"

"I did them myself," I told her. "When I showed them to Towse she said she never 'ad. That always means that if it's just the same to me she'd rather not; and when that happens I just take hold myself. You don't know what you miss, Evelyn, not having a flat, and a kitchen, and a Towse."

"Well," said Evelyn, "I don't see but that I shall have to go on missing it, unless it happens to be dished up for me, like this. I certainly shouldn't find time, in London, to stew anything, either now or at any future period. And I don't know, honey, how you do."

"Oh, I find time!" I told her; "but what will you do if the simple life ever becomes really fashionable, Evie?"

Evelyn sighed, quite a gusty, perceptible sigh. "I expect I shall be back in Roosevelt Towers, Juniper Avenue, Troy, New Jersey, long before that," she said. That was her full address when she was at home.

"Oh, I hope not !" I ejaculated, without thinking. "I mean — you do like it over here, don't you? Why not make it per — why not stay on?"

"I can't import my family," said Evelyn, with a half-tone of gloom, "and you may thank your stars that neither of you know what it is to be an only child. I don't complain of James P. Dicey. He's a model father in his way. But he's very much in charge; and from the beginning he said I could only have six months. Then he's coming over to fetch me."

"Oh, dear !" I sympathised. "And the six months is —— "

"Up in February," said Evelyn.

"We go back then, too," said Graham.

"Parliament opens," I explained.

"Then you are?" enquired Evelyn.

"Are what?" he asked.

"Going back."

"Why, yes," said Graham. "What else, Miss Dicey, did you suppose?"

"Oh, I don't know !" she replied.

"You thought, perhaps, he might have been tempted, too?" I suggested unguardedly.

"Well, compared with this, you won't deny that you're going back to rather a one-horse show," Evelyn challenged him, with a disarming smile.

"It's a one-horse show that is going some day to

pull the Empire !" Graham retorted good-naturedly. "Let me give you a little more of the dressing."

"Yes, I will," said Evelyn, and gave him her plate. "Now, will you tell me whether in any part of the United States of America you ever heard that called 'insertion'? No; nor I. Yet a man apologised to me the other day for saying 'stuffing.' 'I beg your pardon,' he said. ' "Insertion," I should say.' 'Why should you say "insertion"?' I said. 'I think it's rather silly;' and then he produced the usual merry explanation. 'Chestnuts!' I said, and turned the conversation. I'm dead sick of the American myths they keep over here to take the place of wit and humour."

"I know," I sympathised. "Somebody was making me a cup of tea the other day, and asked me archly if I'd have it with all the trimmings. For a minute I didn't know what she meant. But never mind, Evie. Let them laugh at us as much as they can. We can laugh at them a great deal more, because we're made that way, and they aren't, are they?" I used "we" continentally.

"They're too benevolent to be very humorous," Graham remarked.

"Oh, benevolent! I hope you gave a thousand pounds to the West Ham Christmas Dinner Fund?"

"I'm afraid not," said Graham.

"Well, I'm surprised! Not willing to part with a

sum like that, which you could perfectly spare, in order to provide ten thousand indigent families with one square meal! And when the dear Queen has promised to supply all the oranges! That in itself ought to have been enough — the idea of the Queen coming in that way with the dessert. I don't understand it. You're no true Briton, Mr. Trent — you're a Canadian and a foreigner! The true Briton sees to that one square meal on Christmas Day, and gets West Ham off his conscience. I don't know whether it always lasts till next Christmas Day; but he doesn't think about it again till then."

"Oh, no!" laughed Graham. "He's always thinking about it. But it's poor relief run sentimentally mad — or it seems so to us. It's all very well, though, for us to gibe — we can't know the conditions; and we can't feel the claims."

But Evelyn did not want to be taken seriously.

"And you, Marykin?" she said. "Where do you come in on that scheme of the *London Herald's* to provide every poor child in the kingdom with a Christmas stocking this morning? I thought I'd like to do the Santa Claus act to a few of them myself; but just as I'd brought myself round to it I saw in the paper a scare-head 'For Heaven's sake, Stop! Desist!' or words to that effect, and the stream of my benevolence dried up before I'd got it going."

"I know!" Graham laughed. "Not enough kids

for the presents, or not enough vans in the Post Office, or some such difficulty. They're a warm-hearted people."

"The State will be invited to do it next year," Evelyn told us. "Mark my words. Every wage-earner who can prove that he has never been liable to income or any other tax will be entitled to a turkey at the country's expense. You'll see!"

"It would be quite in their general line of pro-cedure," said Graham.

"But what I most love," Eveyln went on, "is the attitude of the beneficees. They know perfectly how valuable they are as an outlet for compassion. I passed a slouch with a red nose the other day in a side street; and as I came near he smiled kindly, and said: 'Lady, would you like to be a friend to a poor man?' It was a handsome offer, and he plainly thought I'd jump at it. I gave him the icy brow, of course. 'I would not,' I said. 'Thank you, lady, thank you,' he replied sarcastically, and the episode closed."

"That's a little like Towse!" I exclaimed, "and the chrysanthemums. I bought some in pots to brighten up the kitchen for her, and Graham happened to be out there and made some remark about them. What was it she said, Graham?"

"'They ain't a great deal in my way, and there, if it pleases Miss Mary!' They're very good and patient, that kind, over here, I notice. They let you do unto others as you wouldn't be at all willing to have them do unto you. It's rather touching, I think; but, phew! It's a choking atmosphere."

"Well, Christmas is an obsession in this country," said Evelyn; "and the imposition of it makes one feel real ugly. I went to see a friend the other day who isn't very well off, and while I was there the parlour-maid came in three times to say different 'gentlemen' were waiting to know if she didn't wish to give them a Christmas-box. The last was the municipal street-sweeper. And these blessed British encourage it. I saw some 'User of Suburban Trains' writing to the paper the other day to point out that while the porters and ticket collectors were always 'remembered,' nobody up to date had thought of the engine-drivers! He hoped his letter would put the engine-drivers into the heart of the travelling public! Is it any wonder they all 'expect'? — every creature that does a hand's turn in any capacity, public or private? If they can't do anything else," Evelyn added disgustedly, "they stand outside your door and sing — out of tune."

It seemed to me that Evelyn was not herself particularly in tune; she wasn't usually so critical of the country.

"It's a pity, isn't it, that they've lost their Dickens?" Graham observed. "What would he have done with the type that is coming out of all this systematised charity? What wouldn't he have done with it? They ought to keep a Dickens always by them."

"It's a pity we've lost our Dickens," I said, with a slight emphasis. I never liked Graham to drop into that objective way of regarding Great Britain, especially with Evelyn.

"How nice of you," said she, "to mention Dickens! After all, here we are spending Christmas in Dickens's London; and that's all right, isn't it? I mean it's worth doing, anyhow. It's a Dickensy Christmas, too; there's snow on the roofs — at least there was this morning. Only I'm sure you ought to have had roast goose, Mary; and haven't I some recollection of punch?"

"Marley's ghost didn't mention what Marley died of," said Graham; "but it may very well have been roast goose. I vote we drink to absent friends, and then 'Long life to Marley's ghost.'"

"You can't propose two toasts at once," said Evelyn.

"Absent friends is quite enough," I said.

"And Marley's ghost is already immortal," Graham acknowledged; so we drank to people who weren't ghosts.

"I wonder what they're doing in Minnebiac," I said. "Do you suppose there's sleighing?"

"If that New York blizzard of Sunday crawled up there probably is," said Graham.

"This was my last year's present," said Evelyn, touching her necklace. "Father went to New York and picked them out himself, at Tiffany's. This year he sent me a check. It isn't so amusing, as they say over here."

"I wish we knew," said Graham, "whether that case got through all right from Montreal."

"I wrote and said I'd bring my season's greetings with me," said Evelyn; "crossing so soon it didn't seem worth while to send."

"What I like," I said, "is a hard frost after a thaw. The woods look lovely then. Did you ever see our woods in the winter, Evelyn?"

"I don't think I've ever seen any woods in the winter," said Evelyn. "I've always lived in a pretty good-sized city at that time of year."

"There's nothing so perfect," I said — "especially by moonlight. Graham, do you remember walking back home from Minnebiac last Christmas Eve, and losing one of my skates?"

Graham said he did.

"Well," I said, "it's the first time father and mother ——"

"So it is, Sis," he interrupted; "but never mind — half Minnebiac will have dropped in before evening to console them."

"Perhaps so," I retorted; "but they won't succeed. And mother wrote me last week that she didn't seem to have the heart for a proper Christmas dinner, and she and father were going to take the opportunity of sitting down to a simple oyster stew."

"And you enjoying champagne and holly," said Evelyn. "I know what you mean. I wish I could imagine my parents indulging in a little self-denial like that, though. It would be very good for them. They do Fletcherise; but that's all I can say for them."

We were having our coffee in the drawing-room, Graham with his privileged cigarette. Outside an omnibus rolled through the void, and the end of a peal came from St. Mary Abbott's. It was raining, and London, from the window where I went to look out, seemed quiet and dark and depressed, in spite of all the lights in all the houses. It was Christmas out there, but it wasn't our Christmas. We were a little isolated group, high in our flat among the roofs and chimneys, that must turn upon itself for cheer. The occasion proved us aliens; we didn't melt into it. In Rome, especially at times of festival, you can do everything but be a Roman. Evelyn, perhaps, was going to be a Roman. I wondered if she would succeed. I thought it would be a good deal to attempt, and I worked out compensations for not being invited to try.

"Marykin," said Evelyn, "you are creating a draught. I can see it."

I pulled down the blind.

"I'm sorry," I said; "I was only looking at London out there, and thinking how little any of us can really have to do with it."

CHAPTER XVI

So long as we were in town it seemed to us that
we might spend a lifetime there and not be able to
say at the end of it that we had had enough of London. Graham used to declare it was the only place
in the world that reproached him with the fact that
he had to die, implying, I suppose, that he would
die unsatisfied. But when at last we left it for Cross-
shire we seemed to have exactly the same greedy
feeling towards the country, except, as Graham
said, that its tranquillity rather invited one to die.

London stands for London, but the country stands
for England; that is what one feels. Or perhaps
one sacrifices to London with the head, and to the
country with the heart. There is no comedy in
the country, but there are primroses in February.
And one seems to taste and savour all English history there. Graham says in the form of a salad,
but he had just the same feeling. England has two
chapters, London and the country; we had realised
London, and now we were going to realise the country.
What is there about realising things — old, often
told, believed-in things — that stirs such a deep
content? Is it the simple happiness, I wonder, of

being so clever as to find it all out? Whatever it
is, there it was for us, in a perfectly delightful form,
when the carriage met us at Little Gorse station,
with the dog-cart for the luggage and the footman
touching his hat, and assuming with beautiful self-
effacement that we were for Knowes, all as it had
been done in novels ever since we could read them.
And not another soul to drive away but ourselves.
That, I think, impressed us as much as anything.
The 4.30 train had run into Little Gorse that afternoon for our sole convenience; we could not help
reflecting what a good thing it was we had come!
I noticed a public-house and a hay-rick and a duck-
pond, and a tousled little boy in a cap, with very red
cheeks, that watched us stolidly out of sight — just
the kind of little red-cheeked, tousled boy that we
had been led to expect — and the elbow of a lane
which apparently concealed some thatched cottages,
and that was all, yet I seem to possess quite a complete impression of Little Gorse. The public-house
was somebody's Arms and it had a hanging sign with
a weather-beaten picture; I asked Graham if he
noticed. And the hay-rick was velvet brown under
the rain, and as round as the tops of the trees
that were everywhere stretched on the horizon; and
we presently met a farmer in his gig, who touched
his hat to us though he had never seen us before in
his life. Broad and apple-cheeked he was, too, and

looked as if he throve. It all added to my delight; but I could see that Graham didn't much like the farmer's salute. He lifted his hat quite ceremoniously in return, as much as to say "I'll show you that I do not feel entitled, as between man and man, to that kind of thing," entirely forgetting, poor dear, democratic Graham, that he was in Lord Lippington's carriage.

I believe we had expected to find something more like winter in the country; but it wasn't there, any more than in London, which it had been possible to imagine kept warm by its houses. The country for that purpose has its hedges and the cuddling lines of its landscape; and the sheep help a good deal, so over-provided as they are. No doubt England owes a great deal of its reputation for solid comfort to the sheep. The air had a pure, still, peaceful chill in it, but there was no look of winter anywhere, only the rain and the rolling ploughed fields, and the grass too ridiculously green; it was a mere withdrawal of summer. One could almost see her anxiously waiting round the corner for the least excuse to come back. Ah! that first drive between the glistening hedges of the English country lanes — who will be the bold person to say at what season it should be taken? The sad, undoubted fact is that it can never be done a second time. One can't discover twice the fields of home. The English are a hardy and an adventurous people; but I wonder if they know any satisfaction, planting their flag in the ends of the earth, that equals the joy of exploring England?

There was a lodge and a lodge-keeper's wife who came out to open the gates, and dropped a curtsey. We were surprised and overjoyed, both of us, to find such things still existing. As Graham said, we had no doubt supposed, without the least warrant, that they had long been supplanted by more modern conveniences. We turned into an ordinary English park, if there is such a thing as an ordinary English park; but it seemed to us, in the wet green dusk, enchanted with privacy and repose. Where the grassy spaces ended in copses two or three little forms with sudden movements broke the stillness, but not the silence. I will not mind being thought ridiculous; it is so pleasant to remember and write down the moment of rapt excitement when I laid my hand upon Graham's knee and exclaimed "Rabbits!" I had never seen them before at home like that, and doing just as they liked in the twilight; and though nobody seems greatly to value the rabbit in England for any reason, I am prepared to maintain that he is the most lovable thing the Lord has put into any landscape.

Tea was going on in the hall, where the firelight flickered on the big staircase and on rows of pictures, one above another. Lady Lippington was there pouring it out, and Mrs. Jerome Jarvis and a Miss Pedlington. It was all dark and vague, with closed doors in the intervals of the pictures; but Lady Lippington made us delightfully welcome, and insisted on tea before anything.

"We own to being the very back of beyond, you know," she said. "No frivolous week-end journey. Yours was a good train — you didn't change at Wofford? — but it takes two solid hours and a half. Or would you like to get a little of the Wofford tunnel off before you even have tea?"

Graham was indifferent to the Wofford tunnel, and begged, if its signs weren't too gross, to be allowed to have tea first; but I elected to go at once to my room.

"I'll send Batchford," said Lady Lippington as I followed the maid up the staircase. "Batchford will take care of you. She is one of our very oldest friends — has been here thirty years, dear thing. But be sure to speak to her right ear. She does weird things if you give directions to her left, poor dear Batchford."

Batchford was already there, busily unpacking me as far as I was unlocked, and referred with grieved patience to the box to which she found no key. Batchford was as agreeable in the room as the rabbits were in the park. She belonged to it, that is all that one can say, was as happily subdued to its solid mysterious old articles of furniture as the conies were to the elms and the laurels. If the wardrobes and the dressing-table could have given orders, one's impression was that Batchford would have taken them.

"And I was to ask, miss, if you would prefer cotton to sleep in. There's linen on, but the cotton ones are all ready, if you're more used to them, miss."

I looked at the big four-poster with its canopy, and decided that cotton would be sacrilege.

"Please don't change them," I said; "I can sleep very well in either."

"It's thoroughly aired, miss — you needn't be uneasy on that account. The 'ousekeeper slept in it for a week before the family came back to take the edge off the damp; and there's been fires in the room every day since Sunday. But since she's been so much abroad her ladyship always orders cotton to be got ready in case it is preferred, miss. But everybody doesn't, miss, do they?"

I had never lived in a climate that wanted such assiduous airing, or heard of the person of a housekeeper being laid under contribution for the purpose, but I concealed my ignorance and said I believed they didn't; and when Batchford asked me what she should "put out" for dinner I indicated my black chiffon quite calmly. I longed to linger and hear

Batchford talk, and look out of the big windows with their rep curtains and gilt lambrequins, that made such great soft blurred pictures at the end of the room; but I longed even more to know what was happening downstairs, so I descended.

The first person I saw was Billy, in knickerbockers, eating bread-and-butter with an air of solidly deserving it. Lord Lippington was there, too, and one perceived at once that he would be more delightfully himself than ever in the country. They had all come in from shooting, that was clear in their beatific looks as well as their clothes, in the peaceful way they sat or stood about, as if the real history of the day were over, and they merely celebrated the close of it. There was another young man, who was immediately introduced as Captain Pedlington, though one would have known at once, by the architecture of their noses, that he and Miss Pedlington were brother and sister. Lord Lippington and Graham, a little aside, were deep in conversation. I wondered if the good news had come that our host had been appointed to Canada. I hoped so, with all my heart.

"I hope you won't mind our being such a very tiny party," said Lady Lippington to me. "Various people are coming next week, but for the first bit of your visit we could make up our minds to share you with only a very few friends."

"We shall appreciate each other all the more, Margot," said Mrs. Jarvis. "Shan't we, Miss Trent? Shan't we, Billy?"

"I hope to be appreciated," said Billy, "I'm sure."

Everybody laughed, and Lady Lippington said, "You always are, dear Billy. And as to other people, we all know you do your best, don't you?"

"I wonder how many of us," remarked Miss Pedlington, "appreciate ourselves properly."

"Query?" said her brother.

"I more than appreciate myself," declared Mrs. Jerome Jarvis — "I adore myself! I find myself a fascinating companion, a person whose opinion I always want, the only friend I have in the world that I positively couldn't get on without."

"But I said 'properly,'" insisted Miss Pedlington.

"You mean I think too much of myself," replied Mrs. Jarvis. "But that's only because you don't know how nice I really can be when I like. Besides, we should all do it. To be pleased with oneself is good for the health; it improves the digestion. There's nothing I wouldn't do," she went on, "to improve my digestion — no crime I wouldn't commit."

"I suppose there is some crime that each of us would commit," remarked Miss Pedlington, holding her chin thoughtfully in her hand, "if we only knew what it was."

"A very good thing we don't know," said her brother; "otherwise we might go and do it."

"There will be all sorts of new crimes soon," said Mrs. Jarvis cheerfully, "won't there? A chance for everybody. With the laws of the land being made by the trades' unions. It will be — what do they say? — cognisable to send out the washing, penal to travel first class. And I think week-end parties, Margot, will be capital."

"Then I must lose my head," said Lady Lippington. "I won't give them up. But people are talking, aren't they, of burying their jewels? Even the dear princess, I hear — ah, here you are, Christopher! Had a good scrub?"

The immaculate little gentleman who appeared offered a striking rebuke to the others, so creaseless was his attire and so frigidly fresh his whole appearance. He was very thin and very bald, with a cold blue eye and a hooked nose and a grey moustache; he looked like a depository of views and archives; one of those people whose chief function in life is to express opinions and quote authorities. I wondered that Lady Lippington dared to question him about his scrub; but he replied with a frosty smile that he had.

"I call such cleanliness disgusting," remarked Mrs. Jarvis to me. "I much prefer the natural man in the others, the dear pigs, don't you?"

I said I hadn't thought about it. "Is he a soldier?"
I asked.

"Was once, a hundred years ago, but resigned as
a lieutenant when the second brother died — had to,
I suppose — things were in a fearful muddle. He's
been appallingly conscientious and economical, and
I believe he has straightened them out more or less;
but it's been practically the work of a lifetime. Not
a bad old boy really, if he were only alive; and he'll
be Duke of Dulwich, you know."

"Then this," I said, "is the only bulwark at present against —— "

"An American duchess. Quite right, my dear.
I see you are beginning to take notice, as they say of
the babies.   Did Evelyn come down with you?"

"No," I said; "I think she was to go to Pavis
Court yesterday. She was going to motor down."

"Isn't it exciting!" murmured Mrs. Jarvis. "Dear
Evelyn! I do hope, for everybody's sake, that it
will come off. I can say it sincerely now; but I once
thought, do you know, that my Billy was rather
épris — I had some very anxious moments. It
never would have done, you know, for an instant.
Evelyn's a great dear; but she has what I call a
sophisticated mind — there would have been no
happiness in it for my poor, tender-hearted Billy.
But I'm thankful to say it was a passing fancy — old
Billy was wise enough to wait."

"I should think he might wait for ages," I said. "Isn't he very young to be thinking of such things?"

"Billy is twenty-four and a half," said Mrs. Jarvis. "His father and I married at twenty-two and seventeen.   And we were so happy!"

Mrs. Jarvis gently stroked my hand.   It was nice of her, I thought, to make so intimate a reference to so new a friend; and I stroked hers back.

It was all very pleasant, the firelight on the silver urn, and the dark polished doors leading I didn't know whither, and the simple talk about the day's doings; and we sat on in the hall until the dressing gong sounded.   It was so much less alarming and impressive than I had expected, that I went up the big staircase quite light-heartedly to dress for dinner by candlesticks.   It is worth going to Great Britain and penetrating to the country, for people who have been brought up by electric light, merely to realise how delightful candles can be, wavering as they do on one's dressing-table in the draughts that no curtain can be wholly drawn against, filling the room with mystery and movement — more interesting even than Batchford.   One of mine melted too fast, sent up a curl of smoke and made icicles over the edge; and Batchford apologised.

"I'm afraid there's a thief in it, miss," she said, sniffing.

"Is there?" I asked, fascinated.   "Then do you

mind letting him stay in it? I rather like the smell."

"Oh, do you, miss!" said Batchford, pausing with the snuffers.

"I truly do. And I am afraid you will think me a very ignorant person, but all my life I have heard of a thief in a candle, but never until this moment have I seen one."

"La, miss!" said Batchford.

CHAPTER XVII

"I'm sorry for your sakes," Lady Lippington said next morning at breakfast, "that this isn't at all really an old house. Early Hanoverian is all we are, I'm afraid, but the neighbourhood is quite rich in historic places, and there are several I can take you to."

"The object of my life-long reverence up to now," said Graham, "on the score of antiquity, has been a communion service presented to a mission to the Massauqua Indians by Queen Anne. Knowes will at all events develop that church plate."

Lady Lippington gave him an uncertain glance, as if she found a little flippancy in his rejoinder, not on the score of the communion service, but on that of Knowes. All that she had meant to imply was, of course, that Knowes made no great pretensions with its two hundred years, beside other domestic monuments she could mention; but it should nevertheless be understood that Knowes was to be taken with all seriousness, especially by persons whose national past was furnished with no domestic monuments at all. Lady Lippington knew those unkempt places in the world, and came back from each of them, I am sure, more than ever impressed with the treasures of her country and her order, and more than ever desirous that the Colonial mind should also perceive them. She thought, quite rightly, that it ought to do us an enormous amount of good, and have no end of an effect in drawing closer the ties that bind. Nor was her feeling at all confined to architecture or to art; it embraced customs, castes, and institutions. It was she, I remember, who hinted that it was better usage, in the fount of usage, to spell honour with the "u," and she who sent her very intelligent maid to take some New Zealanders over the London Post Office. She, too, was an energetic promoter of those Colonial lunches in great houses of London. She said rank had its duties as well as royalty, and insisted that the hostess on each occasion should be present in person. She said it would make all the difference to the warm Colonial heart and was far more important than anything you could give them to eat, which was, of course, quite true. She called it backing up the King.

Lady Lippington confessed to one weakness in the exercise of this virtue —she did look for appreciation. She said she knew the dear old Stoics told one not to, but she could not help it; and the thing that really wounded her was anything like coldness or indifference. To which I saw, by the way she looked at Graham, she would be very ready to add levity.

I longed to tell her that the real Graham was only too deeply impressed, so deeply that I trembled for him; but my apprehensions were, above all, the things I had to keep to myself, even if there had been any way of showing them.

"The worst of Early Hanoverian is that it was so apt to be amateur," continued Lady Lippington. "Knowes was built by an amateur, an ancestor of Lippington's. He was very proud of having designed it himself. His portrait is on the staircase."

"And it's such a bad one," said Lord Lippington from the sideboard, where he was discovering what there was for breakfast, "that we think he must have designed that himself, too. A regular Jack-of-all-trades, that fellow."

"We are afraid poor Knowes is ugly," confessed Lady Lippington. "But, after all, it is English, and it might so easily at that time have been an Italian villa, full of porphyry and inconveniences."

"You only just escaped," said Lord Scansby, taking with precision a chair beside me. "Quite recently I came across letters of his — Villiers Morville, wasn't he? — died without issue. Yes, that's the man. He thought seriously of employing an Italian architect at one time; had the fellow here, and went all over the ground with him. But I don't think the amateurs of those days were altogether to be despised.

One of them built Blenheim; and some people thought Burlington improved on Inigo Jones."

"I imagine there was generally a practical man to look at the plans," said Lord Lippington. "The owner got the credit — more of it than he deserved, I daresay. Just as one gets it for being supposed to run one of these Colonial shows, whereas the real business is put through by a half a dozen old chaps who have never left the country."

"I don't think that is true of your administrations, Amherst," said Lady Lippington reproachfully. "Well, I am very glad that Hanoverian gentleman didn't listen to the Italian's blandishments. What there is to see, though," — she turned to Graham, — "you must see to-day, for to-morrow we are going to Pavis Court, and after that you will have no eyes for anything."

"We are already in love with the idea of Pavis Court," I remarked, and felt as if I had told everything, but nobody noticed it.

"Oh, Pavis Court is one of our wonders!" said Lady Lippington.

"A sadly dilapidated wonder, I am afraid," said Lord Scansby to me. "It used to be shown — the state rooms — and was very well worth showing, too; but of late years my sister has been unwilling to admit the public. It entailed more of an establishment than she cared to be burdened with. Heigh-ho!"

"An American friend of ours, a Miss Dicey, is staying there just now, I think," said I. To my horror I detected a ring of reassurance in the words; but it is hard to hear a British nobleman say "Heigh-ho!" and not involuntarily try to cheer him. Nor did Lord Scansby cast upon me the look of stony reserve I felt I merited.

"She is," he said. "I am supposed to be at Pavis Court myself — only here for a day or two's shoot. My nephew — Doleford — makes practically no attempt to preserve — abroad too much. A very agreeable and intelligent young lady, Miss Dicey. I have no prejudices against Americans myself."

"Has anybody?" I asked.

"Dear me, yes," replied Lord Scansby. "My sister-in-law, the Duchess of Dulwich, is what I call shockingly prejudiced. So are numbers of people. Numbers of people — chiefly ladies, I must say. You yourselves are not Americans, I know. My cousin told me. You are not American; therefore you haven't got indigestion; therefore I see you can eat ham — a thing I haven't touched for years. Let me give you a piece of advice in case it ever does overtake you. Avoid the three P's — pork, pastry and potatoes — you may thank me some day."

Then down came Billy Milliken last of all, except his mother, who did not appear at breakfast, and the conversation at once became so derisive and so personal that I had no chance of discovering how far Lord Scansby's approval of Evelyn was general at Pavis Court. I could only thank Lord Scansby, who was breakfasting upon dry toast and a patent food, for the hint about the three P's, and promise to remember.

It did not take a day to find out that Knowes was not interesting, except when one saw it from the park, a red brick bulk hidden among trees, suggesting solidity and repose, and leading one to think of all sorts of national virtues that would suitably go with it. Nevertheless it yielded, under Lady Lippington's practised hand, a great deal of instruction. I am sure I missed nothing, no ancestor and no episode; the day, as I look back upon it, seems full of the history of very worthy people in archaic clothes. I don't think Lady Lippington had much imagination, and all this moral possession in the past seemed to stand her in stead of it; she drew real happiness and virtue from it. She was most considerate, too, dear Lady Lippington —insisted on one's lying down at intervals, and not beginning again immediately after lunch. Graham had gone off with our host to inspect a newly-opened mound or barrow in the neighbourhood —we found that Lord Lippington in his mild way was an enthusiastic archæologist —the Pedlingtons had driven to a meet a dozen miles away, and Billy had departed early to look for rabbits, so there was nobody to come between me and the full value of the experience.

Our hostess and Billy Milliken and Graham and I were the party next day for Pavis Court.

"We mustn't come down upon the poor things in a cloud, like locusts or trippers," Mrs. Jarvis said, in announcing her intention to stay where she was. Lord Lippington found an excuse, and so did the Pedlingtons. There seemed to be a general desire to spare Pavis Court, as far as possible, the embarrassment of guests, and Lady Lippington wished openly that she could bring the whole party there back with her.

Billy drove Graham in the dog-cart, leaving the landau luxuriously for Lady Lippington and me. I wanted to arrive with Graham. I simply didn't want him out of my sight at such a crucial moment as I had the presentiment that this would be. But I had to let him go, speeding along ahead, with Billy, to his fate. When they disappeared in a curve of the road I resigned him, and gave all my attention to Pavis Court in the dead old past, with special reference to the date at which the Lippingtons had become connected with the family. Lady Lippington produced fact after fact, tradition after tradition, some splendid, some tarnished, all wearing the dignity of long perspective. They were heavy with significance, with indestructible importance, but they somehow would not weigh enough for me — no, they would not — when I put them, foolishly and secretly, behind all my exclamations of admiration and assent, into the balance against Graham's heart.

A grey tower came between some trees. I grasped Lady Lippington's hand. I had to grasp something. "There !" I cried.

"Yes," said Lady Lippington, "that's the Archbishop's tower — built by one of the Archbishops of York in the reign of Henry the Eighth. You see, it is machicolated. The other — you can see it now — and the connecting portal, was added by the first Earl of Doleford, about fifty years later. But the house itself dates from Edward the Fourth."

I think that is what she said; but I was wildly looking, trying, as we say, to take it in. The two grey towers looked lonely and withdrawn and forgotten, as if nobody had time now to listen to what they had to say. They seemed so long shorn of circumstance as no longer even to expect it; they retired before one's eyes into the past. We could see them all the way from the park gates, and if I am not able to relate any more of Lady Lippington's conversation, it is because they made it impossible to hear anything she said. I did not in the least know what to think about them — Graham would have to tell me — but I wanted to get out and walk.

CHAPTER XVIII

We alighted before the portal, and Lady Lippington looked about her. "He's gone, too!" she said, and sighed.

"Who is gone?" I asked.

"Oh, only an old man who used to be in attendance here. When there was a visitors' book he had charge of it — and he always opened the gates."

"But the gates are open," I said.

"Yes, they are open," Lady Lippington replied, and sighed again. "Poor old Andrew. It would break his heart to go."

"But then — this isn't it!" I exclaimed, as we went through into a grassy quadrangle.

"Isn't what — the house? Oh, no! child. We shall come to the house presently. People had to defend themselves in those days," said Lady Lippington, and led the way across a paved walk that took us under another portal, into a stone court, and then indeed I saw the house, but no trace of Graham. I felt as if the house had swallowed him up, as indeed it had. What lives and hearts and fortunes had it not already devoured, that old exquisite stone house!

And all with what an air of detachment, almost of irony, before such sacrifices to its uplifted ideal, an air that said: "What are your foolish human complications to me? I have to do with beauty, not at all with you."

"I needn't say," said Lady Lippington, as we walked across the sunken flags to the door, "that *this* wasn't built by an amateur."

"No," I said, staring; "you needn't say it."

It just caught and seized and possessed one; there was nothing for anybody to say. It put out a wonderful old claim which one answered instantly with love. It was as indifferent as you like, the austere curved gables hardly lifted an eyelid, the single stone rose-wreath that festooned the arms over the door hardly smiled, the narrow paved windows looked dimly into the past alone; but tenderness and worship it would have, the old grey thing, while one stone stood upon another.

"How simple it is!" I said, and Lady Lippington replied:

"Yes, Tudor is simple. All this part is Henry the Eighth."

My heart sang for a moment, in the joy of it, and then went mute with the thought of Graham, giving him up for lost, and we went in.

"Tea is in the banquetin'-'all, my lady," said the servant who admitted us.

"Is it, William?" said Lady Lippington, with surprise.

"Yes, m'lady. There's a good fire, m'lady," the man replied, and opened a door close to us. There it was, the banqueting-hall of the early reigns of English history; one would have recognised it in the planet of heaven. There they were, its inheritors, Lady Doleford, Captain Lord Doleford, Lady Barbara; there were Graham and Billy; there was Lord Scansby; and there, seated in the midst of them all and plainly a little disconcerting, was the Duchess of Dulwich.

There was a fire — a big one — in the wide mouth of the chimney, and rugs on the stone floor, and Barbara was administering some lovely tea-things, yet the occasion did not seem quite normal, or altogether comfortable. The wicker chairs looked as if they had been brought in out of the garden; the Jacobean chest Billy was sitting on had not the air of being put to that purpose every day; the footman came in with a fire-screen, as if it had been forgotten. Lady Doleford, too, had a funny little unusual air of enterprise, which was dashed whenever she met the Duchess's eye. Then she would smile brightly, poor Lady Doleford, and at once relapse into the anxious, slightly furtive, and conscience-stricken expression, with which as a rule she considered life.

"I can't help thinking, Cecilia," the Duchess was

telling her, "that we should all have been more comfortable in the drawing-room, as usual. Fortunately I myself am not subject to colds; but with your bronchitic tendency ——"

"We thought," faltered Lady Doleford, "it would be more amusing, perhaps, for our young Canadian friends."

"Oh, and for us all, please!" Lady Lippington supported her. "I call it a delightful idea. I shall have two cups and a large piece of plum-cake to celebrate the occasion. Is that Mrs. Webb's noble effort?"

"It's from Bunn's in the village, Margot darling," said our truth-telling hostess. "Webb, you know, is ——"

"To be sure she is; I remember!" said Lady Lippington hastily. "Well, I wish we had a Bunn for emergencies. But, Agnes" — she turned to the Duchess — "were we expecting this pleasure? I thought you were at Coldcoombe."

"You were quite right; I was, until this morning. I am now on my way to town and from there to Brighton, for Broad's sake. Broad, you know, has been having influenza — his second attack in eighteen months, but very patient, poor fellow — and the doctor advises Brighton to put him quite on his legs again. So he is taking the motor down to-day. He's quite up to his work, you know, and such a devoted, faithful soul, so I said to him: 'Broad, I think a little sun and sea air would do us all good.' He was so grateful, poor Broad."

"I should think he might be. You spoil your servants, Agnes," said Lady Lippington.

"So people tell me. But they seem none the worse for it," said the Duchess cheerfully. "Then the bright idea struck me — why not pop in upon Cecilia for a day or two on the way? So I telegraphed asking for a night's lodging or so — she has thirteen more bedrooms than I have, so I made pretty sure — and here I am!"

And there she was, unmistakably in command. They are great usurpers of authority in a family, Duchesses. Evelyn was more than usually quiescent in her neighbourhood; Barbara was positively plaintive. Only Peter seemed in his usual spirits. Peter held his own upon his ancestral hearthstone as if he had received reinforcements. I would not imply that he needed them, but I suppose such things are never unwelcome, especially in dealing with disturbances of morals. He was particularly polite to Evelyn, who chaffed him, when the Duchess was not listening, unmercifully; it was her way, I suppose, of asserting sentimental independence. I thought, as I observed, that she needn't have done it; nobody would have supposed her involved in any way that mattered. I could have told her fifty things that she ought to feel before she need give herself a moment's apprehension about her situation, but there was, of course, the look of it; and Evelyn was always a good deal concerned with that. So she fenced with Lord Doleford as if it were all an excellent joke, quite worth going through with on its comic merits; and he was as gallant, on his part, as anybody could possibly desire who was not in love with him. Lady Doleford now and then gave them a glance full of hope and patience and misunderstanding, like a hen who knew how much allowance must be made for ducklings, and was prepared, for an American duckling, to make even more.

I quite started when Lord Doleford suddenly addressed me from behind my chair. He had come round there apparently to sit down on the edge of the daïs which used to raise his forefathers about eight inches above their retainers at meal times. He got up in a moment, to bring me some more tea, and when he had brought it, sat down again in exactly the same place.

"I hope you are coming out with us to-morrow," he said.

"Yes," I said, "I am to. Lord Lippington doesn't know about my following — it will be my very first meet, you know; but he has promised to mount us both. I am to have Cerberus. I've been making friends with him already this morning."

"Oh, but you must follow! Rather," said Lord

Doleford. "Look here— I'll take the responsibility! Your first meet, and not follow! That's a rotten idea. And old Cerberus is as steady as a rock — just put him in charge, you know, don't fiddle about with his mouth too much; and he'll never bring you to grief. There isn't horse in the county I'd sooner trust you to."

"He was very nice to me this morning," I said. "I told him I was a stranger, and didn't know a foot of the country; and he intimated that it would be all right."

"Good horse! And where, may I ask, have you been all this long time? We haven't met since — since —— "

"Since the Gayworthys' concert," I reminded him.

"Yes we did — once. You didn't meet, but I did. In the Park, about a quarter-past six one afternoon just before Christmas. You were walking west with your brother, and he was laying down the law about something, at a fearful rate."

"He does sometimes. I wonder what it was," I said.

"Where did you spend Christmas?"

"Nowhere. In the flat. By ourselves," I said. "And Evelyn came to dinner."

"I call that luck for Evelyn."

"I don't think she did!" I laughed.

This little talk looks almost too simple to put down.

I hesitate for another reason as well; it seems too intimate. If I withstand these scruples it is for the pleasure of remembering and describing, at the risk of being foolish or being bold, the first conversation I ever had with Peter which was quite comfortable on my part, and flowed happily to the end.

"Do you know," he said — I mention this just to show his dear friendliness — "I think England is doing you good. I think, if you don't mind my saying so, you have much more colour than you had."

"Well, when one enjoys every single minute," I said, "it ought to improve one's complexion."

"I didn't mean ——"

"I know you didn't, but I do. I never had any; but in England one would be ashamed not to. It would be unpatriotic," I said.

"You like the old place, too, then," said Peter, as if I were to be admired for liking it. "I know Trent does."

"What old place? Oh — England! I think it's nearer heaven than any other country. And I think if it weren't for the fogs you would all see that it was."

"Perhaps it is — to look at," he said, and sighed. "I sometimes envy people who are free to come and look at it."

"No — to feel — with the kind of feeling one has for what is one's own. Who could feel more about

anything, for instance, than this?" and I glanced
around me.

"I could," he said, as if he were at that moment
convinced of it. "Not about many things, but
certainly one or two. Am I a monster?"

"It depends, I think, upon what the one or two
things are," I said; and after I said it both Lord
Doleford's eyes and mine at once turned, as if for
illustration, upon Evelyn Dicey. It seemed a coinci-
dence, when our glances again met, that left no need
for further explanation; and we had an instant
of very good understanding in silence. There was
no time for more, even if more had been possible.
Lady Doleford was leading the way to the State
apartments, and the Duchess, whose interested eyes
I had already felt upon me several times, was saying:
"Come, Miss Canada, and see Anne Boleyn's sitting-
room. Go on, Cecilia. Peter shall take care of me."

So we began a walk back into English history,
through the old brown oak-panelled corridors and
galleries of the Earls of Doleford. They were all
there, the stout earls, each in his humour as he was
painted, and many of the kings their masters. More
than one of these had been painted in the house during a royal visit, and under the portrait of the first
King Charles stood the rusty velvet-covered chair he
sat in to the artist. There was his bed, too, with
the royal arms, all canopied in tarnished tissue of

gold and silver, of which Lady Doleford told us sadly that it was said to have cost five thousand pounds. There were royal gifts, too, for household purposes — silver door-handles and sconces, cabinets and ivories. Lady Doleford had an unending fund of information about it all; and where she hesitated she turned to Evelyn, who was always prompt, and once or twice put her right, for which Lady Doleford gratefully thanked her. The first time this happened the Duchess looked apoplectic; the second time she contradicted Evelyn flat.

"It was Maurice, the third Earl, not Robert, that ran away with Elizabeth's French lady-in-waiting," she said, with authority. "It is very wonderful of you, Miss Dicey, and most clever, to know so much about it; but you are wrong there. Elizabeth was very fond of Maurice and thought the Beaufoy not a proper match for him. It's a good thing those old-fashioned friends of the family are dead, I sometimes think."

"Sorry, Aunt Agnes," said Peter, "but I am afraid Miss Dicey is right — it was Robert. I was showing her Queen Elizabeth's letter to him only this morning — scolding old cat!"

Peter was the only member of the family who did not invariably defer to the Duchess, and on this occasion he took the liberty of being distinctly angry with her. A line came in the middle of his forehead that made him look amusingly like Robert, on the wall, who seemed to have been painted in the act of defying his Sovereign. His aunt, Duchess and all as she was, saw that he took his male privilege of putting her in her place, and permitted herself to be put there.

"Really?" she said. "Well, well! I apologise, Miss Dicey. I apologise." But Evelyn made no more general contributions to the family history of the Pavisays. She did not shut herself into the oratory, however, and pray for help to bear it, as I think I would have done. She showed, instead, a high magnanimity.

"The poor dear Duchess," she said to me, as we drifted along, "suffers terribly from arthritis. I'm afraid it's pretty bad to-day;" and I found nothing wherewith to reply. There are some kinds of misfortune which words would only seem to aggravate. But Peter the present Earl continued to behave as if Evelyn were by far the most distinguished and interesting authority upon English history in the party; and his aunt the Duchess had to put up with it.

"Isn't it magnificent?" said Evelyn to me as we lingered for an instant in the fragrance of the big Chinese bowls of pot-pourri in the china closet, "the way they have kept it all together! Of course, everything has been mortgaged for years, but in

the time before that it must have been a fearful
temptation to let things go piecemeal once the entail
was broken. They tell weird tales of the bluffs
Lady Doleford put up to get rid of the picture-dealers
the Earl used to send here. It's too tragic, simply,
that they should have to give it all up. I think it
will kill Lady Doleford. I don't think she'll survive
it, really. A horrible person came from town yesterday to arrange to verify the inventory of the
furniture, and this morning at breakfast she looked
like a spectre."

"It seems extraordinary," I said, "that with so
many relations —— Couldn't Lord Scansby do anything?"

"They have all of them their own complications,"
said Evelyn darkly, "and his have been the worst
of all. He is just out of them, at fifty-two, with
seven hundred a year. When he's Duke of Dulwich he'll have a little over three thousand less the
death-duties, and Coldcoombe, which costs at least
that. It's too stupid!" Evelyn reflected aloud.

I suddenly remembered, with remorse, that I had
been for some time too deeply interested in the stu-
pidity of it to think about the person whom it might
most affect, and looked hastily about for Graham.
Lady Doleford — we were in the tapestried organ-
room — encountered my wandering gaze.

"Are you looking for your brother?" she said.

"He has just gone back to the library with Barbara to see the Philip Sidney manuscript — it is only a fragment, but he wrote it in the room. They will rejoin us presently. It has been quite a delight to show all our old treasures to Mr. Trent. He is so sincerely interested in them."

"Yes, isn't he?" chimed in Lady Lippington. "There is something very real about Mr. Trent. You feel that he is not just saying what he thinks you would like him to say."

"What I feel about your brother," said the Duchess handsomely, "is that he's not a foreigner."

Evelyn, where I alone could see, made a little face at the broad back of Her Grace. "I sometimes wish," she murmured, "that I'd struck this village before the Duchess did."

CHAPTER XIX

Two long tables occupied the hall when we descended next morning; and the whole establishment seemed taken up in furnishing and furbishing them, from the page-boy, who elaborately arranged the chairs, to Lady Lippington herself, who hovered over the silver bowls with willow catkins of England and yellow tulips of France. The tables groaned with all kinds of things besides bowls of flowers; beef and mutton and pasties were there, and champagne in bottles and ale in jugs, and at one end of the principal table, pink and smiling and decorated in a very fetching way, that dish of all the legends, that support of all baronial enterprise, the boar's head. A feeling of deep concern and responsibility was plainly in everybody; I am sure Lady Lippington would have entertained ambassadors with less anxiety than she showed on this occasion. Lord Lippington himself walked through more than once with an eye on the arrangements; Billy Milliken seemed to be making himself useful in some obscure way; even Captain Pedlington, though he only stood about, had an air of function. The very portraits on the walls, especially the full-length ones, seemed to look down with interest at the proceedings, as if they would say: "Now this is something *we* know about." I fancied in some of them a critical reserve, which amounted, regarding the French tulips, to positive disapproval, and seemed to suggest that in the authentic days of hunt breakfasts, pink and white were not thought becoming to boars.

"Do you really think, Wimble, there's enough?" Lady Lippington asked the butler, and hung upon his assurance that there was at least double what would be "required." It was more than double what anyone could possibly require, it was prodigious to think of sitting down to at that or any hour of the morning, though one felt that by undisturbed contemplation of the boar's head one could in time coerce an appetite.

"I'm so glad you think it looks nice," said Lady Lippington. "And presently when you hear a solid chump, chump, you needn't be alarmed — it's only that the dear farmers do so enjoy it."

"They save up for it," said Miss Pedlington, laughing. "They really do; they never take anything till they come." As if it were a bucolic habit anywhere to have tea and toast in bed!

"All good trencher-men, the fellows about these parts," said Lord Lippington heartily, and led the way to the dining-room, where, to my surprise, breakfast was ready as usual.

"I don't know," I said, when Billy demanded what he should get me from the sideboard, "I feel very scornful of ordinary breakfast."

"So do I," said Graham. "My imagination asks for cold beef and boar's head. Must I decline upon a poached egg?" So he had expected, too, that the hunt breakfast was a democratic old survival where everybody would sit down together with due respect but no distinction of platters or places. But apparently it was not to interfere with grilled things at nine o'clock. I looked across at Graham.

"Another Colonial illusion shattered," said he, sadly helping himself to toast; and then we were compelled to explain frankly. It is always better, in England, to explain frankly. They will make any amount of allowance for the disadvantage of having always lived out of England; but it is very unwise to pretend you know.

"Well, of course," Lord Lippington said seriously, "here in the house we hardly want it, do we? We haven't ridden ten or twelve miles already, like some of the people who come. And it's the tenants mostly, who make a square meal of it. But it's here, of course, for everybody; and I've had a good tuck-in myself before now, after riding some distance to a meet."

I saw in Graham's eyes that affectionate, acquisitive look with which he often contemplated the nobleman whom he hoped so much we were going to get as a headpiece for the Dominion.

"But how disappointing for you," cried Lady Lippington, "when that was what you were looking forward to! Do have some boar's head, Mr. Trent. Wimble will be delighted to cut you some. Ring, Billy."

"No," said Graham sorrowfully. "Dear Lady Lippington, the boar's head would be nothing, believe me, or a great deal too much, without the occasion, of which I have been for ever bereft. You can't make it up to me with anything on a plate. Pray don't ring, Billy."

Graham was in excellent spirits. A kind of happiness was shining in him that I knew very well. Certain sorts of beautiful things, with which, I suppose, he had some kind of natural relationship, would always kindle it in him, and then he would behave as if nothing in the world existed except his own private kingdom of heaven. I had often reflected, lately, that Graham would find a very special felicity in being in love; and anyone who knew him well enough to recognise his states of mind might have thought, at that moment, of Barbara. But I knew it wasn't Barbara; it was Pavis Court. I confess, with his interests at heart, I approved — as between them — of the object his affections had chosen. It seemed to me the more likely of the two to return them.

s

It was better, I argued — I don't know how rightly, but it was very much borne in upon me — since Barbara did not love him, that he should not love Barbara; and better still, if he seriously and definitely contemplated marriage, that there should be something for him to marry. It was a barren conclusion, no doubt, but nobody could call the situation a very fertile one. And anything was more fruitful, it seemed to me, than an oasis fed by unrequited springs. I thought very poorly of that.

It would not be doing justice to the Lippingtons if I omitted to say that we had prayers, at which persons appeared and sat in a long line with a look of subdued gratification, who were never again visible during the day. Lord Lippington read prayers to his people as the deputy of Providence for that purpose, with dignity and authority, and yet with a reticence on the personal side that almost amounted to humility. I kept thinking that that, no doubt, was the way he would do it for the King, and saw the members of His Majesty's far households sitting in rows in the same gratified and receptive attitude . . . and I thoroughly agreed with Graham, who by this time was losing no opportunity of saying that little word, and getting more important people than himself to say it, to which everybody concerned with the future of the Lippingtons and the Empire seemed to attach such weight.

By ten it was pouring, and by eleven, when we gathered again, it had not cleared. Batchford seemed to think that it would be advisable, nevertheless, to get ready, but I went down with slender anticipations. Nothing, however, had been abandoned; there was the same stir, and one strange lady, planted in front of the fire with her hands clasped behind her, was cheerfully steaming from all the upper part of her person.

"You don't look at all damped," I said to Captain Pedlington and our host.

"Why should we?" said Lord Lippington; "we've been in the house. But I am afraid plenty of people will presently."

"But will anybody come?"

"Oh, dear, yes. It isn't a garden-party, you know," said he, and left us to welcome another dripping arrival.

It wasn't a garden-party, that was clear at once in the appearance of Miss Pedlington, who came down trussed at all points against the weather. None of the farmers, who were now lining the long tables with concentrated attention to the business in hand, could compete, it seemed to me, with Miss Pedlington in this matter of dressing down to the inclemency of the occasion, accustomed as they must have been to such chances. She was quite splendid, a Diana without a flaw; you could not discover anywhere about her an unnecessary wrinkle or a rebellious hair. Mrs. Jerome Jarvis was just as callous to all but the hunting appearance, but wore her indifference with a touch of originality; she appeared, if I remember, in a bright red stock. It was red, because it comes back to me that Billy, who took almost as many liberties as his mother did, asked her if she had a sore throat.

Billy himself was beautiful in a brand-new pink coat. He was not a member of the Famine, but showed me modestly his own button, and as more and more figures emerged from the landscape at the open door, the buttons, varying in glory, of other people. Most of them had the imprint of the Famine, but there were other members of neighbouring Hunts besides Billy, and one or two mandarins without any decoration at all. This was clearly explained to me by Mr. Milliken; at least it was clear at the time, though I hesitate after this lapse to say exactly upon what grounds the button was conferred or withheld. Some day, perhaps, I shall get it up again. But I still feel that not in China, not in Thibet, could more solemnity be attached to it.

Billy, in this connection, showed himself anxious to be a real friend. He clung closely to me, and told me low in my ear that I mustn't say anything about "dogs." Nor, as I loved my life, he said, must

I mention their tails, nor imagine that any sound proceeding from them could be properly described as a bark. He drilled me patiently, as we watched the gathering crowd in the hall and the dining-room, in the substitute for the childish idea that hunting was done with dogs who had tails and barked; and many other things he told me upon which my reputation depended, all with the cleverest imitation of merely talking about the weather. He took so much trouble that I was quite sorry for him when Lady Lippington began introducing me right and left as a young lady from Canada who had never seen a hunt before in her life. Billy looked as if she were making his position unnecessarily trying, but stuck to it gallantly, and never let me get quite out of ear-shot.

"'Xtraordinary country we are," he observed profoundly, as Mrs. Jack Yilke, in all the distinction of her peaked cap, dismounted at the door. "We won't let a woman vote and yet we make her an M.F.H. I'm not at all sure, you know, after seeing Mrs. Jack's management of kennels, that I won't go in for female suffrage after all."

Mrs. Yilke certainly seemed to have an idea of management. People crowded round her almost as the hounds outside were crowding round the huntsman, making much the same demonstration, which I suppose it would be even more iniquitous to ascribe to them. She had a business-like, pleasant, or disciplinary word for everybody.

"Not got it back yet?" she said pointedly to Captain Pedlington, who was in ordinary riding things; and Billy murmured with enthusiasm: "Look at that, now! This is the second time Peddle's appeared without the pink — last time he said he'd lent his coat to a friend. You saw how neatly she dropped on him. He'll have it on next time."

"Plucky little woman, too!" he continued. "Under water for three minutes last week, with her horse on top of her. Rode home all the same, when we brought her round."

"Oh," I said, "there's — there's Barbara! I began to think she wasn't coming. I wonder where Evelyn is?"

"I don't fancy we shall see her. Doesn't ride, you know. But here's Doleford. He'll tell us. I see people are beginning to mount. By-the-way, as you're a bit of a novice at this game, better stick to me when we get off. Don't ride in my pocket, you know, and don't over-ride hounds whatever you do, but ——"

"Cerberus is all ready, Miss Trent," said Lord Doleford, who had crossed over to us. "You might as well get up now, I think, in case he fidgets a bit at starting. Good morning, Milliken."

What happened to Milliken I don't quite know, he

seemed to be in some way temporarily blotted out. I saw him again as we went through the hall. He was following me with an anxious eye, and was speculating, I am sure, in his kind-hearted way, upon the solecisms I might commit in the scandalised hearing of Lord Doleford.

As we went down the steps, Peter and I, a motor came up the drive, Evelyn's motor. Inside sat Evelyn herself, very beautifully dressed; and she was not alone. I have spoken of Evelyn's magnanimity; I have now to mention her hospitality. On the cushions beside her, more formidable than ever in veil and goggles, sat the Duchess.

"You are just in time," I cried thoughtlessly, "to wish us good luck!" and Evelyn, looking at me rather hard, said:

"I believe we are."

Cerberus was all ready, standing with his groom a little apart from the field. I got up rather clumsily. Lord Doleford had something in his hand which made me a little uncertain of my spring from it, something I was afraid of crushing. When I was in the saddle he showed it to me — it was a bunch of rather small, rather pinched and ragged violets.

"Look here," he said — "I wondered if — if you'd care to wear these. They're not up to much, I know — there are practically no men about the place now — but I found them this morning in the Pheasant

Court.   I remembered you said you liked that part."

"And — did you think of a pin?" was all I found to thank him with.

"Yes — I thought of a pin," he said, and produced it.

I am afraid it is only too likely to be thought that I have not done justice to a meet of English foxhounds; but nobody will ever know how badly I have described those violets. It was said that Cerberus carried me very well, over everything, across everything and always well to the fore. I know I wore the violets. We killed after what I agree to have been an exciting run of I can't in the least say how many hours; and they so manipulated matters that I was given the honour of the brush on my saddle. But the thing I possessed was the violets.

CHAPTER XX

NEXT morning it seemed to me that the air still had
an excited feeling, although all traces of the cele-
bration of the day before had vanished. Only the
trampled hoof-marks in the open space between the
drive and the park remained to speak of the great
event. I happened to be out there before breakfast,
and easily found the deep prints of Cerberus where
the dear beast lifted a little in starting; I could even
follow them a short distance, and those of the black
mare Lord Doleford was riding. She was only a
hireling from Wofford, but she seemed to make a point
of showing the way to Cerberus everywhere. Peter
said he was very much inclined to buy her and take
her back to India with him as a charger. I remembered this and a number of other interesting things he
told me. I reviewed the whole day, standing, as it
were, in the prints of Cerberus; and if I do not describe it at length it is because of the impossibility of
making other people understand what a heavenly
thing it is to ride to hounds.

"What are you doing out here?" suddenly said
Billy Milliken behind me.

"Oh, I just dashed out," I said, "to see — to see if it had stopped raining."

"Well," said Billy, "it has, hasn't it? It's a ripping morning. And I say, just as it happens, you know, I was thinkin' about you. I've been round to the stables to have a look at my animal — got rather scratched going through that bullfinch yesterday, but nothing to signify. I noticed you didn't tackle it — very wise, too. So this is luck, you know."

"So it is," I replied. "It must be nearly breakfast-time, too, which is more luck," and we moved towards the house.

"I say, Miss Trent, I say, Mary — have you any objection to my calling you Mary? — I've been thinking things over pretty thoroughly the last day or two, and I've decided that we get on uncommonly well together. What do you say?"

"I can't very well mind your calling me Mary," I said, "because I always call you Billy. It is impossible to help it. Everybody does. Yes, of course we do. Shall we get on a little faster now? Aren't you hungry?"

"Oh, now you're chaffing!" said Mr. Milliken.

"Indeed I'm not," I told him; "I'm starving!"

"Oh, come on, then!" said Billy with the concern that this kind of urgency produces in England, "but I don't know whether you're an admirer of Shakespeare, Miss Trent. There's one certain Shakespeare quotation I haven't been able to get out of my head ever since I met you. There is a tide in the affairs of men which if you're on the spot, don't you know, is as good as the ace. Favourite quotation of my mother's, too. Some awfully true things that old boy said, I consider. I think in that case he meant 'If you admire anybody, tell her so — don't be a dumb idiot !' Don't you ?"

"I think that's rather a free translation, you know, Billy," I said.

Billy pondered for a moment. "Well," he said, "what I was going to ask you, only you put me off, was this. Have you any objection to Englishmen ?"

"Not the least in the world," I assured him. "I am nearly always very pleased with them."

"Then the point is," said Billy — "I yield to no one in my admiration for our Colonies."

"That's right. Don't !" I said. We had almost reached the steps.

"I'd uncommonly like to see them," said Billy feebly.

"Well," I said, "if you'd only do your lessons and get your degree you could run across, I should think, any time, couldn't you ? "

"There's this infernal business of the House."

"To be sure. I had forgotten that. That can't elect you, I suppose, in your absence," I suggested.

"Absolutely impossible !"

"That's a pity. But do try to pay us a visit. It would be real nice to have you, Billy."

A clever beam came into Billy's eyes. "Now I'm going to ask you a simple question," he said. "D'you mean that?"

"Do I mean what?"

"That it would be real nice to have me?"

"I used the language of metaphor — of common politeness," I said coldly. "Didn't you recognise it?"

"There's only one thing I seem to recognise," said Billy, "and that is ——"

"Yes?"

"That you're not on."

"But how did you guess?" I cried with admiration. Unfortunately we had reached the door, and Billy was unable to tell me. I never thought to refuse anybody in these terms; but as I had seen it hanging over me for some time I was in no mood to be particular. Billy was equally inclined, I think, to congratulate himself that the matter had come to an end of some sort. He must have been thoroughly tired, poor Billy, of leading up to it.

"Well," he said with gloomy relief, as he opened the door, "I can tell you one person that will be fearfully disappointed, and that's my mother."

But neither Billy nor I, I am thankful to say, suffered a pang. If we had, it would have been impossible, I am sure, to write about it in this callous manner. I should have been obliged to hint and to dissemble. The question finally came up just, as Mrs. Jerome was so fond of saying, in the day's work, and was disposed of without any tiresome formalities, for which, in connection with a person like Billy, life is, of course, altogether too short. The emotions in Billy's world have become so conventional that I thought it showed great common sense in him to be so superior to them; and on my own part, too, I felt the little episode to have been something of a performance. It belonged, anyway, to the whole remarkable and delightful experience; it helped in its small way to qualify one for that degree in worldly wisdom that is so attractive to the simple mind; and I hope I was right in deciding that it ought to be mentioned here.

We had just finished breakfast and were engaged with prayers when the snort of an approaching motor sounded upon the drive, which the French windows of the dining-room commanded, and I also, since I was kneeling beside one of them. I recognised it from afar to be Evelyn's, but as it came grunting up I saw that the single figure in it was not Evelyn's, but the spare and dejected silhouette of Lady Doleford, who always seemed, in a motor car, more in mourning for life than anywhere else. Lady Doleford also perceived me through the window, and I drew from her glance a queer little chilly ineffectual arrow of antagonism, as if shot by a person who was not in the habit of falling out with the world. I, of course, had a refuge; I could drop my head again in my hands and even convey by doing so that it was rather wrong to cherish animosities towards people preoccupied as I was, a suggestion of which dear Lady Doleford would feel the full force. I had never, I am afraid, been very fortunate with Peter's mother; we had never quite got on. I had thought dreadfully the wrong thing about religious teaching in the schools; upon that essential point I had not been lucky like Evelyn. Lady Doleford and I never had a conversation which failed, it seemed to me, to give her a worse opinion of me. I had shown without meaning to a kind of perversity in seeing where the rocks were with her and running directly upon them. It was as if I must, for my own satisfaction, be at my very worst with her, so that she could at all events make no mistakes about me, with all her unlimited capacity for it, should by no chance be taken in by me. I felt defiant, that was what I felt, towards Lady Doleford and her preferences; and she did not like me one little bit.

None of us saw her but Margot Lippington, with whom she was shut up somewhere for an hour, but she passed the drawing-room door, where I was sitting with Mrs. Jerome, with her handkerchief in her hand, and I was torn by the wildest misgivings. Lady

Lippington joined us almost immediately with all the appearance of a person who has been administering words of sympathy and consolation. And yet the misfortune she announced did not seem, at the first glance, of such a desperate character.

"Peter," she said, "has gone over to Ireland."

"For long?" asked Mrs. Jerome.

"Cecilia hasn't an idea."

There was a full, round moment, a good sixty seconds, of extraordinarily portentous silence. When it was over one thing stood clear. Mrs. Jerome gave it a voice.

"And no announcement ——" she began.

"To be made. Oh, no!" said Lady Lippington.

"You have been so much in dear Evelyn's secrets," she went on, turning to me, "that I am sure you realised that we all hoped — she, too, I am afraid, poor child — that something in the nature of an attachment might grow up there. Evelyn is such a charming creature — such verve, such spirit, and so sweet to look at. But that naughty Peter has shown all too plainly, I am afraid. It's a real blow to Lady Doleford."

I said nothing. I felt unworthy to sympathise.

"How long," asked Mrs. Jarvis again, who was so happily in a position to ask questions, "is Peter going to stay in Ireland?"

"Nobody knows — least of all his poor mother,"

said Lady Lippington. "But I am convinced in my own mind that we shall not see him again until after ——"

"She has sailed for New York," agreed Mrs. Jarvis. "But what a triumph for the Duchess!"

"You may well say so. She and Barbara only are to dine here to-night. Cecilia is too upset. Evelyn — well, Evelyn ——"

Mrs. Jerome nodded with tense intelligence.

"One can understand it. And Scansby has a cold. I must rearrange the table immediately, and tell Wimble. Poor dear Cecilia — it's really pathetic, Janice. So extraordinarily loyal to Evelyn through it all. Says she feels as if she personally had treated her dreadfully, which is absurd, you know."

"Perfectly absurd!" said Mrs. Jarvis. "I could have told her that there was very little dependence to be placed upon Peter. Far too like his father, in a different way. So unlike my Billy."

"Billy is a dear love," said Lady Lippington; "and Cecilia — you know really, Janice, I think it's a little foolish — still clings to the idea. Doesn't in the least give up hope. Says she means to leave it now entirely to a Higher Power. She believes they were designed for one another, and says she is quite willing to trust Providence to remove whatever cause is keeping them asunder."

Mrs. Jerome laughed as if this were the best joke in the world.

"How like her that sounds!" she said. "But it's only Peter, isn't it, who is being kept asunder. Evelyn hasn't been divided for a single minute, I understand."

Lady Lippington looked dignified and serious.

"I am afraid things may have had a little that appearance," she said, "although we in the family have never for a moment taken it for granted that dear Evelyn ——" But Mrs. Jarvis was quite immoderately laughing again.

As soon as I could I took this deeply interesting piece of news to my room for undisturbed reflection. What I wished to remember was whether Lord Doleford had said anything in the course of the long day previous about starting immediately for Ireland; but I could recall nothing whatever. Even when he asked me for the violets back again, which one would have thought a suitable opportunity, he had said nothing about going so far, and at such short notice. There was an estate there, I knew, from which the rents would very nearly pay his travelling expenses if he did not go too often; he had gone to have a look at the estate, to see, I suppose, if it was worth it. I remembered having been told by Barbara that this place in Ireland would be the refuge of her mother and herself when they were finally

T

compelled to resign Pavis Court. It might be, then, that Peter, recognising this eventuality as close at hand, had gone to mend some of the holes in the roof. It seemed, under the circumstances, the least he could do.

CHAPTER XXI

THE Duchess certainly had a great look of elation
that evening. She wore an Elizabethan ruff and a
feather in her hair, which seemed to accentuate it;
and Barbara followed her into the room like some
meek Circassian slave. Barbara was plainly depressed; I suppose she was drawing near to the
coasts of Ireland in imagination, as her brother
was in fact. I panted to know what her feeling was
about her brother, and tried to think what mine
would be about Graham under similar circumstances
— whether I could possibly consider him a monster
of callous selfishness for being unwilling to save the
family fortunes, and so much more than the family
fortunes, at such a delightful price as marrying
Evelyn Dicey. I put the case for the family fortunes,
for dear, lovely old Pavis Court, for Barbara's future
and her mother's past, for the Pavisay place in the
history of England, for everybody and everything
I could think of, arguing it with the greatest elo-
quence, and decided, after all I could say, that it
would be quite wrong and impossible, and abomi-
nably unreasonable, to expect one's brother —
especially when he had a prejudice against Anglo-

American marriages — to do anything of the kind. What I wanted, however, was to hear this from Barbara's own lips, and I found her afflicted demeanour extremely trying. It wasn't as if she did not appreciate Peter. She had the very highest estimate of him. Yet she wished and expected a person of whom she had the highest estimate to do a thing like that — at least, I had every reason to suppose so. It seemed, to my untutored eye, the defect of the system upon which Barbara was brought up.

There had been other arrivals during the day, and various people in the neighbourhood had been asked; it was quite a large dinner-party, a fresh-coloured, clear-eyed, trenchant dinner-party with direct manners and decided views, beside whom the London people looked like exotics. Among the guests was a fellow-Canadian, a gentleman with a stubbly white beard about whom we knew only that he was sent to the Dominion Parliament by the very youngest of the North-West Provinces; he sat next to the Duchess on the other side. Barbara had been taken in by Captain Pedlington, and Graham was next on the other side of her. I had a curate, whom I found particularly intelligent and agreeable, the curate of Little Gorse. There is a great tendency to misapprehend and undervalue curates. They are not exacting and they often have delightful minds. Looking up and down the table I was convinced that I would as soon be taken in by the curate as anybody; it was quite the same to me.

I believed I knew the exact moment at which Graham learned from Lady Barbara that her brother Peter had left that morning for Ireland. I saw him suddenly look very seriously and meditatively at the tablecloth, as if he were possessed for the first time by a full sense of all that was involved, and ask her one or two brief questions. Then it seemed to me that he grew silent and reflective; and I recognised in him a look I knew very well, of having at last a fair field for making up his mind.

"Yes," he thought, "so long as there was any probability that poor Peter would marry Evelyn, you felt, Graham darling, that the situation had no urgency at all — you could see that if you did propose to Barbara it would be for no reason whatever except that it would be a more or less unique and interesting sort of thing to do. But now, with the hammer actually raised, and no succour from Peter, matters wear another aspect, and you can't help seeing a definite opportunity that ought to be heavenly, but is only heroic. . . ."

"No, none at all now. But my grandfather could remember having been chased by wolves in the winter," I told my curate.

"How exciting for him! I have a brother in

British Columbia," my curate told me, "but I don't suppose you ever met him. Canada is a big place — on the map anyway," and my curate laughed.

"Canada is a big place anywhere," I was obliged to say gently; and he begged me not to be severe, as if anyone would willingly hurt a curate.

Besides, I was occupied in asking myself which of those alternatives, if they lay with me, I would bring myself to choose — that Peter should agree with his mother and Providence about Evelyn, or that Graham should follow the promptings of his passion for the beautiful towards Pavis Court, as the opportunity offered itself in Barbara. After all — considering the second — Barbara was really a dear; we had long ago found that out, a warm-hearted dear, with nice ideas about nearly every-thing. And beautifully typical, to look at, of her chances and her caste. Somehow, if she had been insignificant and rather plain like me, it would have been easier to see Graham in love with her — he liked a sketch always better than a finished picture; and Barbara was the finished picture, that left the imagination nothing at all to do. One is dazzled for a moment, but one is bored for all time.

But then there was Pavis Court, and no question of dazzlement or boredom there. Only a long and lovely office of keeping the lamp trimmed and replen-ishing the vessel. Was it or wasn't it enough —

for a person like Graham? It wouldn't have been
at all enough for me; but then I, compared with
Graham, was singularly unworthy to entertain such
an idea. Only one thing I hoped he wouldn't remember, and that was that he was only, as Evelyn
had pointed out, a simple Canuck, whom the world
would probably, when it came to hear of the matter,
think an extremely lucky fellow. It was a view
that was only too likely to occur to him, and except
in the eyes of the world I could not see that it had
any pertinence whatever.

Again I asked myself — I almost asked the curate
— whether it was quite unimaginable that Pavis
Court, and Barbara's future, and her mother's past,
and the Pavisay place in the history of England,
and everybody and everything attached to it should
just — go? I must say a dreadful gulf yawned with
the idea, and I turned, with a kind of fascination,
to the spectacle of my Roman brother plunging in.

I do not know whether our fellow-countryman
from Alberta — his name was Short, Mr. Mackenzie
Short — was unaware of Lady Lippington's ambi-
tion towards Canada, or whether he simply wished
to show himself uninfluenced by it; but presently
we heard him disposing of the Governor Generalship
in quite another way.

"What I ask," he said, "when I come over here,
and business calls me pretty frequently — what I

ask is, what does the Royal Family cost this country? What's the bill? There's one sure thing, you can never know where you are with it. They increase, Royalties do, like — well, I won't say what they increase like, but they do increase."

"For which we all thank God," said the Duchess.

"I suppose there is a feeling of that sort — I suppose there is. But what I say is — why not make them do a little more for it?"

"My good sir, the King works like a navvy," said the Duchess.

"I daresay he does, ma'am — I'm not in a position to deny it. And I may say that over with us the opinion is pretty general that Edward the Seventh is no slouch. But he's got a good many young relatives. They keep coming along, all ready to be photographed, every year; and they all, so to speak, board at home. Now what I say is why not distribute those young relatives among what Edward calls his dominions over the seas? Why not find some sphere of remunerative employment for them and at the same time give us something we can call our own?"

"I don't know what the Waleses would say," observed the Duchess thoughtfully.

"We could certainly cut and come again there," remarked Lord Lippington pleasantly.

"The trouble is, from our point of view," said Graham, "that you're always cutting and never coming again.   Isn't it, Mr. Short?"

"My young friend opposite — if I were at home I should say 'the honourable Member opposite,'" said Mr. Short jocularly, "has hit the nail exactly, to mix my metaphor a little, where we feel it most. There's no sort of permanence about the immediate object, if you understand me, of our loyal affections. Suppose, now, instead of sending over a member of the aristocracy whose time is all taken up trying not to be supercilious while he's putting in his five years, you gave us a king to keep?"

"I shouldn't have thought," said Lord Lippington, "that any fellow who was lucky enough to get the job would have much difficulty in finding the necessary modesty."

"As a matter of fact," said Mr. Short confidentially, "personally nobody has any sort of fault to find with them.   Personally they're all right and a bit more. What we have no sort of use for is the flunkies some of them bring over with them to run the show.   I could tell you a story ——"

"Then tell us," said the Duchess, "perhaps it will be good for us."

"Well, I won't name any names, and then perhaps I won't get into trouble.   And maybe it won't strike you as much of a story.   But not so very long ago we had a Royal visit, and the mayors of the different towns — they're quite plain people as a rule, but they're the best we have for the purpose — presented the usual loyal addresses. There was one special mayor of one special town that was sort of special plain, very ordinary indeed, just a working man; and when it came to be his turn — well, you can imagine what he thought about it and whether he didn't treat himself to a new suit — why, it was the day of his life. And, just before the ceremony, what should one of these young Jack Dandies on the Staff do but suggest to this special mayor that he, being such a specially plain man, should allow somebody more, as you might say, in society, to read the address! That's so — I happen to know about it."

"What an ass!" remarked Lord Lippington. "I hope we may take it for granted that a thing like that doesn't happen often?"

"Oh, I daresay it doesn't!" said our friend from Alberta; "but it isn't hardly safe, under the present system, to take anything for granted. What I say is give us a King to keep, and we'll know how to take care of him. And it seems to me if you can spare female members of the Royal Family to be Queens of Norway and Spain, you can spare a male member to be King of Canada. What do you say, Mr. Trent?"

"Why, I say," said Graham, smiling, "that if monarchy isn't too old a tree to transplant, it would be an ideal arrangement."

"Then I give you a toast," said dear Lord Lippington. "The future King of Canada, coupled with the name of the nursery at Sandringham!"

"A branch of your Royal House to be grafted on to our Canadian maple!" cried the Member from Alberta with enthusiasm, and waved his glass.

"What are you all so excited about at your end of the table?" enquired Lady Lippington from the other; and when it was explained to her she said: "By all means. We'll drink, too. To the King of Canada — all in good time."

After dinner the Duchess, making room for me on the same sofa, asked me some pointed, personal questions, based upon the fact that among all the colonies she had the highest opinion of the one I humbly represented. The Duchess observed you might say what you liked, there was nothing like family ties.

I don't know whether we owed it to Mr. Mackenzie Short and his ardour for monarchical institutions, but the country seemed suddenly raised, in the point of view of the Duchess, from the geographical to the practical; she seemed literally, as she sat on the sofa and considered me, to come, like the early discoverers, within sight of land. Even in that momentary embodiment I felt honoured, and when she enquired whether we had any Indian blood in our family I was sorry to be unable to gratify her intelligent curiosity in the affirmative.

"But are you sure?" she said. "There is something so very dark and distinguished about your brother — quite the young brave."

"Our father came from Yorkshire," I interrupted, "and our mother's people emigrated from Massachusetts."

"Ah, well, perhaps it came in there," said the Duchess. "Not that I have personally any particular objection to it — rather a noble strain I should consider it. And I shouldn't at all wonder, Miss Canada, if there was more of it in your part of the world than you think."

At that point the men came in, and I saw Graham walk straight to where Barbara was turning over the Academy pictures of the year. I saw, too, that he had made up his mind. Without seeing any more I was aware that they had contrived a disappearance together somewhere; and with a queer, only half-sincere feeling that there was at least nothing to suffer for him yet, I gave my attention to the curate, who had rewarded my politeness during dinner by coming to seek me out again after it was over, as curates will.

The Duchess and Barbara were spending the night; and Barbara's knock came, just when I thought it would, about ten minutes after we had all gone to our rooms. She shut the door with perfect composure, and took a serious and collected seat near the fire.

"I thought you would like to know, dearest Mary ——" she began.

"I do know.   I'm sure I know!" I said.

"That ——"

"Graham ——"

"Has asked me to marry him," said Barbara.

"Of course he has," I told her. "And — are you going to, Barbara?"

"Yes, I think so," said Barbara equably.

Neither of us said anything for a moment, and then it struck me to put a question.

"Tell me, Barbara, are you happy?" I asked.

"I don't know," she said honestly.   "I'm pleased."

"Oh!" said I.

"Aren't you pleased?" she suddenly demanded, and at that of course I kissed her.

"Darling Barbara," I told her, "I would rather have you for a sister than anybody in the whole world."

As a form of congratulation this was perhaps a little egotistical; but I saw that it perfectly satisfied Barbara.

CHAPTER XXII

"A MARRIAGE has been arranged, and will take
place early in July, between Graham Trent, Esq.,
D.S.O., late lieutenant of the Connaught Yeomanry
Regt., son of the Hon. Mr. John Trent, of the Senate
of the Dominion House of Commons, and Lady Barbara Pavisay, only daughter of the late Earl of Doleford, of Pavis Court, Crosshire, and Long Water,
County Antrim, Ireland."

There was only one thing I didn't like about it;
and that was that the *Morning Post* should know it
would take place in July before I did. That seemed
to lift the matter into a cold, far, official sphere, to
suggest that the warm, human, domestic interest
had very little to do with it at all. I could almost
have wondered, if he had not been at Pavis Court at
the time, whether it had been thought necessary to
consult Graham.

I was not at Pavis Court; I was in town with Mrs.
Jerome Jarvis, who was staying with me at the flat
while her house was being painted. There was this
to be said about Mrs. Jerry, and I had often heard it
from others — she never let anything make any

difference. You might break any number of the commandments and as long as it suited Mrs. Jerry to continue your acquaintance she would not for a moment give you up; and I had only been foolish, and not sinful, about Billy. So when the little awkwardness arose as to what was to become of me while Graham took his privilege of falling more deeply in love than ever with Pavis Court, Mrs. Jerome most magnanimously said she would come and stay. As we had Billy too almost always for dinner, nothing seemed really to have been affected by anything, which was very much Mrs. Jerry's view, I believe, of ideal relations; I wished I could make it mine. To be lifted above sentimental vicissitudes of any sort, as Billy was, would simply, I thought, be too happy and delightful a fate.

The awkwardness at Pavis Court took the obvious form of there not being another habitable bedroom. Evelyn was still there, and Lord Scansby, and with Graham every corner that was decently comfortable was occupied.

"If you had been a King or a Queen," said Barbara regretfully, "we could have done you quite well."

She meant, I suppose, that I could have had a State apartment with silver sconces, and slept under a canopy powdered with centuries and heavy with bullion. I wasn't qualified for these honours, that was very clear, but it was no reason why I should feel,

as I nearly always did with Lady Doleford at Pavis
Court, like some stray cat that she didn't want to
encourage about the place. No doubt there is exag-
geration in that way of putting it; but the hostility,
or antipathy, or whatever it was that chilled the air
between Lady Doleford and myself, was so slight
that I am obliged to use a strong term to bring it
out, as it were, at all. I very much doubt whether
anybody was aware of it except me; but it was one of
those things that are not an atom the less clear to
oneself for being imperceptible to other people.
After the departure of Peter, and especially, oddly
enough, after the engagement of Barbara and Graham, it seemed unaccountably to intensify. She fully
accepted Graham, more fully, I thought sometimes,
than Barbara did, and made a great deal of him; but
her attitude to me plainly indicated that though
Graham might be, under the circumstances, a very
good thing, he was in himself enough of it.

Evelyn stayed on through everything at Pavis
Court. It might have been thought that Barbara's
engagement cut the ground, so to speak, from under
her feet; but nobody who knew Evelyn could suppose that she could be made uncomfortable by the
loss of a mere trifle like her *raison d'être*. Besides,
she had not altogether lost it, she remained to comfort and support Lady Doleford through the be-
reavement, if one might say so, of the daughter of

her choice. I don't know whether she counselled
resignation, or shared Lady Doleford's ardent faith in
those wise over-rulings which in the end were bound
to bring about such announcements under the *Court
Circular* as were to her taste, or whether it was just
out of bravado that she went on holding a position
that might be considered to have fallen twice; but
there she remained. When Mrs. Jerome read Graham's engagement out of the *Morning Post* at breakfast — Mrs. Jerome always had the *Morning Post*, it
followed her about like a sheep, and naturally she
brought it to the flat — I said it must be getting nearly
time for Evelyn to sail.

"I must say I sympathise with Evelyn," said Mrs.
Jerome. "Very deeply."

"Do you think she has been badly treated?" I
asked.

"I think Cecilia Doleford has made a goose of her."

I reflected for a moment, and then I said: "Do
you know, I don't think anybody could quite make a
goose of Evelyn."

"It's all right being sent upon approval," remarked
Mrs. Jerome, "if you are approved, isn't it?   And it's
pretty clear — however, she is a clever little person,
as you say. She and Cecilia may have their way
yet."

"Lady Doleford," I said, "must be a delightful
person to have for a real friend."

U

"Too clinging," said Mrs. Jerry, "for modern life. No time for all those stores of affection."

"I haven't seen that side of her," I remarked.

"Well, of course," said Mrs. Jerome enigmatically, "she considers herself pledged to Evelyn, you know. She's tremendously what you might call a woman of honour, Cecilia Doleford. And very patient, very persevering. Rather stupid, too — she can only see one thing at a time. Never has more than one string to her bow, you know — there are people like that. Although, in view of dear Barbara's having saved the situation the way she has, I am inclined to agree with you that she might as well give it up."

"I never said so!" I cried. "I only meant that if Lady Doleford seemed to like me better it would be pleasanter meeting her in society."

"Never allow your personal feelings to interfere with your social relations," said Mrs. Jerome Jarvis. "That's a cardinal principle, for London, at all events. You find me useful, don't you, putting you up to dodges of sorts? Dear me, what a romance it is, this engagement of your brother and Barbara Pavisay! I was one of those who indicated it, you know, from the beginning. I saw he adored her from the first. Aren't you very pleased about it?"

"I love Barbara," I said.

"Yes, isn't she a dear? And a lot of principle Barbara has, too — she gets that from her mother.

So much better than taking after her in looks, when you could choose to be a Pavisay.   Thinks out things for herself, Barbara does — surprises you sometimes. And she has not only behaved very well over this affair, but your brother Graham will get a good wife into the bargain, which might have been by no means to be taken for granted."

"I think he will," I said furiously, "and I know Barbara will get a good husband."

"And that's not to be disregarded, either," said Mrs. Jerome Jarvis.

Barbara was in town for a week just then, staying with her Aunt Agnes, who had accomplished Broad's cure at Brighton and had now returned to London, for whose sake in her establishment I am not certain, possibly for her own.   Graham did not take the opportunity of coming too — as Barbara explained he had so little time left now to be at Pavis Court, planning repairs with her mother, and being introduced to all the silly old things there, that it would have been inhuman to drag him away.

"Aren't you ever," I asked her desperately, "the least bit jealous of Pavis Court, Barbara?"

She looked at me thoughtfully.   "I see what you mean," she said.   "But, no — I don't think I am." "Perhaps," she added presently, "I ought to be."

"Oh, I don't know!" I said.   "If he's satisfied, why should anybody worry?"

"That's your point of view," said she calmly, indicating that there might be another. It was so surprising to find Barbara specialising in this way upon her situation, that for a moment I had nothing to say. Hitherto she had seemed to take it as she took most things, as an essential part of a general scheme, prescribed by circumstances and sanctioned by authority, to which it would be tiresome of her not to conform. Barbara's wasn't, whatever Mrs. Jerome might say, an analytic mind, and wouldn't be at all likely to decipher a problem for itself without some suggestion from outside. When I saw that she was really pondering her engagement, I wondered greatly what influence had been working upon her. Could it be Evelyn, I speculated, who had taken toward such unions a high moral tone? No; Evelyn, however otherwise she was equipped, had a sense of humour, and besides, Evelyn approved. Could Peter have written anything? That wasn't likely either — Peter was only human, and it must have been a weight off his mind. Probably he approved.

Barbara broke in upon my thoughts. She had come to tea.

"Mary," she said suddenly, "I like Graham."

"Well," I said, "I know he likes you."

She gave me a dissatisfied glance. I don't know what else she expected me to profess.

"It's a very good foundation, isn't it?" she said. "Mutual liking."

"Oh, yes!" I said, but in my heart I was thinking, "What a forlorn pair of people!"

"You know, of course, that he has secured Pavis Court."

"I hope so," I said. Without that, it will be admitted that the prospect would have been a little bleak.

"Mother looks ten years younger. But what I was going to tell you was, he has promised — has offered — to hand it over to Peter, if Peter should ever be in a position to buy it, on very easy terms. And Peter easily might, you know."

"Yes, but do you think he would?" I asked. "Unless it just happened so?"

"Well, it might just happen so," said Barbara.

"Yes, I suppose it might," I agreed.

"Or he might get a post — Peter might — out in India or somewhere, and save up on his own account. He has ideas," said Barbara. "But anyway I think it's splendid of Graham to be willing to give it all up like that; and so does mother."

"Well," I said, "I don't suppose Graham would feel very comfortable in King Charles's bed, with the Earl of Doleford walking up and down outside."

"He won't want to sleep there," said Barbara. "It's too stuffy. Though, of course, he could if he liked. Especially as we shall only be in England for the summers and not every summer;" and she sighed.

"Mother will be longing to see you," I said. "And you will try to like Minnebiac, Barbara."

"I've had the sweetest letter from her," said Barbara, and sighed again. "And I do mean to try to like Minnebiac. That will be something for me to do. Evelyn says ——"

"Oh, how is Evelyn?"

"She's very flourishing indeed, and very well occupied. She is saving Uncle Christopher's life — at least he says so. She is teaching him to Fletcherise — chew, you know."

"Why, what a good thing!" I exclaimed. "If he doesn't happen to know."

"Isn't it? They sit opposite one another, and cheer one another on. Mother and I stick it out at dinner, but at other meals, when there are things to do, we often have to abandon them — just leave them at it. It's noble of Evelyn, for she does love talking, and her digestion is all right."

"Evelyn is a person of great resources," I said. "If she had to chew, she would just chew, but she wouldn't be wasting her time."

"Especially when it's supposed to be so good for one," said Barbara. "What has Towse got there — oh, a telegram!"

"It must be from Graham," I said. "I wonder what he wants."

"He's hunting again to-day," remarked Barbara; "I hope he hasn't had a spill."

At that I opened the telegram quickly. It was from Graham.

"What a relief!" I cried. "And what good news. 'Watchett wires Lippington appointed Canada.' How very, very nice, Barbara."

"I was perfectly certain Margot would bring it off," said Barbara. "Margot brings everything off."

"Now when you go to Ottawa with Graham you'll have to be presented to her," I said.

"Presented to Margot?" said Barbara. "How ridiculous that seems!" and she sighed again.

CHAPTER XXIII

IT was then the first week in February, and winter was over, at all events for the lilacs in the Park. There had been two postponements in the arrangements of people interested in this account. Graham and I were not to sail until the twenty-first, and Mr. James P. Dicey would not arrive in England until March 1st. Evelyn had wrested a fortnight's extension of leave from her parent. On the other hand Lord and Lady Lippington were to sail for Canada rather earlier than had been anticipated. Vice-regal honours had begun to press — rather inconveniently, Lady Lippington was explaining, the day I went to see her. I had meant to express something like congratulations, with a suitable mingling of happy reflections on the good fortune of Canada; but the general tone of what was being said made me pause abashed.

"There is hardly time to get Lippington's uniform made," she was telling Miss Pedlington, "though luckily I had a hint some weeks ago that this might come upon us; and I knew upon what short notice one *can* be whisked off to the ends of the earth, so I made him go to be measured. If they had found somebody else to appoint no harm would have been done — he acknowledges the wisdom of it now.   But isn't it too inconsiderate of them to give us only till the tenth?"

"I suppose we never know what we are equal to until the trial comes," said Miss Pedlington; "but I must say I think you are very brave about it all, dear Margot."

Margot smiled pathetically.   "We are to have the boys out for their summer holidays," she said, referring to members of her family whom I have not mentioned before because, being at school, I never saw them. "Amherst thinks it will be good for them.   That is my great consolation.   But it is rather soon to uproot us again, isn't it?   I should have been glad of just one little peaceful year."

"It will be simply exile, of course, for you both," said Mrs. Jack Yilke, who was also there.   "Couldn't you take out a bobbery pack, or start harriers or something?"

"Oh, we try not to look upon it in that way at all," said Lady Lippington brightly, "and of course one's own pleasure is the last thing one must consider! But I am sure we shall find a great deal," and she smiled graciously — already — at me, "in the simple amusements of the country."

"You have one thing to be thankful for," remarked the Duchess of Dulwich, who had dropped in unexpectedly as usual — it was, I believe, Her Grace's substitute for the satisfaction of travelling incognito. "You can depend on the loyalty of the people. Once you get hold of their affections. No sedition there, eh, Miss Canada?"

"I hope not," I said.

"You must attach them — you must attach them," continued the Duchess. "That is what we are sending you out for, remember. Take a bobbery pack by all means, but no puppies on your Staff, please, like the one that Mr. What-you-may-call-him was telling us about the other night at Knowes. You and Amherst laid that to heart, I hope," and the Duchess helped herself to more tea-cake.

"We did indeed, dearest Agnes. Though I'm sure the poor man hadn't a suspicion into whose ears he was pouring that most distressing story. And we do indeed mean to win their hearts if it can be done," Lady Lippington went on plaintively. "That is my great anxiety always — the social side. I make one strict rule — no favouritism. If I dance with one Minister I have a little talk with another, or sit out with the Leader of the Opposition — ordinary tact, and it's really quite easy."

"And what," asked the Duchess, "do the Canadians pay you for all this? What's Amherst's princely salary?"

"I'm ashamed to say I don't remember," said Lady

Lippington; and I do not think she did. The Duchess turned to me.

"I'm ashamed to say I do remember," I murmured, "but nothing would induce me to tell. It's so ridiculously small," I added to Lady Lippington, "compared with what you think you ought to do for us — I'm humiliated."

"Ah, well!" said the Duchess; "you mustn't expect too much of us. We're only human, you know."

I longed for the audacity to say: "Dear Duchess, you are far too modest!" but I didn't find it; and presently, as more people arrived, the air became so thick with condolence that I felt compelled to come away. All this is only important because it explains why I had taken a short cut into Piccadilly on my way home on that particular afternoon. That is what I am leading up to, my being exactly in front of Apsley House, walking, with a drove of Londoners, toward a lovely sunset that was going on in the direction of Hammersmith, thinking how little matters are ever arranged in this world to our entire satisfaction, and coming unexpectedly face to face once again with Peter.

He had turned round and was walking beside me before either of us realised, it seemed to me, quite what had happened, exactly as if we had met by appointment, instead of its being the most astonish-

ing thing that could possibly have taken place, as
I said it was.

"I thought you were in Ireland," I remarked.

"One can't always be in Ireland," he explained.
"Shall we ——?"

"Yes," I said.   He meant should we turn into the
Park, out of the noise of the traffic.   We went rather
a long way in, where it was almost green with
lilac-bushes, and then turned west again.   The
landscape, I remember, seemed to slip away on both
sides, and the path to disappear under us and behind
us, by the mechanical necessity of walking.   It was
a heavenly exercise, walking, that had very little to
do with the ground, and yet enormously helped the
real matter in hand, whatever it was.   Whatever it
was seemed more possible and easier with every step,
and yet every step had a rhythmic value of its own
that made it, looking back, indescribable.

I learned from Lord Doleford that he had just been
seeing Mrs. Jerome Jarvis at the flat.

"I generally look her up," said he, "when I'm in
town.   But she said you were out.   So it doesn't
seem so very wonderful, meeting you here."

"No," I said; "it doesn't.   Not now."

It is incidental to the Serpentine that little boys
throw sticks into it and that brown and white spaniel
dogs plunge in and get the sticks.   Or else it is one
of those things that you remember from a previous

existence; I think, however, that we spoke about the brown spaniel dogs; I am almost certain we did. If you take it for granted that what we said was very clever I shall be pleasantly surprised, but should hardly think it mattered. The actual quality of a conversation may have so little to do with its importance. I know I mentioned having been at the Lippingtons', but forgot to explain how amusing it had been there. One doesn't remember everything at the time.

We passed a number of people sitting upon the benches, mostly young people, sitting there in pairs. Some of them would not bear looking at — at least they would bear it, that was the horrid fact — but I was fascinated by the aspect of one group of two. She was nice-looking and tastefully dressed; and she had a pathetic expression, and poked the gravel path with her umbrella, while he, at a proper distance, as melancholy as she, hung upon her slightest movement. It seemed even more reposeful and beatific than walking to elucidate whatever it was, and I had an instant of wishing that Peter would suggest sitting down somewhere so that I might poke the gravel with my umbrella and he might watch me doing it. Presently, however, I saw that this was no isolated case. The gravel was being poked in all directions to such an extent that I wondered the caretakers didn't interfere; and I perceived a confession in the poking that made it impossible to dwell upon even in thought. The melancholy, however, we could make our own, and we did, walking along as if our hearts were breaking instead of being simply too full for utterance, as they were, at least for more than utterance about the dogs.

It might be thought that one special topic would have absorbed us, that we would have rushed to discuss the engagement of our several brother and sister. The event had happened since we met; it had been thought interesting and important by all our friends, widely talked of, and celebrated in the newspapers. It was impossible to deny its interest and importance to us as well, and equally impossible to suppose that for one moment we forgot it, yet the difficulty of approaching it seemed insuperable. It ought also, in the nature of things, to have drawn us cordially together, yet when at last we managed to drag it in, we mentioned it allusively and looked at it askance, as if, once it were fully recognised, it would have rather the effect of keeping us apart. But it could not, of course, be ignored, taken for granted, or treated with other indignity, indefinitely.

"I think it was uncommonly sharp of them to discover that they liked one another," said Peter. "Uncommonly sharp. I never saw any traces of it, — did you?"

Then Peter suspected, Peter understood, Peter criticised, too. I cannot explain the unexpected comfort and support that there was in this discovery, or the insight and power of arriving at just conclusions upon very slight data that it seemed to reveal in Peter. Compared with mine his opportunities of observing what I suppose I must call the love affair of Graham and Barbara had been very small indeed, yet here he was saying things, venturing in his unvarnished, British way to say things of exactly the kind that I had for weeks been thinking. Yet I did not agree, immediately.

"Oh, well," I said, "so long as they have discovered it!"

Why I took the line of appearing to suppose they had is inexplicable to me to this day. I may have wanted Peter to insist that I was wrong. But he is one of those Englishmen who always suppose that people mean exactly what they say; he never gives them the benefit of the doubt.

"Then you think it's all right? Good business?" he said gloomily.

"I'm afraid that's a very proper way of describing it," I replied, with prudence.

"You're afraid — oh, I see! Well, personally, I hope there's more in it than that. Your brother's such a good chap — I should be sorry ——"

"And Barbara is such a dear," I responded. "One would hate to think ——"

"It's so fundamental, isn't it?" said Peter.

"Yes," I said, "I think so, too." I did think so.

"Barb isn't much of a judge of human nature," he went on thoughtfully, "but she ought to like him."

"And I don't believe Graham is much of a judge of — of love," I said, quite clearly, "but he ought to adore her, of course. Darling Barbara."

We passed three lilac-bushes in silence, during which I felt that Peter was perceiving the situation in a further aspect. I wondered if he would find it improved.

"Then do you mean to say," he said at last, "that you think neither of them ——"

"Oh, never mind!" I replied recklessly. "I daresay it will come out all right in the end."

"But in that case," he went on seriously, "what, in heaven's name, are they doing it for?"

"Don't ask me!" I disclaimed.

Peter turned red, I could see without looking that he did. "I suppose I've got to understand it from Barbara's point of view," he said unwillingly; "but what Trent is thinking of — what is he thinking of?"

I reflected for a moment. "Graham is simply charmed!" I said.

"I do not understand that," he replied obstinately, "and I'm pretty sure poor old Barb doesn't either. I won't believe that of her, anyhow. She must imagine he wants her more than that."

"I daresay she does," I said cheerfully. "I am sure Graham could do a courtship that would take them both in beautifully."

As Lord Doleford considered that, our eyes met.

"It hasn't taken us in," he observed; and I did not know whether I wanted most to laugh or to cry as I answered "No."

CHAPTER XXIV

"Evelyn seems to be taking it very much to heart," said Mrs. Jarvis, whom I must, before it is too late, begin to call Janice, as I had been doing on and off chapters ago in real life; she liked it so much better. As I had met Mr. Jarvis only twice, she excused me from calling him Jerry — it wasn't really unfriendly in me, she knew, only shy and silly and Colonial. Mrs. Jarvis — Janice — was never at a loss to explain anything, especially by adjectives.

We were still in the flat, though Miss Game threatened on the horizon, and Towse kept an increasingly anxious eye upon the mantel ornaments. It wasn't that she thought our honesty wouldn't stand the final strain; it was, now we had got so far, that she didn't want no cracks, 'ouse-agents, as we might or again we might not know, being that artful. Term had begun and Billy had once more gone "up." Janice often said she was sure I missed him almost as much as she did, to which I agreed with pleasure. Peter had again disappeared, leaving, his and Evelyn's friends were all afraid, no sort of doubt about the future. Graham was still at Pavis Court — there was so much to arrange — and the party there remained unchanged, with the exception of Lord Scansby, who had left again for Yorkshire.

I asked Mrs. Jerome about Evelyn's taking it to heart — if she really thought so.

"Yes, I do," said she. "It isn't like an American to bury herself in the country. The hunting is no good to her, and the weather is beastly. She's simply pining."

"If she were pining," I remarked, "she wouldn't pine there, Mrs. Jarvis — Janice. I think she's just staying on to show that there never was, from her point of view, anything in it."

"Of course, so far as the general position is concerned, it matters less now than it did," pursued Mrs. Jarvis serenely. "Peter has only now, one may say, his own interests to consider. Your dear lucky brother has set him free from any other obligation. By the way, aren't we to see Graham to-day?"

"Yes," I said, "he has business in town, and I am to meet him at Euston. Evelyn is coming, too, but not Lady Doleford; and Barbara was doubtful."

It was the tenth, and we were all to rally at Euston to speed Lord and Lady Lippington on the Liverpool special for Canada. The hour of their departure had been duly published in the Court Circular column of the *Times;* and there was every prospect of one of those distinguished gatherings that are always reinforcing, at London railway-stations, the prestige of Greater Britain. I was looking forward to it with the interest one has for a typical occasion, as well as nursing a secret throb in the prospect of seeing off a Governor-General of my native land as if he were an ordinary person. Presently the Lippingtons would be as the sun in the heavens for splendour and remoteness; the dazzling consideration was whether it would make the least difference being distantly connected with them by marriage. Of one thing I was proudly certain — Senator and Mrs. John Trent would never impose upon that connection, or any member of their family.

We rattled into the outer court of Euston in a line of shiny carriages and motors; there was a sense of informal function even there. The already drawn-up coachmen and footmen were enough by themselves to impart it — how representative they always are with their immobility and their decorum and their cockades! Almost capable, I could not help thinking, of conducting such an occasion with perfect propriety by themselves. However, they were putting down numbers of even more important-looking people — the unexpected legs of a Bishop descended just before us — in whose train we, too, presently found ourselves on the platform beside the steaming special, placarded "For the Canadian Pacific S.S. *Empress of Britain.*"

The distinguished travellers had not yet arrived,

but a quantity of luggage, luxurious yet travel-stained, with a man-servant and a couple of maids hovering over it, seemed to speak with a high sense of duty of other viceregal departures, and to claim a certain precedence in the van. That and an ordinary first-class saloon carriage labelled in blue letters "Engaged" were the only outward and visible signs; the engine had not so much as a flag or a wreath on it. The station was full, too, of people who were obviously bent upon their own affairs and hardly aware of what was transpiring among them — running after porters, buying newspapers, or establishing mere relatives in corner seats. Among these the Lippingtons' friends stood in groups of very chosen silk hats and frock-coats, groups that had greatly the air of being repositories, and of uttering permanent, undeniable truths to a heedless and struggling democracy. I picked out Graham at once, walking up and down with an Anglo-Canadian Liberal M.P., discussing perhaps the respective fields of usefulness for legislators in an old country and a new one, or perhaps just general political probabilities, as people do in England when they have finished the weather. I noticed what a difference sat upon Graham — something in his step and his shoulders and the outlook he expressed upon life — from the Lippingtons' friends who were native to the island, and even from his fellow-Colonial member of Parliament, who seemed already, as they walked together, to have assumed the insular yoke. He, Graham, was more free than they, more free of a thousand things — traditions and conventions and responsibilities, privileges and commandments, interests and bores, advantages and disadvantages and fearful indispensable sign-manuals. That was the great thing that was published in him as he went swinging up and down the platform with the other man; and surely it was something as precious in its way, I reasoned, as any opportunity or any possession, something which gave even Pavis Court one aspect of a mess of pottage. That Graham should cherish his freedom seemed indispensable and necessary. My own sex, I found myself thinking, were more or less born into a state of bondage — it would not have mattered nearly so much if it had been me. I even — I might as well own and be done with it — had begun to wonder why, as things were turning out, it couldn't have been me; but I can honestly, honestly say that I was sorry for Graham only on his own account.

Evelyn came up and greeted us in that happy expectant American way which always seems to say "What next?" in England.

"Then Barbara hasn't come?" I asked.

"No, she hasn't. We left her writing what she called an important letter to Peter. She complains fearfully about being out of touch with Peter, but so far as I can see nobody is in touch with him particularly at present. Nobody in his own family, at all events."

There was the funniest implication that Evelyn was involved in the family injury, took the family's point of view; and I thought of all I had heard of the American power of adaptation.

"Tell him, if you happen to see him, not to come back to Pavis Court next week, unless he specially enjoys the smell of fertilisers. Otherwise he may find it dull. Graham is coming into town and the rest of us go to Ponds from Monday till Saturday."

"To Ponds," I said.

"Christopher Scansby's place in Yorkshire," Evelyn explained. "Where I hope we shall not be compelled to live entirely upon grape-nuts. Poor darling Lady Doleford can do her duty on a crust but she loathes patent foods. Luckily, Barbara says, there's always a chop to be had in the village."

"How is Barbara?" I asked. I had felt more than a usual interest in Barbara's state since her engagement; I hung upon it as if I expected it to develop something critical, in spite of knowing that she was the most normal person it was possible to meet. However, it is natural enough to ask after even the most normal person in her absence.

"Oh, bursting with health as usual! She was quite funny about it the other day — for Barbara. Envied me, if you please, my American digestion.

Said it was very hard not to be able to look interesting when you felt interesting."

"I wonder," I said, "why she feels interesting?" without intending, in the least, to imply anything to her detriment.

"Exactly! That's what strikes me. Isn't she engaged? She ought to be feeling as dull as ditch water. Once Graham said the fatal word the element of interest, in my opinion, dropped out. The rest is mostly candy, isn't it? Candy and chaff," said Evelyn pensively.

"How late they are," said Miss Pedlington, coming up. "I don't think they ought to keep people waiting like this — they aren't Governor-Generals yet."

"Perhaps they're practising," said Evelyn.

"Well," continued Miss Pedlington, "Margot has her heart's desire at last. I wonder if she is really happy — I wonder if any of us are really happy when we obtain our heart's desire."

"I don't think one ought to want anything too much," I remarked, "for fear of getting it." The idea came to me quite suddenly, looking at Graham.

"Oh, please say that again!" cried Miss Pedlington. "I must have it for my commonplace-book. Is it a quotation? To want a thing too much is to be sure of getting it! How true!"

"Here they come," said Evelyn; and at the booking-office end of the platform we made out the entry of Lord and Lady Lippington. A porter preceded them with light articles on a truck, and beside the truck danced a young man with a happy supervisory air, restoring matters, as he danced, to an inside pocket, no doubt tickets to Liverpool. By the fact that the luggage was in no possible danger one saw at once that this was the A.D.C. I could not, to my surprise, take much interest in him; but I thought he looked equal to all he would have to do.

They moved with becoming viceregal modesty along the platform, especially Lady Lippington. Dear Lord Lippington looked impressed and pleased and dignified; but it was she who really wore the honours of the occasion. One would say that while he was Governor-General elect, to her it had actually happened. The Colonial Secretary and Lord Selkirk accompanied them, and we all converged, in groups, upon them; but not with frisky rapidity. A kind of shyness settled upon us, and it was felt that the Bishop was quite within his province in making the first farewell. Bishops are never shy. This one looked at his watch, the kind of thing, as Graham says, that one envies anyone under such circumstances the capacity for doing. Then everybody crowded about with such warm handclasps and affectionate wishes that Lady Lippington broke down and had to retreat behind her handkerchief to the saloon carriage.

"I thought she would collapse," said Mrs. Jerome

Jarvis. "What can you expect? It's frightfully trying, and she has wept for three solid days already at having to go. Poor dear Margot!"

"Oh, dear!" I said. "If only she had let it be known earlier! But I suppose nothing can save her now."

My good-bye was negligible, but my roses were lovely, and I had to deliver them, so with one or two other friends I followed into the railway carriage. Our worst anticipations were confirmed; Lady Lippington was sobbing in a close circle of exquisitely-dressed and deeply sympathetic ladies, to whom, for obvious reasons, she could not relinquish both her hands.

"I don't believe anybody loves England as I do!" cried the poor lady the King was sending away because somebody had to go. "If I could only take it with me!"

The engine whistled and Lord Lippington appeared smilingly in the door. There was a tumult of embraces and then it was our turn. Miss Pedlington rose to the occasion, leaning tenderly over Lady Lippington.

"Don't cry," she said nobly. "It's for the Empire."

I wished I had thought of that; but I could only thrust my roses into the unhappy exigency and say: "It is a shame!" Lady Lippington gave me a pathetic smile and a hurried damp kiss.

"Do I look too horrible," she asked, "to present myself at the window as we go out?"

The train slid away amid a forest of black silk hats, and a dropping chorus of "Bon voyage!" "Good-bye!" and "Good luck!" to which Mrs. Jerome Jarvis added in a high key "My love to Canada!" which, from so complete a stranger, I thought kind. An instant later we had turned, from an Imperial occasion, into a mere dissolving platform; and I managed to attach myself to Graham.

"Well," he said, "come along. Shall we go and get rid of lunch first, and where?"

"You are Anglicising," I said bitterly. "If you don't mind paying, I'll take you to my club. I've only got sixpence ha'penny."

"I don't mind paying," he replied, but he said it quite seriously. There was even, I fancied, a half-tone in it that said with humble acceptance "What else am I here for?" It made me turn hurriedly to find Mrs. Jarvis and part with her for the day. I wanted to part with everybody, to get away from all those people.

"We won't go to my club," I said, remembering that it would be full of them, "I'd rather go somewhere with you, Graham. Any little old place — Lockhart's or the British Tea-Table — the kind of place we went to when we first came and didn't know anything, and enjoyed ourselves — don't you remember?"

He did not reply as we elbowed our way out of the station. Most of the occasion disappeared into carriages, but we found ourselves presently in Euston Road and looking anxiously, as we did in the beginning, for a right 'bus.

"Would you rather have had a cab?" asked Graham, as we hurled ourselves into what he used to call the most entertaining spot in London, the front seat on the top, next to the driver. I said no indeed, and for a minute or two we lurched into the traffic of North London in silence.

"I've been considering motors for a week," Graham said, and settled luxuriously into his corner. "Barbara would like one, I think, to play with while I'm away. There's a lot of fun to be got out of them in the country. Which do you prefer, a brougham, or one of those big open things?"

"I hate them all!" I said. "Heard from father this week?"

"Oh, well, that's foolish, you know!" returned Graham, but with a shade of depression. "Yes — I've brought the letter. Father's just tickled to death," he added a little more brightly.

"Mother is rather frightened, I think. How is Barbara?" I asked.

"Quite all right, thanks."

"And Lady Doleford?"

Graham smiled.   "Lady Doleford's positively blooming!" he said. "It's a pleasure to see her. We get on capitally."

"Then you're lucky," I said.

"Lucky?"

"In your mother-in-law," I explained.

"Oh! Yes, indeed; we have great talks. She's fearfully interested in her village; and I've got her to see that it isn't a live proposition as it stands — her village. All gone to thatch. As a matter of fact, it doesn't do much more than keep the rain out, though, of course, I don't tell her exactly that. But she goes down to the cottages and argues it one way, and I drop in at the pub and argue it another, and between us we've got about three-quarters of the able-bodied population tickled to death with the idea of Alberta. I'm transplanting three families myself. Lady Doleford picked out the men. I wanted to have them vetted; but there wasn't any sort of necessity. She knew exactly how they were geared — how Crupp had broken his leg in two places when he was fifteen and Stobbs had had rheumatic fever the year before last, and the other Johnny never suffered from anything since he had the measles. You would think they belonged to her!"

"She has all the virtues of her class," I said, "I'm sure."

"That's very much it.   And it's a lot to say, mind. We can't care about people just because they are people, on our side, the way they do here.   It isn't in us — yet."

"I suppose she's very pleased with the — repairs and all that," I said.

Graham's face ever so slightly clouded.   "She naturally likes to see things being done," he said.

"Isn't it a little unusual — beforehand?" I asked. "Things being done, I mean?"

"Possibly.   But they just had to be.   The poor dear old place couldn't wait," he went on, "another half-hour."

He reflected for a moment.   "They're tremendously considerate, you know," he added.   "Lady Doleford, Scansby — all of them. They consult me at every point.   More than they need, really. I sometimes wish they would just go ahead and have it as they want it.   They are so much more likely," he amended, "to get it right."

"And Barbara," I asked — "is she as deeply interested as the others?"

"I'm not sure," said Graham candidly, "whether Barbara cares as much as she ought to care.   She gives me the idea sometimes of a person taking great pains to do something that wasn't really important to her."

"Her heart isn't in it?" I hazarded — and I could

swear that the answer that jumped into Graham's eyes was, "I'm afraid I don't know where her heart is." But what he said was as different as possible.

"You ought to try to get to know Barbara," he replied. "Now that I'm engaged to her I find her very well worth knowing. If the Criterion will do as well as the British Tea-Table, here it is."

"'Old tight!" said the conductor, as we approximately stopped the machine and got down.

CHAPTER XXV

About this time, the decorators having gone out
of the house in Rutland Gate, Mrs. Jerome Jarvis
returned there, and when the Pavis Court party
left for Ponds, Graham came back to the flat, to
Towse and to me. Towse had a critical eye on him
when opportunity served, and confided to me in
the kitchen that she didn't find him as 'earty as he
should be considering that he had been in the country.
He reminded her, she said, of Bargus's pore nephew
who went off in a decline from having been treated
badly by a young lady. Fair 'eart-broken he was
when she forsook him, and never got over it. I
couldn't agree that Graham showed indications of
a decline, but neither could I contradict Towse when
she remarked that his spirits didn't seem to be what
they was; and we both noticed that the discovery
that Billy had tilted a Heppelwhite arm-chair to its
ruin brought hardly a groan from him. He seemed
"off" Heppelwhite and Adam, even off the fifteenth
century, implied that he had been living in so perfect
an atmosphere of the Renaissance that fragments
of it in a little modern flat had somehow lost their
spell.

It seemed to me that he suffered, without knowing it, in this advantage, and that for us the true joy would always lie in fragments or approximations wherever they might be. It depresssed me beyond words, this loss of interest in his own things, especially as I could not see that it was replaced by any special appreciation of treasures likely before very long, to come, in a manner of speaking, into his possession. I say "in a manner of speaking," because any property in them was the last thing that seemcd to occur to him. In the beginning — the early stages, I mean, of the transaction — he used to suggest to himself with the dearest modesty, a kind of wardship over them. He was going "to take care of" the beautiful old repository; but nearer to it than that he never seemed to see himself, and now he did not talk of it at all. On the other hand, he had far more to say about Barbara, Barbara's ways and ideas and favourite authors, and Barbara's character; above all, her character. He would explain her character to me for half-hours together, and I could see that he spent even more time in thinking about it. He seemed to have settled that Barbara at all events was going to be his, and he sought anxiously for his duties and privileges in her connection. He wrote to her every day, quite long letters, upon the subjects in the newspapers; his presents to her were truly charming; he seemed

Y

to expect her to be the central figure of his life. It was really as if, having lost his captivity to Pavis Court, he turned to Barbara to forge new chains for him.

With my ideas about the whole affair I suppose I ought to have found this an improvement. Upon all principles I had to prefer seeing Graham more anxious to be husband to Barbara than curator to Pavis Court. It was certainly a move in the right direction, if in such matters one could move. And no doubt Barbara would see it and respond. She had the sense of obligation — she would recognise a claim like this. She would say: "Poor Graham, has the old place come rattling down about your ears, like a house of cards, after you've bought it, too? Well, here am I — if I can be of the slightest use ——"

At least that, I was convinced, was what Peter would say in her place. They were a good deal alike, Barbara and Peter, and both Pavisays. . . .

And all would yet be well. It was merely my imagination that would find the whole thing such a pathetic muddle. It is fatal to bring too much imagination to matters of sentiment — they are imaginative enough in themselves. At least it was so with Graham. How far imagination would influence a person like Lord Doleford was more difficult to say. Perhaps a good deal — though he was so like Barbara — since hadn't we seen, didn't we know for a fact, that he had refused to avail himself of the most valuable and charming advantages for no other reason that could be made out except that she — the advantages — had once laughed at the caricature of an old horse? It was absurd. People may have extremely good qualities, and yet be unable to see that an old horse is the most poignant and touching spectacle in all the animal creation — as Peter said — and that people who enjoy a caricature of him are not fit for decent society, as Peter hinted. And since this was the only fact he had ever been able to produce against her, his behaviour must have been based upon imagination, as it plainly was in connection with dull and insignificant people who seemed so curiously, now and then, to please him. Was it also imagination that kept him, in spite of this, so constantly resident in Ireland? It is impossible to decide about the value of such a gift, but one thing seems clear — that it should always be exercised with a great deal of common sense.

I spent a good deal of time in reflections like these, and I was thinking about nothing else when Barbara came. She was quite unexpected, and the first thing I remembered when I let her in — Towse had gone for an outing, to see a relation of Bargus's in the hospital — was that she must have known Graham was not in town. I said at once how disappointed he would be, and Barbara explained in the passage, rather lamely, I thought, that she had taken the chance of motoring in.

"And I am lucky to find you alone," she said with agitation — for Barbara. "I wanted to find you quite, absolutely alone."

"Let me go first and put the kettle on the spirit-lamp," I interposed. "It's almost tea-time."

I spoke collectedly, but in the kitchen I had to strike three matches. Barbara was not herself, and if you knew her you would realise that to move Barbara from the normal a matter must be very serious indeed. Her eyes looked bigger than usual and all her colour had gone into a square of red in each cheek.

"Be as quick as you can," she said as I went, with the forced composure of a person who can't wait very long to get something over or out. I flew to the conclusion, as the matches went out one after the other, that Peter had broken his spine in the hunting-field. He was not killed; she would not be there if he were killed; but he had had a serious accident. Otherwise why should a person like Barbara behave in such a dreadfully emotional way?

I brought the spirit-lamp in and set it on the hearth. "There," I said. "In here, if it boils over we shall know. Now will you please tell me at once whether he is likely to get over it?"

Barbara gave me a surprised glance. "I hoped you wouldn't take it that way," she said. "I am sure he'll get over it. I am sure we shall both be much, much happier."

"Barbara," I said, "what can you mean?"

Barbara looked at the floor and then she looked at the wall, and then at Miss Game's mantel ornaments, and by the time she got to the mantel ornaments two large tears had made their way to the edge of her lower eye-lids. She is a person who hates crying, so she took no notice of them, only stared at me rather fiercely through them.

"I mean Graham," she said.

"Oh!" I said. "Graham!"

"You see," she continued, "during this last month I've naturally got to know him much better. And — I don't know what you'll say, but I've irrevocably decided ——"

"What?" I panted.

"That I can't marry him."

"Barbara!" I cried. "You darling angel! But why?"

"He's such a dear," she explained, and added firmly, "It's impossible!"

"He is, isn't he?" I said. "I see." I did see, in a flash, but Barbara went on.

"I don't mean that I ever thought him horrid, even when I said I would. But not nice enough to matter.

I really didn't know him at all," she confessed. "But now I do, and I like him so much that unless I liked him awfully you know it seems to me that to marry him or anything like that would be perfectly abominable!"

"It's curious," I said, "but he has been talking so much lately about getting to know you better, and finding so much more ——"

"In me than he expected?" asked Barbara modestly, and reddened. "That was nice of him. We have got, really, quite fond of one another."

"Do you think so?" I asked doubtfully. "I don't mean, you know, that one saw anything like that in it. Necessarily, that is. Nothing, I mean, that need change your point of view."

"But I have two," said Barbara with self-respect. "There's another."

"Do tell me."

"In the beginning I did think — I really and truly did — that he liked me. He *might* have liked me, you know."

"Of course he might."

"And it seemed such a useful — that sounds too vile! But — everybody thought so. And it seemed to me that it was just the most fortunate thing that could happen — his liking me. On those terms I don't know — it wouldn't have been right, but I don't know that I couldn't have gone on. You see if he liked me particularly and I only liked him — ordinarily," said Barbara with consideration, "there would have been something on my side, wouldn't there?"

"You mean," I said luminously, "a *quid pro quo.*"

"Exactly — exactly! And imagine my feelings when I found I wasn't even a *quid!* When I found I was being thrown in! How would you like to be thrown in?"

"Like a pound of tea," I sympathised.

"Not even like a pound of tea," Barbara insisted. "I thought of that. But the pound of tea is thrown in as an inducement. Now in my case, I'm not an inducement, am I, Mary?"

"Darling!" I murmured.

"I know I'm not clever," Barbara went on, "but the most dull person can find a thing like that out, if she is at all anxious about it. "Mary," she added tremendously, "Graham doesn't care a bit more about me than he does about mother. I knew it in a fortnight. It puzzled me frightfully — not being clever, you know. I used to lie awake thinking about it. That being so — well, what was there?"

I listened attentively, but suppressed the reply, "That is what I always wondered," which rose to my lips.

"I had to think it was the old place and — all that, you know. Don't be furious — I am not clever. Well, then I said to myself, 'That's something, any-

how — if he likes it.' I thought he wanted it for
himself. It was quite natural to think that. Everybody is mad about it. And then, as I tell you, I
began to find out that he is really nice and doesn't,
and of course one can't let him, you know. So I've
written him a letter — here it is. Would you mind
giving it to him?"

"I think I would, a little," I said. "Couldn't you
drop it in the letter-box?"

"Perhaps that would be better. But you will see
that he gets it?"

"I won't take it out of the letter-box," I promised.

"I don't write a very good letter," said Barbara
earnestly. "So I just tore out here to make it all
perfectly clear to you, dear; and then, I thought,
you could explain to Graham anything he doesn't
understand about it.   And, of course, to ask your for-
giveness and all that.   I hope you forgive me, Mary?"

"I'm afraid he will hardly consult me," I said, a
little stiffly. "You see, Barbara, for Graham, it
isn't altogether a business matter."

"I know," said Barbara simply, "it isn't. It
ought to be, and it isn't. That's just it. So it
mustn't be for us either — for me, or for mother.
Poor mother — that's the only thing. But you do
forgive me?" she insisted.

"Yes, I do, dear Barbara," I told her. "I would
have forgiven you anyhow."

Barbara embraced me. "I wish I wasn't going to lose you," she said affectionately. "But we shan't, shall we? And you'll promise to come and see us in Ireland?"

"Oh, dear!" I said, suddenly remembering complications. "Ireland! Poor Lady Doleford! And who is to live at Pavis Court?"

"That's the nice part of it," Barbara replied cheerfully. "Graham can keep it if he really wants it, and if he doesn't, Hofmeyer wrote the other day offering five thousand more than it came back to us for. I'm so glad you gave me the chance of telling you — it wasn't a thing I could write to Graham."

I suppose it was reasonable that Barbara should consider this a lucky circumstance; but I could not help feeling a trifle offended.

"I don't think he will sell it to Hofmeyer," I said.

Barbara looked at me. We had reached the door. "Because of the five thousand pounds," she said, and I nodded. She opened the door.

"You don't know what it is to want five thousand pounds," she said. "But — I don't think so either. He's funny!"

"He is funny!" I agreed, and as Barbara sank down in the lift I turned to contemplate the communication in the letter-box that would tell him how funny he had been.

CHAPTER XXVI

"THE marriage arranged between Graham Trent, Esq., and Lady Barbara Pavisay will not take place."

When the *Morning Post* said it, as briefly, as finally, as that, one might dismiss the idea that there was any sort of doubt about the matter. On further consideration, the *Morning Post* could hardly refer to it in terms less brief or less final — could hardly say, for instance: "The marriage arranged between Graham Trent, Esq., and Lady Barbara Pavisay is not quite so likely to take place as it was." It would have no way of hinting at the dreary week of fuss and talk and expostulation that had gone over all our heads since Barbara went down in the lift, leaving her letter in the letter-box. It would have been the height of impropriety to inform the public of how Graham posted off to Pavis Court at the screech of dawn next morning, openly and devoutly wishing that the place and all that was in it would burn down in the night, and so enable him to marry the girl he wanted with no idiotic complications. Of how Lady Doleford carried the matter, quite in vain, before the Lord and the Duchess. Of how Peter declined absolutely to come near the scene of disarray or

even to express an opinion; of how Barbara was
spending her time in the arms of her friends and
the reprobation of her relations.

All this I realised; in the Court Circular a thing
must either take place or not take place. Still, the
two lines of the announcement seemed brusque and
uncomfortable and damaging, as if it only lacked that
to complete the wretchedness of everybody concerned,
which was now quite public and perfect. I did not
see why Graham should be further depressed by it,
with a fire in the room. It was a paper he seldom
asked for, anyway, the *Morning Post*.

We were to sail in two days. Everything we had
become possessed of was already packed and shipped.
I noticed with regret that Graham entrusted the task
to strangers — did not even superintend it. I was
in no anxiety about him; but I never knew him so
dull. He had long periods of meditation, out of
which he would come with a baffled air, and straight-
way bury himself in the Toronto papers. He was in
no sense heartbroken — how could he be? — but his
heart, all the same, appeared to have suffered a
reverse. He was living, I suppose, in the reaction
from his high attempt. There was a kind of flatness
in the check he had received which was more disconcerting than the sting of defeat. He was not to
be allowed to immolate his heart on the altar of
Pavis Court; that was how it summed itself up to me.

Dear Barbara, the priestess of the occasion, would not allow it. How it summed itself up to him there was no way, after his first outburst over the letter, of finding out; but his spirits did not seem to indicate a very lively appreciation of his escape. It was odd that only Barbara seemed able to cheer him. He saw her two or three times, and always came back refreshed and heartened for his task of abdication.

Well, it had proceeded to the end, and there in the back of the fire, was the announcement to the world. We were having our last breakfast in the flat. Towse had put it on the table and left the room, again wiping her eyes on her apron. To do anything for the last time affected Towse in that way toward her apron. She had felt the same earlier about Graham's boots and taking in the milk. I tried to cheer her with the thought that she would presently be beginning everything over again for Miss Game; but she would not see it in that light; she said Miss Game was a very peculiar lady, almost too particular, and it would not be at all the same. We had to infer that whatever we were we were not peculiar and not particular. We tried to find it as flattering as we could.

"I'm dead sick," Graham was remarking, "of reading that the fine weather tempted a great many people into the Park yesterday." He put down the paper. "I believe I shall be glad to get back, Sis."

"Wouldn't it be rather curious," I said inclusively, "if we weren't?"

"Here is another interesting announcement," he returned. "Lady Halleigh, whose beautiful house in Curzon Street is really too big for her now that both her daughters are married, is trying to dispose of it, and if she succeeds will in future live almost altogether in the country, which she adores."

"Is it an advertisement?" I asked.

"I think it is," said Graham. "Well, I don't want her house in Curzon Street."

I suppose what the poor dear boy thought was that a house in Curzon Street, acquired to enable Lady Halleigh to live in the country which she adores, was all that was necessary to make him perfectly ridiculous.

"Certainly not," I said vaguely, wishing to be sympathetic.

"I expect they like it — the British public," said Graham, "being taken into Lady Halleigh's confidence in that way. Being told it is really too big for her just in that confidential tone, and for such natural reasons. Here's something about the Duke of Barnstaple on the Riviera — very kindly written! 'Warmly wrapped up' they say His Grace motors somewhere and back every morning before breakfast. They pet and pat and cajole these people like tame animals. I wonder how long one would be obliged to live in England to care whether the Duke of Barnstaple were warmiy wrapped up or not?"

"I don't know," I said. "I'm afraid we shan't do it this time," but there was no great spirit in my reply.

"This is a country of lofty traditions," continued Graham; "but like the horse which is a noble animal it does not always do so. Of the five men I dined with last night — the conversation at dinner turned upon clothes — three of them took me aside afterwards and recommended their tailors. Well, Sis, some of our Colonial ways mayn't be pretty, but when we recommend our tailors we don't do it privately."

"I was present," I reminded him, "when Lord Doleford recommended his to you. So was Evelyn and Billy Milliken. Isn't he giving satisfaction?"

"Oh, yes, in a way. But I'm waiting now till I get home. I'm tailored to death already; and half the things won't be wearable there."

This, I reflected, was exaggerated; the island's tailors at least were pre-eminent. "I thought it wasn't a thing you minded much about — clothes," I said soothingly.

"I'd rather not look more of a fool than I need. These things, walking down King Street, would shout aloud," he persisted.

"King Street, Toronto?"

"That is the thoroughfare the name suggests to me," said Graham, rather severely.

"I have been told how many King Streets there are in London," I observed, "but I forget."

Towse brought in our last eggs. I sliced the top off mine properly. Graham turned his into a wineglass.

"Somebody," I remarked, "I can't think who — told me not long ago about being proposed to on board ship, and while she was considering it they went down to breakfast and she saw him eat an egg — like that. It had such an effect on her that she had to tell him she really couldn't."

"She must have been attached to him!"

"It hadn't got as far as that. Here is such a nice letter from Miss Pedlington, Graham, to say good-bye."

"The last time I met that woman I inadvertently mentioned the fiscal outlook. I must have been hard up for something to say; but I asked her whether she was a Free Fooder. 'My great-grandfather,' she informed me, 'was the only Bishop that signed the Reform Bill. We are not likely to hold any other views!' I told her she was a credit to her country."

"The Bishop was, anyway," I said. "Have you any interesting letters?"

"Here's a bill of five pounds fifteen from the fishmonger," he replied. "I thought we had some game of a weekly book."

"We had," I said, "and I paid it every week up to ten days ago, by the man who called for orders, and he signed the book. But now they say they've lost the book. Do you think we're likely to have had five pounds fifteen of fish in ten days?"

"I have no way of knowing. But if you haven't got the receipts you must pay the bill."

"It's unlucky," I said, "but the same thing has happened with the laundry-book. Do you suppose they have done it on purpose?"

"Oh, no!" said Graham grimly; "but you'll have to pay. We can't stay to discuss it, unfortunately."

I did not like his tone, but I was willing to make every allowance. "Are they all bills?" I asked, referring to his letters.

"No," said he. "Some of them are dilapidations. Do your remember the young man from the agent's?"

"I remember a young man," I said, bringing him back with difficulty as if from the other side of the Flood. "A young man who represented that he was there on my behalf. A very unnecessary young man."

"I'm afraid you didn't encourage him enough. He wasn't altogether unnecessary," said Graham. "He was here again two days ago looking for damages. He seems to have found a lot."

"I know of only three," I declared. "One tumbler, one kitchen plate, and the handle off the dresser drawer. I told Towse particularly to show them to him. Did she?"

"I have no doubt she did, in spite of every natural instinct, if you told her to. But he doesn't seem to have needed showing. Did you know, for instance, that we had put the spring roller blinds in this room out of order?"

"Towse must have concealed it."

"We have — hopelessly it seems. Eleven and six."

"I'll speak to Towse."

"There are four further serious offences against the dining-room. We have marked Miss Game's table, scratched her chairs, chipped her mantelpiece, and removed one of the wooden apostles from her blessed Armada-oak sideboard."

"Removed one of the wooden apos——! But that was Luke and he never was there! Don't you remember pointing out to Peter that Luke wasn't there, and Peter said he must have gone down with the Armada?"

Graham looked at me critically.

"You mean Doleford," he said. "I would not lend myself to this fashion of Christian-naming every Tom, Dick, and Harry if I were you. It's one of the decadent things about England."

There was no use in saying that I meant Peter the Apostle on the sideboard, so I merely reiterated, "He never was there."

z

"The most interesting item in the kitchen," said Graham, "is the linoleum. 'Holes burnt in several places. One pound five and sixpence halfpenny.' The halfpenny is touchingly honest."

"Towse may have done it," I confessed, "but she always stood on that place by the range, and it was impossible to see."

"Bathroom — ceiling discoloured."

"Could we help her old water-pipe bursting?"

"Principal object of water-pipes in this country. With us they don't burst, no doubt because we have so much more frost. But that is not the point. Twenty-seven and sixpence."

"Do they just charge at random?" I asked.

"They charge at anything they see. I can't go into all they've found in the drawing-room, but I notice a considerable sum for calendering the furniture covers."

"But we weren't to ! She didn't for us — and they were anything but fresh, and it was agreed !" I cried with indignation. "Miss Game herself ——"

"Has left it entirely to her excellent agents," said Graham calmly. "And do you remember what you signed?"

"I signed the list."

"And a statement to the effect that everything not otherwise described was in good order," said Graham.

"Never!" I cried.

"To do you justice I don't think you did. But the statement was there — this thing came in yesterday and I went round to see the people — between the end of the list and your signature. They probably stuck it in afterwards."

"They could," I said with conviction. "There was plenty of space. What a contemptible trick!"

"It's a certain way of doing business," returned Graham, who seemed to be enjoying himself, "to which we don't happen to be accustomed — that's all. But I could wish we had taken better care of the mantel-ornaments."

"The mantel-ornaments!" I exclaimed wildly. "There are forty-two, and thirty of them are in the closet."

"One match-holder — toad design — cracked."

"It was done before!"

"One yellow cat — chipped behind the ear."

"We never chipped it behind the ear!"

"One green dog, right paw damaged; one ditto pig, left leg ditto."

"Ah!" I cried with triumph; "but I put all the green animals in the closet. So that proves it."

"Not a bit," said Graham, "since you have stated that the whole forty-two were in good order. The list totals up handsomely. Twenty-one pounds, ten shillings, and elevenpence."

"That was what he meant by being there on my behalf! And worrying me to pick holes in things! What shall we do about it?" I exclaimed with excitement.

"Oh, we'll pay it!" he replied contemptuously. "What else is there to do?"

This was not at all my inclination. I did not wish to pay the twenty-one pounds ten shillings and whatever it was. It seemed to me improper, almost immoral, to pay it; and I would have rushed into the courts rather, or submitted to be dragged there, whichever the circumstances required. I would even have been willing to postpone sailing for a week or two to do it. I said so. Indeed, the more I thought of postponing sailing the more desirable and necessary it seemed not to be trampled upon by the young man from the agent's. But of course my frame of mind was different from Graham's. I had not evolved an ideal and chivalric project and had it returned on my hands as not quite ideal and chivalric enough. I wasn't suffering, in the most delicate and high-minded region of my consciousness, from a fearful, fearful snub. And poor Graham was. It was quite enough, what Graham was suffering from, to impel a person to wash his hands of everybody and everything involved, with just the criticism that such a demonstration implies, a hint that departure was cheap at any price. I was obliged to let him wipe them, as it were, there and then, upon a cheque.

Still I had to put in my word on behalf of the island.

"It seems to me," I said, "that if people allow themselves to be overreached like that they have no business to complain of it."

"Oh, it isn't worth complaining of!" said Graham. And I daresay, by comparison, it wasn't.

Towse came up for the last time to take away, and as Graham gathered up the newspapers a letter appeared under the *Times*. "It's for you," he said. "Sorry; I didn't see it."

"I don't know the handwriting," I remarked; and this was not surprising, as it turned out to be from the Duchess of Dulwich by a new secretary. It contained a kind invitation to spend my last whole day in town with Her Grace.

"I know I must not expect your brother," said the note. "He will have a thousand things to do and must keep every moment free. But it will be very nice to see you. I have an Empire First tea-party in the afternoon, and we shall expect you to explain to us all this trouble about Newfoundland."

"Shall you go?" asked Graham dissuasively. "You're not in the least obliged to."

"Oh, yes, I think so," I said. "But I don't know anything about Newfoundland. How shall you spend the day, dear old man? Mooning about West-minster?"

"No," said Graham, "I'm a landed proprietor now, and I don't moon as much as I did. I shall spend it with my agent."

CHAPTER XXVII

His Grace was in the country; the Duchess and I lunched alone. I had not seen her since the evening she motored over with Barbara to dine at Knowes, the evening of the day we all learned that Peter had left so irretrievably for Ireland. It was Evelyn's motor, I remembered, that brought the news in the forlorn person of the Countess in the morning; and Evelyn's motor again which delivered the Duchess, in plain triumph and exultation, in the evening, while Evelyn herself remained in accepted grief and seclusion at Pavis Court with her darling Lady Doleford and the Marquis of Scansby, who had a cold. I remember thinking at the time that this use of the motor was not altogether delicate on the part of the Duchess, though it was just like Evelyn's American magnificence to lend it, even to an enemy.

But this was not so very long ago; and there seemed very little necessity for the Duchess to explain having seen nothing of us during the past month, on the ground that she was a woman of business, that she had had no less than two cases of appendicitis "downstairs," and on the top of all had herself been in bed three days with a chill.

"That extraordinarily mild week we had, you recollect, at the beginning of the month."

"Oh, yes!" I said. "Do you remember the lilacs in the Park?"

"I do not. They weren't in bloom, were they? But they must have been extraordinary, for someone else was speaking of them to me not long ago in exactly the same way. Who could it have been? Ah, to be sure — my nephew Peter. Well, I don't know how foolish the lilacs were, but they couldn't have suffered more than I did for leaving off my chamois-leather vest. At my age I should really have known better, whatever the weather was. 'Change ne'er a clout till May be out!' is no new saying in my ears, whatever it may be in yours."

"Lord Doleford is in Ireland, I — I hear," I said.

"Oh, yes, in Ireland — more or less. But he looks us up now and again. He talks of cutting short his leave and getting back again to India — great nonsense, I tell him. But with no home to go to——"

"Oh!" I exclaimed. "But ——"

"You mustn't pick me up too literally. The place is there, of course, but who do you suppose has taken it? Who but Miss Evelyn!"

"Taken it!" I cried. "Graham never told me! Why —— Duchess! Taken Pavis Court — Evelyn!"

"Oh, for no great period — only six months, I believe. Your poor foolish brother has been most anxious that Cecilia and Barbara should stay on there for the present. He seems to have the most extraordinary ideas of what is possible. And into the breach steps Miss Evelyn, with her long purse. Mind you, I don't say what he's getting for it. No great sum, I daresay, for our little friend has quite a notion of a stroke of business."

"Then Evelyn ——" I gasped, deprived of words by the new situation.

"Is mistress of Pavis Court — after all!" completed the Duchess, not without a chuckle. "And that fool Cecilia Doleford gratefully accepts until May, thinking no doubt — well, that is neither here nor there. When she learns that she has driven her son back to those intolerable climates before there was the least need, perhaps she will realise her folly."

"It does seem a pity!" I murmured.

"I was sure you would think so. Meanwhile," continued the Duchess with the last accent of disgust, "we are to have the pleasure of welcoming Henry Q. or Thomas K., or whatever his alphabetical distinction may be, to Pavis Court next month for as long as he cares to stay. His daughter told Barbara, who told me, that she could not imagine anything that would entertain him more. So there he is to be."

"James P.," I ventured. "He isn't a bad little man."

"Oh, don't praise him to me. Not a bad little money-bag, I daresay."

"I can't think," I repeated, "why Graham didn't tell me."

"He is still considering it, I believe, though there can be no kind of doubt as to his agreeing in the end. He must think himself lucky to get people to stay there upon any terms, with the place full of workmen. He couldn't go off to his native wilds with a very tranquil mind, leaving such a house to the care of two or three servants, could he?"

"Yes," I said, "I think he could."

"Then," said the Duchess severely, "he must be very indifferent to what is rare and old and beautiful. And quite the wrong person to have bought the place."

"There I do agree," I hastened to say.

"He was led into it, no doubt, poor fellow," continued the Duchess, relenting, "by his infatuation for Barbara. Perhaps it was not unnatural, considering the undoubted encouragement he received. This is very frank of me, but we have all been, haven't we, so much behind the scenes together? And if Barbara has suffered any mortification in being obliged to dismiss him, I consider that it was entirely her own fault. The Pavisays have always treated marriage a great deal too light-heartedly. However, it is much better to repent a whimsical choice before it is too late — better for all parties."

"I think so, too," I said, "and I am afraid Graham wouldn't have repented — at all events in time."

I felt exactly like David and Goliath, and I am almost sure I got the Duchess, just a little to the right of her Early Victorian hair-parting. Perhaps it was lucky for me that the butler at that moment re-entered the room.

"You may tell the cook, William, for the third time this month, that I will not have cold mutton cockered up in any form," said the Duchess.

"Yes, your Grace," said William, without blenching. "Sweetbreads, your Grace."

Oh, dear, how funny it was! I can't describe how funny it was. I despair. I mean not myself at all, just the Duchess and William. The way William, coming innocently in at the door, received this broadside, sacrificed his proper person to enable the Duchess to recover her equanimity — it was feudal. I realise that nobody could find it quite so amusing as I did. Only I must be forgiven if, looking back, I laugh irrelevantly and to myself, which is, perhaps, not good literary manners.

"But he is young, and we have every reason to hope he will soon get over it," she resumed easily, as William disappeared to ricochet into the cook.

"Every reason," I agreed.

"And I think, candidly, he would be wiser to

marry in his own part of the world. We are not intended to know everything, and for some inscrutable reason it docs not seem desirable that the men of younger countries should look for wives to England. Providence does not appear to approve of such unions. Look at the Billingers — Lady Marjorie married Australian mutton. They have no family. Nature is against it," pronounced the Duchess.

"Dear me!" I said.

"It is different with women. I am no traitor to my own sex, but with women I admit the case is different. It is my opinion, as you know, that American marriages have been grossly overdone; but a certain number of the daughters of our own kith and kin beyond the seas" — the Duchess smiled at me benevolently — "might very well help to replen — might very well make good English wives. I should not object to being quoted as thinking so, if it would do any good. And if such ideas seem in any way sordid or grasping, it should be remembered that the Colonies pay nothing, or almost nothing, for the protection afforded them by the British navy."

"Yes, indeed."

"And I understand," continued the Duchess, "that the preference they are supposed to give us commercially does not amount to a row of pins."

"Oh, yes, it does. It does really, Duchess. Ask Graham," I urged. "He can tell you."

"Oh, well," said the Duchess skilfully, "all the more reason for a little Colonial preference on our part when a choice is to be made; that is my view. Now shall we go upstairs for our coffee?"

My day with the Duchess was memorable even in detail, and I must here note that I was sent to lie down before the party, while her Grace was engaged, I believe, with her secretary. I understood that she wore out secretaries as other people did boots and shoes, but to repeat the simile she used on her own behalf, she always sent them to be mended. She had two, she told me, at the cobbler's at that moment. I saw the current secretary later. She had a distracted air, having just dropped a sheaf of dinner invitations out of a Blue-book at the head of the stairs, on her way to tell a deputation that the Duchess would be with it shortly. I have forgotten what the deputation wanted, but the Duchess dealt with it between three and four, and by the time people began to arrive it was quite cleared away.

CHAPTER XXVIII

The Empire First tea-party was really a function, with flowers and lackeys in profusion and refreshments on a lavish scale, although the Duchess declared that her Imperialism stopped short of strawberries, with which she told us the American Ambassador had already announced the coming of June. "Things like spring chickens," said she, "that one had to carve." There were no strawberries, but there was everything else, and the Blue Hungarian Band, and the Duchess, imposing in grey silk and cameos, doing her duty as England expected her at the head of the staircase.

It interested me very much to notice the different kinds of people with whom the Empire was first. There were so many — it seemed to place our Imperial future on a very various foundation. One had not expected them, of course, all to be Duchesses, but one had looked somehow for a certain similarity of demeanour among them, an appearance of concern that would correspond at least with her grey silk and sense of responsibility. And there were several examples of this. I remember two or three ladies whose mien and whose bonnets showed them to be of an importance quite different from anything recognised in smart circles, whose high-bridged noses spoke distinctly and austerely for principle and for that alone; and in whose hands I felt sure all national issues would be safe. They were trenchantly Gothic, those ladies; they abased the most sumptuous in their neighbourhood; one was glad to think that they were still here to reckon with. But there were hardly enough of them to make a back-bone for the gathering, which fell away from them in every direction. The men, I thought, were no doubt solid for the ends of Greater Britain, though some of them looked young to have made up their minds. The Bishop of Medicine Hat was a natural prelate to the movement — the Duchess was unaffectedly proud of him — and an ex-Viceroy of India unconsciously appropriated the occasion wherever he happened to be. I was shown lieutenant governors in retirement, who seemed to shrink from publicity, and somebody very important from the War Office. There was also a tailor-made type of elderly young woman with pleasant, rather short manners and "interests" written plainly all over her, moving about in small numbers, and a sprinkling of impressed, alarmed, delighted persons whom I recognised by these feelings to be fellow-Colonials. But most of the ladies must have considered Imperial interests from very complicated points of view; they were so charming and so deeply interested in quite different subjects. They must always, for instance, have had before them or behind them their adorable clothes; and from those of one radiant being who had the courage — so gracefully — to embrace the Duchess, I for one could never have permitted my mind to stray to the Bengalis or the Rand.

It was too new a party, I feel, to introduce at the very end. No Lippingtons, no Mrs. Jerome Jarvis — and how one missed her in the few places in which she didn't appear! — no Billy or Barbara, not even Graham or Evelyn. But that is quite like London; up to the last minute there is always a new party. I felt a little lonely and lost in it, though several people asked me in a friendly way how I was enjoying myself in England. It seemed to me too that I did not want to meet so many strangers, or even any strangers, at the very point of departure. For me too this story was to end on the very next day as for you on the very next page; and I wasn't at all keyed up to the Empire; I wanted more than anything else in the world to see my mother. There, I remembered, all this time had been the dear shelter of my own home in Minnebiac, and the fact that it was in Greater Britain did not thrill me in the least. I only wondered whether I had not been rather silly in staying so long away. It seemed to me that I was in that house in London, that had been a great house in London for three centuries, on a kind of false advantage, and that it would be easier, if that was my lot, to be rich in Minnebiac where it mattered so very much less. Perhaps this showed the advantage not to have been wholly false; but when one is very depressed one is not always strictly logical. I could not imagine why I was at the party, why I was being introduced as the Duchess's little Canadian, like something she had just caught, why I was not in mourning with Graham somewhere, as a sister should. And then — the party was almost over — a door opened from the more private part of the house and admitted — Peter.

There is no use in pretending that I was quite composed and nodded nonchalantly, as I longed to do. There is no use in pretending anything. My heart suddenly began to pound so violently as almost to drown the Blue Hungarians, and it seemed to me that if I should by any chance meet Lord Doleford's eye he could not help hearing it. The prospect of meeting his eye was terrifying; I could not and would not face it. I turned my back and risked, with a pang, his again disappearing into Ireland. Fortunately there were still twenty or thirty people left; and near me stood a tall, lanky girl with a nice face, wearing a white fox boa and waiting to be

2 A

taken home, the way they do wait in England.   Her I hurriedly addressed.

"I have just remembered," I said, "that the Duchess wanted me to tell people about Newfoundland."

"Have you ever been there?" asked the tall girl.

"No, never."

"I was born there," said the lanky girl.   "My father had a post there."

"What kind of a post?" I asked with unnatural curiosity.

"He was the Governor of the island.   There was constant trouble with the Americans even then."

"Was there?" I asked.

"Yes, indeed.   They would come within the three-mile limit for bait.   There always was a Bait Act of sorts, you know."

"I'm afraid I didn't," I said, "know, you know."

"Oh, yes.   The trouble was our people would sell to the Americans.   We were always prosecuting our own fishing-smacks.   But trespass and illegal recruiting are as old as Newfoundland politics, father says."

"Oh, really."

"And so are these purse seines they will persist in using.   They catch the baby herrings as well as the grown-ups — isn't it horrid?" said the nice girl. "How do you do, Peter?   This is my cousin, Lord Doleford — I'm afraid I didn't hear your name."

Peter had already bowed to me distantly, so distantly that I wondered why he had come within bowing range. At the lanky girl's introduction, however, he smiled with apparent relief, and warmly shook hands with me.

"We are old friends," he said, as if he dared me to deny it. "What are you two talking about so solemnly?"

"Herrings," said the girl who was waiting to be taken home.

"I was telling — I mean your cousin was telling me about Newfoundland," I said. "I know what you think — you think I ought to know myself. But Newfoundland isn't Canada, you know. They won't belong to us, so we don't pay much attention to them and their herrings."

"Quite right too," said Peter earnestly, looking at me with the most extraordinary scrutiny.

"My father always opposed the idea of Newfoundland's entering the Dominion," said Peter's cousin, "because, you see, it would have abolished us. Nobody likes to be abolished. My father thought it was much more likely to be well governed as a Crown Colony."

"I'm sure he was right," I replied vaguely.

"Rather," Peter assented, with an absent hand on his moustache; and together we bent upon the lanky girl a serious and preoccupied gaze.

"Between the Americans and the French," she continued, "father used to say the Governorship was no bed of roses. France had special fishing and drying privileges on some parts of the coast, secured to her by the Treaty of Utrecht. Very annoying it was."

"Fishing and drying?" I repeated, for politeness' sake.

"The Treaty of Utrecht, eh?" said Peter. "Most mischievous things, these treaties."

"Very annoying indeed, it must have been," I assured her.

"But that is all settled up now. There is only the question of the herrings and the Americans. And, of course, other fish."

"Odd fish," said Peter.

"Well, principally cod. The other principal feature about Newfoundland," continued his cousin cheerfully, "curiously enough, is ponds. It is said that about a third of the whole island is covered with fresh water."

"Fresh-water ponds?" said Peter, with a renewed effort at attention.

"Yes. But don't think that I know all this of my own knowledge. We came away while I was a baby! But I have heard father talk about it ever since I can remember. And I hope you won't mind my saying the Americans are — that about the Americans.

Father says he is sure it will straighten out some-how," and the cousin gave me a friendly apologetic smile.

There was an instant of silence. I saw what she thought; but it didn't seem worth while to explain.

"Are there any fresh fish in the ponds?" I asked weakly.

"Ah, there you have me! I've never heard papa say. I should suppose so — shouldn't you? But I see mamma making signals — good-bye! It has been so nice meeting someone from the part of the world I was born in."

And there she left us stranded. Such is the con-sistency of human nature that I at once longed for her back again. While she was there I was at least not obliged to look at Peter.

"I'm late," said he — "unavoidably. It was almost impossible getting here at all; but Aunt Agnes sent me a reminder, and she doesn't do that unless she really wants a fellow to turn up. She's fearfully keen on these Imperialist shows of hers. Do you think they do any good?"

"Oh, yes," I said. "Don't you?"

Peter looked at me with sudden enquiry, and we exchanged recognisances in a smile. After that there was no use in saying, "I don't mean what you think I mean," was there? Especially as I did.

"Let us go and sit down," he said. "Unless you are just off too?"

"No," I said. "I have my hat on because I happen to look better in it, but I am spending the day here."

"Oh, are you?" We had gone and sat down.

"Yes. To help the Duchess with this party, and tell people about Newfoundland. I don't know why I'm dining here, unless it's to tell them about Alaska."

"I'm dining too," said Peter. "I understood I was to meet the Aga Khan. You were not mentioned."

"No," I said. "Why should I be?" We exchanged another recognisance.

"People have such queer ideas of comparative attractions," said Peter, after doing this. "Though the Aga Khan is a very good sort. I don't know why Aunt Agnes should have found him so formidable."

Here the part of intelligence would have been to ask to be informed about the Aga Khan; but what I said was, "It's our last day, you know. We sail to-morrow."

"Yes, I know," said Peter. "I was coming to the station."

It was a small fact to make one at once happy and comfortable.

"That was very kind," I said. "But now we shall have an opportunity of saying good-bye here. Euston is so far from everywhere."

Peter's face fell, ever so little. It was a joy to me to see his face fall, even ever so little. "Yes," he said, "we could do that."

"If you are dining," I continued, "there will be plenty of time."

Lord Doleford appeared to reflect and to defer his decision; and there was a pause.

"And so," he said, "I am not to have you, even approximately, for a sister-in-law?"

"A sister's sister-in-law," I corrected, "not a legal sister-in-law."

"I said approximately."

"I'm sorry," I said. Why did I say that when I was not? But I may safely repeat it here, as I know I shall not be believed.

"It would have been something," I added.

"Do you think so?"

"Why, yes. Something nice and friendly. I regret it — for that."

Peter, his hands thrust in his pockets, looked gloomily into space. "I'm not sorry," he said, "even for that. I think it was a poor sort of idea, you know — those two; I didn't think old Barb would go through with it, once she realised how things were."

"How did she realise?"

"Oh, she arrived at it, I imagine — she worried it out by herself. I didn't say anything." Peter twisted himself round to tell me this as if it were important.

"Dearest Barbara," I remarked quite easily, "says that nobody ought to marry a mere nice old place."

"And she's as right as possible," said Peter controversially. "Isn't she?"

"Oh, I suppose so. But architecture is very plausible," I added rather sadly. "Especially Tudor. It seems to stand fearfully on its merits."

(Remembering that I have fully disclosed what I really did think about such pretensions, I am ashamed to report this conversation.)

"Believe me, Trent's much too good a chap to be married for a coat of paint," said Peter. Then most unexpectedly, most alarmingly he added, "And so are you!"

"Oh!" I replied, suddenly thrown into confusion. "Nobody would ever think of marrying me for a coat of paint."

"On the contrary — plenty of people," said Peter darkly. "Don't ever lend yourself to anything of the sort."

"I won't," I promised.

"I hope I know you well enough to offer such advice without impertinence," he continued stiffly.

"I am sure you would always advise me for my good," I told him; and we looked at one another very straight.

We were in the hall near the bronze figure of Frederick the Great on horseback and more or less behind the azaleas. The silhouette of the Duchess crossed the arched entrance to the ballroom, as if exploring the scene of her function for more duties to perform; but there was nobody left except an Agent-General and his wife, who had secured seats together on the other side of the statue and had not yet noticed that they could be safely given up. No doubt the Duchess was reconnoitring on the Agent-General's behalf, for presently the secretary appeared and invited them to have some tea, at which they got up and went away.

"About Americans," Peter went on with extraordinary candour, "I haven't the same feeling. They have their eyes open — they know what's involved and what's understood. If they care about that kind of bargain, by all means let them make it."

"Then if I were an American ——" I began.

"I should not be advising you," said Peter.

"No, of course not."

"But you — you belong to us," he continued in a voice which anyone would have found penetrating. "You are our own people. We can't marry you on that principle."

"Can't you?"

Peter hesitated. "I would rather not do it myself," he said.

"It would be nicer not to," I reflected.

"I don't yet see my way to tariff-reform."

"You will," I interrupted confidently.

"But I'm a fool about the ties of sentiment."

"Aren't they," I said, "the only wisdom?"

Peter looked at me very thoughtfully. "If there were any way of finding out," he said.

I could not think of any way; and so we sat, for a full and wonderful moment, waiting for the sun to rise.

"There's a suggestion you might make," he resumed in a pained tone.

"Is there?" I said. "Well — I'll make it."

"That in our dealings with the colonies the heart is supposed to have more of a chance," said Peter.

"I think that is a thing that ought to go without saying," I told him.

And then the sun rose.

*   *   *   *   *   *

Next day saw us embarked, nevertheless. There was time for only one practical measure before we sailed — the desperate and final relief of Pavis Court. Whatever happened, that hardly defended seat should not suffer even temporary capitulation. Dear old Graham was easy to convince about that. It was distressing to seem to take everything, to leave our friend Evelyn not even her vestige of victory; but it was reasonable to suppose that she would understand. In matters of business Evelyn's understanding could always be relied upon.

Graham received the news of Peter's and my engagement without marked enthusiasm, but he gradually warmed into satisfaction at the thought of this happy attendant circumstance. It was not the old ardent flame, but it was a glow from the same source. There was in his demeanour just a hint that it would have been simpler if we had thought of the arrangement sooner, in which case, I might have reminded him, there would have been no story; but those are the things that one thinks of afterwards. I could see too that he liked enormously the idea of being a kind of brother-in-law to Barbara; and I was glad to think that he had at least to thank me for that.

Peter travelled to Liverpool with us. He would thus, the Duchess told him, learn the proper Imperial route across the ocean; and, besides, he wished to come. The *Empress of Britain*, after depositing their Excellencies Lord and Lady Lippington, had kindly come back for us; and we were standing on her deck near the gangway, when a steward approached Graham with a telegram. It was not for him, but for Peter, in his care; and I had an intuition that the news it brought was intended to interest us all. It was. Peter considered it in silence for an instant, and then read it aloud:

"'Dear Evelyn has consented to marry your Uncle Christopher. — Mother.'"

After one incredulous second, inextinguishable laughter overtook us. It really was, at that instant, too clever and too funny of Evelyn.

"Poor old chap!" commented Peter feelingly, in a voice that still trembled.

"She has taken an heir presumptive with grape-nuts," said Graham brokenly, and added, "We have never done her justice."

"She can hardly call him ——" I began impulsively.

"What?" asked the others.

"A dear and precious lamb," I murmured. "It is an expression of Evelyn's when she is fond."

"I suppose we must congratulate mother?" said Peter. "She is really attached to her."

"Oh, congratulate everybody," said Graham, going off again.

There was one person, however, who could not possibly be congratulated; one person to whom indeed it would even be difficult to offer any form of consolation. It was left to me to realise where the blow, delivered with such grace and precision, would most tragically fall. I am proud to remember that I was the first to feel a pang of sympathy with the august lady at whom, I am convinced, it was really aimed.

"Your mother has telegraphed to you," I said to Peter, "but who will tell the Duchess?"

"I will," said the Earl of Doleford sturdily, as the

last bell rang to clear the decks. A moment later he stood upon his native shores. Looking back at him as the Atlantic widened between us, I noted once more with pride how like he was to the ancestor who held out against Elizabeth.

Mr. WINSTON CHURCHILL'S NOVELS

Each, cloth, gilt tops and titles, $1.50

Mr. Crewe's Career — Illustrated

" Another chapter in his broad, epical delineation of the American spirit. . . . It is an honest and fair story. . . . It is very interesting; and the heroine is a type of woman as fresh, original, and captivating as any that has appeared in American novels for a long time past."— *The Outlook*, New York.

" Shows Mr. Churchill at his best. The flavor of his humor is of that stimulating kind which asserts itself just the moment, as it were, after it has passed the palate. . . . As for Victoria, she has that quality of vivid freshness, tenderness, and independence which makes so many modern American heroines delightful." — *The Times*, London.

The Celebrity. — An Episode

" No such piece of inimitable comedy in a literary way has appeared for years. . . . It is the purest, keenest fun."— *Chicago Inter-Ocean.*

Richard Carvel — Illustrated

". . . In breadth of canvas, massing of dramatic effect, depth of feeling, and rare wholesomeness of spirit, it has seldom, if ever, been surpassed by an American romance."— *Chicago Tribune.*

The Crossing — Illustrated

"'The Crossing' is a thoroughly interesting book, packed with exciting adventure and sentimental incident, yet faithful to historical fact both in detail and in spirit." — *The Dial.*

The Crisis — Illustrated

" It is a charming love story, and never loses its interest. . . . The intense political bitterness, the intense patriotism of both parties, are shown understandingly." — *Evening Telegraph*, Philadelphia.

Coniston — Illustrated

" 'Coniston' has a lighter, gayer spirit and a deeper, tenderer touch than Mr. Churchill has ever achieved before. . . . It is one of the truest and finest transcripts of modern American life thus far achieved in our fiction."— *Chicago Record-Herald.*

THE MACMILLAN COMPANY
PUBLISHERS, 64-66 FIFTH AVENUE, NEW YORK